INHUMAN

HUNTER BUREAU #4

BLAZE WARD

KNOTTED ROAD PRESS

Inhuman
Hunter Bureau #4
Blaze Ward
Copyright © 2022 Blaze Ward
All rights reserved
Published by Knotted Road Press
www.KnottedRoadPress.com

ISBN: 978-1-64470-253-6

Cover art:
Illustration 136611110 © Ilya Shalkov | Dreamstime.com

Cover and interior design copyright © 2022 Knotted Road Press

Reviews
It's true. Reviews help. Even a short one, such as, "Loved it!" So please consider reviewing this book (and all of the ones you've read) on your favorite retailer site.

Never miss a release!
If you'd like to be notified of new releases, sign up for my newsletter.

http://www.blazeward.com/newsletter/

Buy More!
Did you know that you can buy directly from my website?

https://www.blazeward.com/shop/

The Jessica Keller Chronicles

Auberon

Queen of the Pirates

Last of the Immortals

Goddess of War

Flight of the Blackbird

The Red Admiral

St. Legier

Winterhome

Petron

CS-405

Queen Anne's Revenge

Packmule

Persephone

Additional Alexandria Station Stories

The Story Road

Siren

Two Bottles of Wine With A War God

The Science Officer Series Season One

The Science Officer

The Mind Field

The Gilded Cage

The Pleasure Dome

The Doomsday Vault

The Last Flagship

The Hammerfield Gambit

The Hammerfield Payoff

The Bryce Connection

The Science Officer Series Season Two

Alien Seas

Buried Among the Stars

The Lazarus Alliance

Escape

Return

Rebellion

Revolution

Liberation

Retribution

Alliance

Shadow of the Dominion

Longshot Hypothesis

Hard Bargain

Outermost

Dominion-427

Phoenix

Princess Rualoh

The Handsome Rob Gigs

Can't Shoot Straight Gang

Can't Shoot Straight Gang Returns

Hunting Handsome Rob

Handsome Rob, Assassin

Earth Force Sky Patrol

Birth of the Star Dragon

Flight of the Star Dragon

Call of the Star Dragon

Shadow of the Star Dragon

Trial of the Star Dragon

Hunter Bureau

Mirrors

Latency

Pleasure Model

Inhuman

Fairchild

Fairchild

Strawberry Dragon

ONE
SYMPATHETIC MIRROR

Greyson Leigh considered his reflection in the bathroom mirror. Skinny man, just past middle-aged or something. Fifty, but in better shape than most men half his age. Being an alien impersonating a Human helped. The Phrenic could live for centuries if nobody shot them dead with a nerve scrambler first.

He figured his day was coming.

Still, the mirror was just a reflection. He hadn't bought himself a sympathetic mirror, like some folks did. Greyson wanted to know what he looked like, not how he could be made to look better with a little technological magic. You got what you got.

Well, technically not. You got the Human named Greyson Leigh. Detective/Hunter, Eastern North America Division, Earth Police Special Missions. *The Hunter Bureau.* Toughest, meanest, nastiest son of a bitch to ever wear a badge, according to some of the folks he worked with.

Greyson didn't necessarily dispute that. He'd need it. Shortly, they would be departing Earth to travel to Brees, homeworld of the G'schtack as well as the financial and political capital of the Illymus Merchants Guild, the trade network that bound the whole known galaxy together.

The aliens had only made it to Earth a little more than sixteen years ago, back when Greyson was still in the US Army doing things he wasn't legally allowed to discuss with civilians. Back when the US was still more of a thing, as opposed to today, when it was slowly oozing down the sink, replaced by the various Metroplex Districts.

Greyson was a Hunter. Had been one before. Now he was dead. A Phrenic infiltrator named Ethen Boli had snuck in one night, killed the man in his sleep, and assumed his identity. Turned out to have been a mistake, because even though he was dead, Greyson had been too much for Ethen to handle.

So they presented as Greyson now. Used a mental projection inside their combined mind to *be* Greyson. It was so complete, so deep, so powerful, that Greyson had functionally returned from the dead, and Ethen had been able to go hide in a closet from the evil shit she'd done over the decades.

Greyson would protect her. Did. Would continue, right up until someone realized what he was and killed him. Or his partner Rachel told them it was time to die.

Then he would. Simple as that.

But not today.

Today, he had to meet her downstairs in a few minutes. Get some breakfast, then travel to the starport. They were only a few hours from leaving Earth at this point.

Greyson wasn't sure he'd come back. That he would be allowed to come back. The G'schtack had scanners that were supposed to find people like him. Except that Rachel had a friend with even better equipment.

Last night, it had sworn that he was just Greyson Leigh. Human. Anglo. Excellent shape.

Not a Phrenic infiltrator.

He'd ride that luck as long as he could, because Greyson Leigh had some folks on Brees that he wanted to chat with. Smugglers, at first, until they rolled over to indict the people behind them, hoping that they didn't end up in jail forever. Cop like Greyson might even let some of them get off easy, if he thought they might help him take down some of the big players.

This morning, the mirror wasn't any more sympathetic than ever, but he wasn't surprised. It never was. Unlike Greyson, who might still decide to be.

He moved out of the bathroom and killed the light. He'd already had one coffee early. Read the news. Caught up on a few things. Filed an update on his case for the Captain to read in two weeks, that she might be emotionally prepared if one of her Hunters happened to bring down the entire, fucking Illymus Merchant Guild in fire and wrath because of what they'd done.

The thought warmed him occasionally.

He moved to the kitchenette area and assembled his life. Palmstunner, hardly ever used. Nerve scrambler that had seen more use. Wallet. Keys. Passport. Tickets. Cash. Everything into its correct pocket.

Greyson didn't know what season it would be on Brees when he and Rachel arrived, so he'd packed a warm coat in the suitcase by his foot. Greyson Leigh had never been to Brees. Never walked on a surface 0.88G equivalent of Earth. Never watched green skies as first the brighter star Udoth rose, followed a few hours later by Vaad. The Hound and the Hunter.

He was a Hunter chasing someone, so it felt doubly right.

Ethen had told him about the place. Showed it to him to prepare for this mission. The US Army had prepared him emotionally and psychologically to kill total strangers for no reason at all. The Hunter Bureau had honed him into an Officer of the Court.

The Law.

Interestingly, while he didn't really know jack shit about Illymus Trade Law, his partner was a walking encyclopedia. But he'd been training her to be the best Hunter ever born. Better than him. The Best, at least until she found a student one of these days who could surpass her.

Greyson Leigh might be dead, but Ethen had decades of penance to do.

And the people of Earth, those silly monkeys everyone else laughed at, deserved better than the Guild had given them.

He'd see to justice there, too. Both of them would. All three of them.

Because somebody had fucked up and pissed off Greyson Leigh. Outraged his sense of fair play.

He would see them pay for it.

He had everything settled, so he went out and locked the door behind him, taking the stairs down to the street.

Greyson Leigh had a job to do.

TWO
IN THREE DIMENSIONS

Patrolman/Hunter Rachel Asher was driving the government-issued Skycruiser disguised to look like a late-model Chandler Jouster. Ugly gray. Four doors. Seating six. Capable of hovering flight using alien tech she still didn't fully understand, in spite of asking her gearhead partner to explain it a few times.

Greyson always drove on manual. Everywhere. Never trusted the computers to handle it unless he was so tired that they would be safer. And even that was a judgment call. He expected her to drive, too, so she was on manual, cruising slowly up the block to his place.

In the distance, the sun was just thinking about starting to rise. She spotted him standing on the sidewalk out in front of his building, suitcase resting against his feet and eyes tracking every jogger, feral cat, and vehicle like his life depended on it.

Rachel didn't complain. His paranoia had kept her alive more than once.

She pulled close and popped the locks. He was already in

motion, opening the rear door on his side to toss in the bag, then climbing up front.

He buckled himself in and she drove.

They had two kinds of days in this job. Sleep in late because they were going to be up all night chasing bad folks, or up before dawn to catch the silly gits just coming home from a night of dancing, when they'd be too tired to keep their guard up as they approached their front door.

Today was the early kind. They just weren't after anyone around here.

Hopefully, nobody had warned the folks back home what was coming.

It helped that the ship they'd be flying on was the first to leave the Earth System since the news had broken about Armstrong Base and the death of a Phrenic Infiltrator, plus the arrest of the Human Administrator.

Moon bureaucrats running amok like chickens with their heads cut off.

Rachel glanced over at her partner.

"We still doing this?" she asked as she headed into one of the oldest neighborhoods of Boston.

"Working in three dimensions, kid," he growled back, just as surly as usual until you got some food in the boy.

"Which one takes precedence?" she fired back.

"The only one that ever does," Greyson said. "I understand that you were raised with the moral and we were both trained for the legal, but this will always be the ethical."

She grunted and let the conversation slide. The car was a giant radio with wheels, constantly transmitting data to various places. They'd had to get creative about where they could talk and not risk being overheard. Breakfast today was a joint down near the harbor, where the fisherfolk would be leaving about the time the two of them wandered in, so they'd have it largely to themselves for an hour before the early birds started shuffling in.

She got them there, parked, and chirped the locks. Waitress put them in their usual spot away from the bathrooms and removed from a few old captains that still hung out with friends but remained behind reading the paper rather than go face the north Atlantic.

"You have been a terrible influence on me," Rachel announced as they got coffee and their orders started cooking.

Greyson grunted something noncommittal and rude.

"I was raised a good, little Catholic girl, Leigh," she continued. "Even though we all know just how horrible those people have been for centuries these days. Can't help my parents and grandparents."

"It's still child abuse, if you ask me," he muttered quietly. "Let them study it as adults and join if they want, but keep impressionable children away from pederasts and rapists."

"Well, yeah, but if they did that, nobody would join and the Church would collapse in a decade," she fired back. It was an old discussion.

"Not seeing a downside here, Rachel," he said, sipping his coffee with a hard, planar face.

He'd lost weight. It was there in the face and hands. Hard living and too much stress. Plus, he ate as much as he always did, but she suspected that the transformations into his base form and back to Greyson in the last few days had burned a lot of extra calories.

She started to speak but he interrupted.

"Plus, if you read the damned book, you'll see that it favors slavery, rape, child murder, Human sacrifice, genocide, and a whole bunch of other crimes," Greyson reminded her. "I'd think more highly of them if they actually followed their own book about punishments for the shit they did. Instead, they indulge all the sin, and ignore all the penalties, in favor of social control and extraordinary wealth that doesn't ever seem to help poor people, even as Popes wear cloth-of-gold and expensive shoes. Have them put Matthew 18:6 into the law books and we'll talk. Until then, they're all just a bunch of scurrilous hypocrites."

Worst part? He was smiling as he talked.

"So, okay, I get it," Rachel nodded. "The Moral Axis is more fucked up than anybody wants to admit in polite company. I suppose you're more one of those militant Buddhist points of view?"

"Close enough for this conversation," he shrugged.

"So how about the legal?" she asked. "We're cops. This is a violation of the law."

"Is it?" he asked, eyes boring into hers now.

"What do you mean?" she countered, trying to see his angle.

"The Guild has only been down here since 2042, Rachel," he offered. "Sure, people been talking about little gray men that look a lot like G'schtack since World War Two ended a century before that, but they refuse to admit to anything."

"And?"

"And someone was able to create a Pleasure Model, Rachel," he ground on. "A perfect replica of a Human. A *perfect* Human woman, by the way. Everyone noticed that. Even dead, she was amazing. I'm a guy most of the time, so I can have that opinion. You think they went from zero to modified, vat-grown, perfect clones in sixteen years?"

Rachel felt the bottom of her stomach fall out. Gravity seemed to be dragging her down into the bench extra hard this morning.

Shit.

"Exactly," he said, either having heard her speak or

reading her mind. "So let's just assume for now that this is a research project dating back a long time. All those folks supposedly abducted and anally probed in the last century, and that sort of shit. Give a scientist a tissue sample and tell him to make you a copy. That's going to take a while, even their tech. How long?"

"You think they've been lying about things?" Rachel asked.

The two of them were about to go to the very soul of the Illymus Merchant Guild in pursuit of a perp and a case. How many cages was Leigh looking to rattle there?

"Until someone proves to me otherwise, yes," Greyson said sternly. "If you're feeling rude, here's a research topic for you to consider as we travel. I know you are getting close to completing your degree, so maybe we can consider this Master's level work. The cop I intend to turn you into will need to know these things."

"Hit me," she said. He scowled at her hard. "Sorry, figure of speech."

He'd accidentally given her raccoon eyes, saving her from his other partner, back at the start. She'd teased him about it at the time by getting cupcakes made up that said *Happy Makeup Sex*, because too many of those fuck-wits at the office thought they were sleeping together, when she had two extremely deadly big brothers. Though it turned out one of those brothers was actually her deadly big sister.

"I'm willing to bet you a Sammie, Rachel, that the project would have been covered under General Agricultural Research when it was started, because Humans hadn't been contacted yet and admitted into the Guild," Greyson said.

Usually, they bet Twoonies.

A Sammie meant the boy was serious. $20 Canadian coin with a salmon on the front and First Nations/Native American art on the back, rotating every year to a different culture or tribal band. You still ran across American dollars from time to time, but they'd turned into Weimar Marks eventually. That was part of the reason the aliens had come down.

To save the Humans from a global economic collapse that might have brought the whole damned planet down.

"Okay?" she asked, not sure where he was going with this. "Implications?"

"Cloning sheep, like they did when I was a kid, Asher." He turned deadly serious now. "Nothing in the law to stop it. Maybe even Guild money to start it, so they got a leg up on us. You know, in case they needed to turn Humans into an entire species of perfect assassins. Or harems of pleasure models. Or Manchurian Candidates. Or maybe just a new food crop."

"Most of them are vegetarians, Leigh," she countered.

"Sure."

He didn't sound convinced. She leaned back now and considered sheep.

They'd pulled a con job on Virgar Andell, the G'schtack Engineering Master of Armstrong Base, before they left the moon. And gotten that being to more or less confess to knowledge of such biological programs, but he'd obviously not considered perfect soldiers or perfect assassins.

She and Greyson had spent the whole trip back to Earth discussing it quietly.

"Okay, so maybe the project is legal at the top," Rachel allowed. "Or was. Understand Human biology so well that you can inoculate everyone from everything, and that sort of thing. Heal us if we get hurt. All that makes perfect sense. Then what?"

"Then we cross a line somewhere," Greyson said. "It had been legal. Maybe it still is, but I don't read Guildlaw like you do. That's your assignment. The Moral Axis is fucked.

The Legal Axis might be, depending on classifications and security clearances. That leaves the Ethical Axis, Rachel. Right and wrong at a fundamental, Socratic level. Somebody out there is creating assassins and using Humans to do it."

"And you're going to take him down," she breathed, as their waitress approached with food.

"Down doesn't even begin to describe it, Rachel."

THREE
BLACK SKIES

GREYSON, when he'd been Human, hadn't been off the surface of Earth any farther than a few Low Earth Orbit stations for vacations and business trips. The two trips to the moon were new personal records.

Ethen, on the other hand, hand been born in a different solar system several thousand light years away. Greyson could dream about those places. And he spoke accentless G'schtack, but as Rachel had pointed out, he had a reputation as a irresistible force anyway. That ruthlessness was why Andell had originally pressured the Bureau into reinstating him from an enforced retirement. And why the same man had called Boston when they had a murder on the moon.

Phrenic, both times. Dead Phrenic, both times, too. Justice served, long ways around the back of the track first, maybe.

Now, they were in LEO again. Low Earth Orbit. First launch from the surface with all the tourists on a busy space plane. Hundreds of Humans and a few dozen aliens. Last time, he and Rachel had crossed over to a section of the station that let them travel on to Armstrong Base with a few dozen people.

This trip was going to be a bit more interesting.

He'd looked everything up and had it on his phone, like a proper tourist. Greyson Leigh had never been through this process. Ethen Boli had been impersonating someone else at the time.

First things first, they went to the security booth at the middle of the station. Long hallway concourse, with a booth off to one side, like a concierge, with a low console in front and one person seated.

Human rent-a-cop on duty. Male. Fifty-something. A little pudgy. Looked like a cop who'd retired from the streets to just about the softest gig Greyson could imagine that let you keep a gun.

Greyson pulled out his ID. Beside him, Rachel did the same. They were plainclothes. Detectives. Travelers. He hadn't even brought a uniform on this trip. Only wore it annually anyway, for the awards banquet when he couldn't find a way to avoid that night.

"Leigh and Asher," he said. "Up from Earth. We have flight reservations."

Fellow looked at them owlishly for a moment, then typed something into the keyboard on his side of the counter. Looked at that for a moment. Flinched suddenly when he got to the part about who they really were. Paled a hint. Looked up.

Greyson smiled at the man.

"Yes, sir," the cop stuttered now.

He turned to his right and gestured. A door next to the booth buzzed and opened inward.

"Right that way, Detectives," the cop said.

Greyson nodded to the man and they went through. Luggage was already going. Rachel had a small messenger bag with stuff she wanted handy, plus her reader forever tucked into the pocket on her thigh. Mostly, she carried those damned erotica books the girl read in her spare time.

At least she'd outread the one woman who wrote alien/cop porn. At least for now. Rachel was on to the stuff where sequential members of a Late Nineteenth Century Russian aristocratic family somehow got seduced by pretty peasant girls and they lived happily ever after, but only after several bouts of wild sex in every possible gymnastic position a gravity field allowed.

He had his phone to watch videos on, plus they had an extremely generous expense account from Andell for this investigation.

Helped, when you had a Guild bigshot's balls in a vice.

Through the door, they were in a much nicer lounge that the outside might have suggested. Carpet, thick and lush in a muted maroon. Furniture for Humans, near-Human architecture, and a few alien species that didn't fold the same way. Physics had settled on a standard galactic design close enough to Human, but a few planets still had to be special.

Nobody here right at the moment, but that was fine. They had a nearly seven hours until their interstellar flight boarded. Time for dinner and a nap. He'd slept some on the flight up. He'd nap more as he needed it. Too many years in the Army.

A hostess appeared as they sat on a couch to one side. Comfortable enough to fall back into, if he'd wanted.

"Detectives," she smiled and nodded. "Can I get you something to drink or would you like a menu?"

"Coffee, black for me," Greyson said. "And a menu when you have a chance."

"Orange juice," Rachel added.

He looked around. Greyson was amused and impressed by the room. Ethen's memories were more prosaic.

Another rent-a-cop entered now, carrying a small anvil-style briefcase as she got close. Attractive woman in a generic kind of way. Short, blonde hair. Station security uniform that was tight enough to show off her lack of curves.

"Detectives Leigh and Asher?" she asked as she approached. "Could I see your IDs, please?"

He pulled his and flipped it open. Rachel did the same. The woman took them both and studied them closely.

"Thank you," she replied, handing them back.

Greyson watched her set the case to one side and unlock it with a thumbprint. Inside, two palmstunners and two nerve scramblers, along with holsters and power packs, packed separate for the trip up from Earth. She handed them over, smiling at him in a flirtatious way.

"You are familiar with the regulations about carrying weapons on starships?" she asked.

"We are," Rachel kind of growled possessively at the woman. "We are also sworn Officers of the Court on an investigation."

Greyson liked the way the woman's eyes flared a little. That hint of excitement that most cops never really got, because the job tended to be twenty years of boredom, maybe with two or three days of excitement. These days, most cops could go their entire career without drawing their sidearm.

Greyson rarely went a whole month. Hunters.

The woman departed and Greyson stripped his jacket. Rachel did the same. He'd be lying if he said he hadn't felt naked without a nerve scrambler under his left arm. From the look on her face, Rachel felt the same way.

"I'd ask if they were really going to let us do this," she said as they got jackets on and settled again. "But I already know the answer. Cops are cops."

"They just didn't expect Hunters when they wrote those

statutes," he agreed. "At the same time, they've never, to the best of my knowledge, actually dealt with Human Hunters anywhere outside this solar system, so everything we do will be judged on a new scale."

"I'm planning on setting the bar so high that everyone who comes along after us ends up looking junior varsity," she smiled back at him.

"Same," Greyson agreed. "Helps, having the kinds of knowledge we possess about what's coming."

"They really going to let us just waltz in there and go to work?" Rachel asked.

"Kid, they don't have a choice," he fired back. "Well, they do, technically."

"Oh?"

"The Guild has something like an Official Secrets Act, if they want to claim executive sovereignty," Greyson smiled now.

"That do them any good?" she asked innocently.

Greyson felt his face turn feral.

"No," he said. "I'll find a reporter and tell them everything, complaining that I was pulled off a major case, then leak enough details to grab the most salacious attention possible. I'll let the court of public opinion destroy those people if I have to. They'd be wiser just letting me arrest them at that point."

"Burn it all down?" she asked.

"Don't hire me to enforce laws you want to ignore, Detective," Greyson stated coldly. "I'm not fooling around here."

"Helps that I have an expert assassin on call as a technical resource." Rachel's smile matched his. "Hopefully, I won't have to use him."

"Yeah," Greyson licked his lips. "Hopefully."

FOUR

OUTBOUND

RACHEL HAD STAYED up late last night after dropping Greyson off, just so she could take an immersive video tour of the ship. Getting to orbit was like an airplane or semi-ballistic. Rows of seats, jammed together as efficiently as possible.

Traveling between stars, on the other hand, drew inspiration from cruise ships. She supposed physics was physics, at the end of the day.

Couple of days to get far enough out from the Sun's gravity field to transition to hyperspace. A week to get anywhere, mostly because Earth was so far off the beaten path from the rest of the Guild.

Something about an original expectation that Humans wouldn't start seriously traveling in space for maybe a millennium or something. Hell, powered flight had only first occurred in 1903 CE. Less than one Human lifetime later, Armstrong and Aldrin had landed on the moon and walked around. Less than a full Human lifetime later, the Guild showed up to say hello.

There would be several stops to get to Brees. Rachel

thought of them as islands in the Caribbean, a bit farther apart, but similar mentally. She might even hop off at a few of them, if the ship was going to be in port long enough. Still, call it six weeks in flight from here.

The ship was huge. Luxurious, too, but part of that was the fact that Greyson had leaned on the Engineering Master of Armstrong Base for Business-class tickets. Not quite First-class, because Leigh didn't need gold-plated champagne glasses with dinner. At the same time, he wasn't getting prefabricated fast food out of a freezer pack, warmed just before consumption and comprised of calories, protein, and, if you were lucky, taste. Nor were they crammed into spaces smaller than her closet back home.

They had cabins on a deck with the corporate warriors. Travelers going to and from Earth to handle business. The Guild specifically prohibited most things being imported to Earth, in order for factories to absorb all the folks thrown out of work in various militaries and military-industrial complex jobs.

You didn't need to build ICBMs or tanks if war was illegal and the Guild could enforce that. By now, most of that gear had been dismantled, so folks needed other things. Exports from Earth were churning to try to keep factories moving and people from going hungry.

In her lifetime, all of Earth had taken on most of the trappings of those developing places in Southeast Asia and Africa. So men and woman needed to go find markets for Human goods. Helped that Humans were way more inclined to just go somewhere than many of the other species. They shared that with the G'schtack, but not folks like the Minbe or Xaniea.

She had checked out her room when she dropped her messenger bag. Confirmed that her luggage was there, along with the instructions for laundry. Again, everything was covered, along with food and some entertainment. If she was careful and frugal, Rachel might only have to dip into her own resources occasionally when she really wanted to splurge.

Greyson was outside his room when she emerged.

"What do you want to do first?" she asked, wondering how he was taking the transition from Earth-bound cop to galactic traveler. He'd been pretty stressed the last week, and that was just the moon.

"You want to watch Earth recede?" he asked back. "Departing in about an hour. Enough time to find a lounge with a view."

"You care?" Rachel probed.

Greyson shrugged. About what she expected. Much of him was an act for others to consume, but underneath it all Greyson Leigh really didn't give two shits about what other folks thought. He wasn't as depressed as he'd first been, but not much else was different. Other Hunters in the building hadn't seen any difference in the man.

"Let's eat." She stepped close, poking him in the side. "You've lost about ten pounds in the last fortnight, if I had to guess. I'll get a light salad. You'll eat dessert."

On the one hand, it would have been interesting if Emmy had joined them for this trip. She'd keep a close watch on the boy and would have noticed the weight loss as well. Plus, she'd have distracted him with sex, dancing, and overall living.

Flipside, the woman was so deeply enmeshed in business that disappearing from Earth for three or four months would be detrimental. Rachel knew how much the woman was actually worth. Better than Greyson did.

It was a frighteningly large number. At the same time, much of it was on paper. Stocks and valuations that were valuable because Emmy held them. Folks respected her business acumen. Trusted her.

So Rachel had the boy to herself for the trip. And probably needed to mother him a little, because drawing Ethen into the sunlight, so to speak, had really done a number on the two of them.

"Dessert, huh?" he asked as she took his elbow in hers and started forward to where the nicer business lounges were.

"I know this is stressful for you, Greyson," she murmured as they walked.

He grunted, but didn't resist.

Around them, Humans and other species were moving. The corridor was wide enough to accommodate everyone. Again like a cruise ship, which really was what the thing was, at the end of the day. She caught a Dyarnan staring openly at her, aqua-colored scales and gills. They'd originally been an aquatic species in the same way that Humans had once been arboreal tree shrews.

Past a corner, she nearly ran headlong into a Nese who wasn't paying attention as he walked. Taller than Humans, but skinnier than even Greyson. Purple skin. This one was male with maroon hair.

In the dark, she supposed that they might be mistaken as a skeletal Human.

Not that she was interested, even when he smiled at her.

"Am I supposed to chaperon or something?" Greyson asked when they got clear of the guy. "Or turn a blind eye to any shipboard romances?"

Rachel growled up at the man and dragged him forward. The lounge she wanted was close.

They both had fobs worn like old-fashioned wrist watches that contained all their traveler information and let them in there. Would keep them out of the ultra-elite places without invitations, but those were up another deck for the most part.

Carpeted deck, but more like astroturf than anything. Friendly green, too. The walls were distant, but pillars upheld things, both done in a sedate baby blue. The mob in here ran the gamut of fashion and color, but she generally ignored them.

Rachel wanted to see the food. Troughs of stuff for putting on small plates and standing around while chatting people up and doing deals. She'd never *done* business, but had dated a girl once who was all about that shit. Forever hustling.

Eggrolls. Samosas. Taquitos. Human finger food that doubled as comfort food in most cultures. Everything labeled by ingredients, so you didn't eat something bad. Useful when a quarter of the folks in here weren't Human and probably had to pay closer attention to things.

"You need fattening up," she announced, pointing at the hot stuff.

Rachel moved to the salad bar and went heavy on protein with some chicken and bacon over her greens. They ended up at a standing table off to one side. Got drinks delivered from a waiter wandering around. Observed.

Sixty people in here roughly, as folks came and went. Nobody but staff wore black, but she and Greyson were dark enough in charcoal gray to blend in if they wanted. Others were bloody peacocks and peahens.

Whatever.

She was concentrating on the dozen or so non-Humans she could see. G'schtack, certainly. About half, because they were the most common aliens in the solar system. None she recognized personally.

That one Nese was back. Looked around and spotted her

standing there, but apparently decided the scowl on her face wasn't foreplay, so he ended up across the way.

A Mooz, just like Zentra Izelth who had died on the Moon and caused all this craziness to occur. Tall Humanoids, but with far more body hair. Wide faces with small jaws. Teeth that were mostly points for eating meat, like a dog. Ears that stuck out straight sideways to points about six inches long, like some fantasy character come to life.

She'd heard them called *Bugbears* in her time, the same way Phrenic were usually referred to by Human cops as *Freaks*.

A G'schtack in a fancy, blue uniform entered the lounge now and looked around. Female, so even shorter than Rachel's five-foot-two. Gray skin. Cartoon ears that were lower on the head and stuck out farther than a Human's.

The woman spied them and immediately moved this direction. Rachel felt Greyson become aware of her by the way he did the opposite of tensing up. It was like he turned completely liquid, standing next to her, ready to flow into any new form necessary.

Weird, but she'd been around the boy long enough now to understand that as a danger signal.

Greyson Leigh, preparing to kill extravagantly if it became necessary.

Rachel smiled at the woman to draw the fire down on her instead.

"Leigh and Asher?" the woman asked as she got close.

Rachel noted that while she had a bit of an accent, her voice could have gotten her famous if she'd had a gig on radio anywhere. Smooth, sultry, rich. Coming from a short, gray, alien, mammalian biped.

"That's right," Rachel answered first.

"I'm Captain Boppa Sheedo," she said. "Commander of this vessel."

"What can we do for you, Captain?" Rachel asked politely.

"I'm given to understand, from my legal departments, that both of you are currently armed," Sheedo replied in a crisp voice right on the verge of angry now.

"That is correct," Rachel nodded. "We are sworn Officers of the Court, currently on an investigation for Virgar Andell, the G'schtack Engineering Master of Armstrong Base, and working at least tangentially under his authority."

Shit, studying Guildlaw was going to get her into so much trouble, wasn't it?

Rachel didn't smile at the woman, but wanted to. She and Greyson had talked, and come to the conclusion that Andell must be so much more than he seemed, if he could make the Hunter Bureau do things against their will. Or any of the other Human governments that came into shape over the last sixteen years.

Was he maybe the top-ranking Guild Member around? Nobody could say. Nobody they'd talked to, anyway.

Sheedo grimaced. That spoke volumes.

"I am instructed that the Human Hunter Bureau has precedence in this situation, as you are on a case," the Captain said. "I would greatly prefer not to have any incidents before delivering you to Brees."

"As would we, Captain Sheedo," Rachel said, noting that Greyson was relaxing some, but still silent and utterly still. "However, Guild criminals are on the run from us and even think they might manage to get away, so we are currently, technically, in hot pursuit, with all that those statutes imply."

She didn't know if G'schtack ground their teeth like Humans, but that was the sound coming from the woman now.

Not like Rachel hadn't *specifically* prepared for this conversation at some point. Or anything silly like that.

"Just so we understand one another, Detectives," Sheedo said.

She gave them a cursory scowl, turned on her heel, and departed. Rachel watched her go, noting that from behind, she looked Human enough.

Just completely hairless, like many Guild species. Humans and Mooz were the ones with body hair, as a rule. G'schtack and Balo had none, anywhere.

"That was interesting," Rachel noted as they were alone again.

"Bureaucrats," Greyson muttered, as if that covered everything.

It might, as far as he was concerned. Rachel wasn't as cynical and hoped she never got there.

"Eat," she instructed him, returning to her salad and watching him cram an eggroll into his mouth as an excuse not to talk.

They had a long flight to get to Brees. Hopefully, it would be a quiet one.

FIVE
BREAKFASTING

GREYSON HAD SETTLED into something of a new routine. The coffee sucked, but that was him. He had a complicated ritual for his mornings, and the beans here, like everywhere, tended to be roasted too dark for his tastes. Plus, he made each mug by hand back home with individually picked ingredients.

Pushing a couple of buttons and having a super-advanced coffee robot spit out a mug was too much like being back at the office. It had taken him nearly two days and six tries to get the programming even close to right.

Next time, he was going to download the robot specs from the machines on the sixth floor and just carry them around for machines like this.

Next time? You think you'll turn into the scourge cop of the spaceways, old man?

Greyson listened to that cynic growl in his mind. Wasn't Ethen. She had a different tone, most of the time. More curious, though less frightened these days.

No, that was an old Master Sergeant he'd had to deal with, back in the assassin days. Not the drill instructor who created Greyson Leigh, but the later man who made sure Greyson kept his qualifications up later.

Old killer, which was a rarity in their business. Even older than Greyson was now, which put the man into an elite and lonely category. One where he'd watched most of his comrades die or be too broken to continue.

Greyson didn't know what the future would bring him. Just over a year ago, Olek Zielinski had come walking out of the mist to offer Greyson his old life back. Virgar Andell had been there that day, though Greyson hadn't known him then. Before that, he'd been retired with his two pensions, his classical music, and his cheap, synth whiskey.

Now, he was a cop, on a case, tracking a perp halfway across the civilized galaxy. And introducing Rachel to the folks that would make Scotland Yard look like a kindergarten class.

And that still didn't make his top ten list for weird this year.

Morning. Way early, because it had taken him about six hours to adjust to ship's time, which was set to Brees City, on Brees. Starships were constant things. Especially civilian cruise liners like this.

But Greyson had his rituals. That included a cup of robot juice and the news. They were still close enough to Earth to read it in real time, lagging just a few hours.

There were few stairs to run up and down on this ship, so he had too much pent-up energy. Caused him to wake up before the roosters.

Greyson finished his coffee and decided to head out. Rachel would ping him when she was awake. Find him in the commons, either eating or reading the latest news.

He needed to move.

Ritual was acceptable, but predictability was not. Greyson went down a level and aft to a small restaurant tucked in a quiet corner. A shade upscale for Third-class. More like a mom-and-pop diner in a small town in Oregon. Honest portions. Simple food. Mostly Americanized, so fried instead of a Continental or Asian style.

He got three eggs and extra sausage because Rachel had been right. Transformations burned a lot of energy, and he tended to eat the same amount of calories every day. Fighting trim, as the Master Sergeant had always said.

He was alone right now. Not even other customers because it was so early. The fishing crew would have been here with him, but the civilians and vacationers were operating later in their day.

Just how he liked it.

Greyson looked up when she entered the room. Captain Sheedo. She'd left them alone after delivering her canned lines and implicit threats. That was good. He knew the statutes Rachel had been quoting to the woman, and could cause this woman all sorts of grief when they got to the next stop, if he needed to.

Or just wanted to.

The look on her face was not promising. Worse, she flagged down the Human waitress for a menu and ordered some aniet. It was the G'schtack equivalent of weak coffee or strong tea, depending on how you took it. Hot water infusion through vegetable matter to impart color, flavor, and certain trace chemicals. Coffee-like because it had the G'schtack version of caffeine in it.

She moved to the space Rachel would have been in and gestured.

Greyson shrugged. Eggs, sausage, and toast didn't take long to cook. He expected them about the time her aniet arrived.

They stared at each other for a few moments. Greyson drank his coffee. The waitress delivered aniet and fixings.

Captain Sheedo had her own ritual similar to Greyson's. No honey or coconut milk, but all the same touches and motions.

She doctored her mug. He sipped at his. The waitress delivered his food, plus his Cholula hot sauce. He couldn't eat eggs without it, nor much else. Too many years of Army commissary food and questionable meals in questionable places. A few dots of hot sauce killed most nasties you might eat.

Kept him alive. Even Ethen just grunted at Greyson's rituals, though he supposed she might be able to handle just about anything that came along. And she was closer to the surface than she had been for a while.

Eggs over easy and runny today. Four links. Sourdough toast. A few more days and he'd be back to a weight that Rachel would stop nagging him. Hopefully.

He made a mess, cutting up the eggs and flopping them on the toast. Then stuffing it in his mouth. All they were missing around here were breakfast burritos. He'd have to find a place that did them. Pretty soon, they would be to the first stop, and Greyson expected the Human population of the ship to decline significantly as a percentage, so food options would shift.

Sheedo sipped her aniet and watched his performance. He supposed it was a performance. Better to eat than talk. Words to live by.

"You don't talk much," she announced.

Greyson stuffed another bite into his mouth and chewed, washing it down with fresh coffee as the Human waitress refilled his mug.

Needed stuff. He paused and fixed it up with more honey and milk. Then took another bite.

"I had a conversation over the line with Virgar Andell," she continued, once she decided he wasn't going to engage in verbal fencing with the woman. "And I read about the Phrenic infestation on your moon."

He sipped and watched her. Short, hairless, gray. Bald Human woman in the dark. None of Rachel's muscles or hard curves, but also the G'schtack equivalent of middle-aged.

Greyson ignored her and went for a sausage.

"You killed the Phrenic impersonating the Legal Affairs Officer with the nerve scrambler under your left arm," Sheedo announced quietly.

"Rachel did," Greyson said around a mouth of spiced pork. Not bad stuff, either. Better than the Army, anyway.

Never let someone give you credit for another's kill. Old Army lesson, too. The truth always comes out.

Of course, the real truth would get him killed. He sipped some coffee.

"Andell told me exactly enough to guess that you are still on that case," Sheedo continued after long enough that he could have added something. "Pursuing some other avenue he would not discuss."

As if Greyson wanted to discuss things with her.

He washed down the sausage with some more coffee. She had some aniet and waited.

Greyson went back for more eggs. He had a lot of toast to enjoy.

"What do you expect to find on Brees?" she asked now.

Greyson speared her with a scowl good enough that he got a defensive flinch.

"Criminals."

Then he speared another sausage and gnawed on it.

"I do not understand you, Detective Leigh." She tried a new tack. "The crimes occurred on your moon, orbiting Earth. The criminals are all dead or facing trial. What else is there? You have no reason to go out-system."

He wondered if she was just fishing, or was maybe bent enough that she thought she could sell someone a warning to flee before he got to them. The ship was moving slow enough, and stopping a couple of places along the way. It would be possible to get a letter to Brees on a courier if you wanted to pay the expense.

Or had a reason to fear the truth coming out.

Greyson had finished his eggs. And two of the sausages. He had jam and more toast to stretch this out all day if he wanted. Plus coffee.

She looked like the kind of woman who had patience to sit here that long. He would admit that she might be almost as stubborn as him. Like Rachel.

And few others.

"My current jurisdiction contains the entire Illymus Merchant Guild," he said in a slow, ugly voice. "Every single inhabited planet admitted to date. Plus anywhere else somebody thinks might be far enough away to escape me. Your job is to get me to Brees. Nothing more. Maybe the bad people don't see me coming. Maybe I have to chase them on to R'Onar or points farther."

He went back to his sausage as she gasped. R'Onar was the original homeworld of the G'schtack, before everyone important moved to the more central world of Brees. Kind of like the drive from Plymouth Rock to New York City, back home.

She waited. He held up his mug for more coffee from a waitress watching the whole thing with her jaw dropped open. Quiet room. She'd heard his words over there.

Sheedo sipped her aniet. Greyson adulterated his coffee. Dug the jam out of a glass jar and slathered something purple on the sourdough. Didn't know the flavor. Didn't really care. Carbs and sugar. Fattening him back up so he had the energy to chase people forever.

Because that was what he did.

She ran out of patience before he ran out of food. Stood her tiny self up and nodded. Almost a bow. Silent. Turned and walked away.

Nearly ran into Rachel, coming through the door, so his partner had assumed he'd be up early and asked the ship's systems to find him. They did that, as long as you didn't have a reason to block it. That was how Captain Sheedo had found him, no doubt.

The two women danced briefly, separated, and Rachel headed this way.

"I miss anything interesting?" she asked as she sat across from him and noted that the chair was warm. "She seemed…flustered."

Greyson shrugged. He still had food to consume. And little patience for games this morning. Even Rachel, though she got a lot more slack than a G'schtack stranger.

"She had questions," Greyson offered.

"You give her any answers?"

"None that mattered."

"She a friend or an enemy?" Rachel asked as the waitress came with more coffee.

"We'll see," Greyson nodded.

SIX

LITTLE MISS PERFECT BOOBS

RACHEL HAD READ MOST of the various genres of romance in her time. They filled a hole in her mind by stroking just the right emotions. She'd even wandered down the rabbit hole of cop/alien romance for a while before she'd realized how it must have looked to Greyson. Or Ethen.

Icky, in retrospect. So she'd swapped sub-genres sideways. Still hot and extremely heavy, but historical stuff now, back before the aliens came along and carbonated everybody's hormones. The books were mostly about power relationships, anyway.

Rich guy in some fancy and exotic culture that let the writer nerd out on historical details. Poor girl with a pretty face. Fish out of water sequences as they each explore the other's world. Separate when they decide they can't span that cultural divide. Come back together at the end with the help of some friends convincing them to gamble on happily-ever-after.

You never read for the plot. Those were almost paint-by-numbers simple. You read for interesting characters and fascinating places, ignoring the historical inaccuracies where nobody bathed and dentists hadn't been invented yet. Gods, the smells must have been horrible.

Rachel liked getting lost in the setting. And the sex. The new stuff included some good kinks that occasionally involved a woman riding on the back of a horse, bent over nude as she was being taken from behind by the guy in the stirrups. Something about the rhythm of the hooves.

Rachel flashed back to Captain Sheedo and the look she'd seen on the woman's face as they nearly ran into each other at the door. Flustered. Hot and bothered, even. Horseback, at least in her mind.

She could see that. Greyson Leigh, when he'd been Human, had had lots of women chasing after him. He'd even let a few catch him, like the future Metropolitan of the Eastern Metroplex or the powerful businesswoman and Argentine Tango dancer Emmy.

These days, he made her hand out business cards on an investigation, just so nobody tracked him down later. And being born again had just made it worse. Now, he had so much competence porn going on that Rachel could occasionally *hear* tongues wagging as they walked away.

He, however, had a really good grumble going today. Top shelf stuff. Sheedo must have made a dumb power move and messed it up. Rachel would find out later, when he was in a less-grouchy mood.

She couldn't say a good mood. She doubted he'd hit that level at all until he got back to his flat and Emmy. His cheap booze from the corner shop. Something to cheer him up. At least good enough at some point.

She ordered some breakfast.

"Sheedo apparently talked to Andell," Greyson said out of the blue when they were alone.

"He tell her anything?"

"No, but she's smart enough to put two and two

together," he groused. "Not like this case is even that complicated right now."

"Not until we hit Brees," she nodded.

He agreed and finished his last sausage. She might have stolen it, but he needed to eat. Greyson had even stopped arguing with her on that point.

"What happens when we get there?" she asked. "News going to travel with us?"

"Might already be there," Greyson shrugged. "However, certain information should have supposedly died with our friends, so folks back there might not expect us to swoop in. We still won't have long. Anyone else with a modicum of smarts can also put two and two together when we arrive."

"Any chance they can get away?" she asked.

"They can run," he offered.

Not the same thing. You could always run. Greyson had an expense account paid for by the Guild. At least for now. At some point, they might decide to jerk his chain short. Especially if he started getting too close to things they wanted hidden.

That was when shit would get serious.

Several years ago, this same man had been rolling up criminal networks with odd and dangerous connections to folks in the Hunter Bureau itself. So a bent captain and his crooked friends had framed Leigh, gotten him thrown off the force in trade for scaling up his pension to twenty years, and then figured they'd gotten away.

Until two Phrenic infiltrators somehow got through immigration controls and were running loose on Earth.

Rachel had seen the scanners on the station behind them. She had reached out to Dave to scan Greyson ahead of time to make sure what they should expect. Might not have mattered, considering how cheap the Guild equipment was.

Still, better safe than sorry.

"So if this is an officially-sanctioned thing, then what?" she asked.

They'd chewed on this bone for a week now.

"Can't be," he smiled in a frightening manner. His voice dropped. "I've been looking at the statutes, and they forbid research on intelligence species, intelligence having been defined in a footnote of a footnote as Guild Membership. They could do it until 2042. After that, we got promoted."

"So Little Miss Perfect Boobs was absolutely a crime, in and of herself, separate from the programming?"

"Indeed." At least his smile got nicer. "Be interesting to see if they have brothels of her, somewhere on Brees."

"Oh shit, Greyson," she muttered. "Sex slaves?"

Now, he shrugged.

"It gets messy," he countered. "If you program them to like it, which is even worse, could we free them without doing emotional damage to the clones? Anais was programmed as a counselor, and did a fantastic job at it, from what we've read, so they got that part of Human psychology correct. But in spite of the plumbing involved, was she really Human? Do they get Guild membership at that point, or have they been modified enough to not count?"

"Yuck."

She hadn't really considered that the laws might protect the creatures. Keep them in slavery. Maybe addict them to it. Yeah, Moral was fucked. Legal might be working against them.

That left Ethical. You could always count on Greyson Leigh to come down on the side of Ethical behavior. Usually with a ton and a half of bricks accompanying him like rabid badgers.

"So what happens if we can't?" she asked after a moment.

"Assassins and Manchurian Candidates are still on the

table, even if they somehow make prostitutes and soldiers acceptable under their code," he said. "If nothing else, I'll tell everyone. Fucking *everyone*. File briefs demanding Freedom of Information Act shit and depositions. Not quite the same legally as back home, but all I have to do is tell a judge when we get there that smugglers haven't been paying taxes on things and I suddenly gain a whole raft of allies and carnivorous accountants."

"Those smugglers are going to have a case of the blues at that point," Rachel grinned. "Maybe blue balls, while we're at it."

"I think if there are brothels, they are likely to be extremely high-end and private," he said now. "I've spent too much time wandering down rabbit holes instead of sleeping."

"Talk to me," she grinned.

The man was intent on making her the best Hunter ever. In her case, he had a thirty-year head start and a career as an assassin for the Army, so Rachel was already learning things far beyond the beat cop shit she had originally signed up for.

"They sent her to Earth," Greyson said. "Programmed to kill specifically one person, then destroy herself before anyone could interrogate her. Hell, it might have been possible to steal some of her memories, like I did Wailos Gritchkan and see the beginning, but that would have created more problems than it was worth."

"So they know the Human form and mind well enough to do this," Rachel said. "What's that get us?"

"They had to know she'd end up being public," Greyson replied. "If folks on Earth found out, they might ask questions, so we can be pretty sure that the general public back on Brees and other places has no idea these things exist. If they do, mind you. Still speculating. At the same time, the folks behind that end of things are advanced enough in their knowledge that someone could call in a favor from someone else on R'Onar, to have a Pleasure Model delivered from Brees after having it programmed to kill Zentra Izelth then itself."

"Shit," Rachel breathed.

Her breakfast was coming, so she shut up at that point to think and eat. Across from her, Greyson had those eyes that said he'd gnawed that bone hard, but they wouldn't—couldn't—know anything until they got to Brees and raided somebody's shop.

She'd hope that something like that would be endgame. Sounded like just the beginning, though.

Like they had a full conspiracy going somewhere. Research the basic Human form. Replicate it in a test tube or something. Perfect it. Program that. Send it under the table to Earth, knowing that it would be destroyed as soon as it completed its mission.

Nobody had counted on Greyson Leigh being put on the case. Worse, Ethen Boli was involved, and that *chicka* had some serious anger issues over sexual slavery things. Seen from the inside, as it were, in more ways than one.

They were alone again. Rachel paused mid-bite, fork halfway to her mouth.

"We could really end up bringing down the current Illymus Merchant Guild, couldn't we?" she asked him.

"That option was always on the table," Leigh replied.

Rachel couldn't help her shudder.

Maybe it had always been there, but now it looked like that might be the single most ethical solution.

And she had the kind of hammer in Greyson Leigh that might solve that problem.

SEVEN

STRANGER

Looking around the tiny bar, Greyson kept his scowl and snarl internal only. Nobody else in the tiny, dark space deserved it. It was his problem, not theirs.

He simply had absolutely no interest in socializing with complete strangers on this trip. Hell, some days Rachel was a little much, but that was a professional relationship, and he could manage that sort of thing. Too bad he didn't have Emmy hissing and biting at any woman wanting to get too close to him.

She'd do that for him, if he asked, as opposed to seducing them herself. He'd even considered asking Rachel, but for now Greyson figured that his natural surliness would be sufficient.

It had been for most of the last forty years.

Except that the ship didn't allow take-out from the bar.

Back home, his usual habit was to refill a one-liter bottle of the cheap synth whiskey he'd gotten hooked on in a previous lifetime and take it home with him. That was usually good for a week or more, depending on things.

He'd sit on his couch at the comfortable end, lights down

and music up. Sip a highball glass while letting the ancient classics envelope him. Tune his mind out and let backbrain ruminate on some topic, usually related to a case he was trying to solve. If he was really into it, he might have a second glass after a few hours.

The ship didn't like that.

He understood. Fears of passengers getting blackout drunk and maybe even surlier than him. Dangerous enough that goons and bruisers would have to be called.

And he was too grumpy about it to walk back for a second glass, considering the number of steps involved from his cabin to the nearest bar. Booze was to be savored with music. Even if someone else was paying for it.

So he was in a space best described as a corner pub in a small New England town. Not the hard-core honkytonk down the street, nor the biker bar the other direction.

The place where Mom and Dad might pop out for a quiet drink after work and before dinner, or after putting the kids away.

This ship—the name translated into English out of G'schtack something close to *Cirri Heavy Irregular*—made regular runs to Earth. He'd gotten lucky enough to find a ship that went all the way to Brees on a spoke run, instead of the smaller ones that usually just went as far as Beahrnz, pronounced almost exactly like the Scottish poet Burns.

Because the ship called on Earth and then headed back to Brees each time, about half of it was decorated and outfitted for Humans, including spaces like this. There were other decks far less comfortable for his type. And that flipped back and forth. Non-Humans weren't likely to be as relaxed on these decks, so weren't all that common.

Thus, the woman walking in and looking around stood out. Balo. Aliens from way the hell across Guildspace, but that didn't mean much when you had a single political system spanning so many light-centuries in every direction.

Nature had settled on a pretty basic design. Physics were physics, after all. Erect biped with tool-using hands. Guild bipeds went from eight fingers all the way up to fourteen on the Xaniea, who had two opposable, opposing thumbs on each hand. Otherwise, the exteriors were all similar. Height, weight, and scale varied, but Humans already did that, from Rachel and smaller up beyond Quinton Laux at six-foot-ten.

Balo were maybe the closest to Human for overall design. Same exterior shell. Ten fingers. Everything arranged in a similar pattern. The only real difference was the complete lack of body hair and the fact that their skin tended to range outward from a kind of lime green a little brighter than the old disease called jaundice.

They didn't have the ethnic range of Humans. Not many species did, though neither Greyson nor Ethen had ever really spent the time to find out why. He supposed that after a few millennia of space flight, all Humanity might settle into a light brown somewhere a touch softer than Rachel's Puerto Rican heritage. Would take a while.

The woman looked around and Greyson felt the surge of interest when she saw him. He considered just getting up and walking out the door right now, glass only half empty, but figured she'd chase him through the corridors if he did.

Predatory. That was what her eyes promised.

He wondered just how dumb that made the woman.

Still, he studied her like he would a victim on a slab. Which brought Anais Manel's utter perfection to mind. No woman wants to be compared to that. She couldn't compete.

Stranger couldn't either, but it wasn't as big a stretch as some women might find it.

Tall and leggy. Maybe five-foot-ten, with dancer's thighs and a bigger chest than Humans normally got when they worked out that hard. Greyson wasn't sure about Balo physiology, so couldn't tell if her chest was normally that size, or she'd had them modified later.

Lots of women did. It was right up there with changing hair color frequently. And mattered about as much to Greyson, other than it would give him insights into her psyche later.

Later?

She looked like there might be a later.

Intent.

Ship's temperature was comfortable for Humans on this deck, so she wore capri pants in a bright copper color, like a new penny. Silver blouse that shimmered with glitter or something in the fabric itself, fortunately thick enough to obscure colors.

Tight enough to show shapes.

No hair, which threw him off a bit, but her skull had nice symmetry and seemed to glow with some inner light he supposed was either good health or better cosmetics.

Greyson wondered what sexual signals Balo gave each other. Humans had so much communication wound up in hair, of all the options in nature.

She moved from the bar to a nearby table that let her sit facing him. The blouse was unbuttoned strategically, showing the valley of her cleavage and promising more if you wanted to move close and stand over her. She seemed to be inviting it.

He sipped at his whiskey and wondered how long he could string this out before he had to get up and order another glass, or make a break for the door and try to evade a slide-tackle.

She smiled at him as if reading his mind. Or at least his discomfort.

Greyson doubted that she knew anything about him.

Only the Captain and a few of her officers knew that he and Rachel were cops. The rest would see them as traveling business companions, with separate cabins and connected lives.

Let them make of it what they would.

And he'd heard all the stories of sordid, shipboard affairs. That transcended Humanity and seemed to come with travel on any kind of ship, anywhere in the galaxy. Hell, there was a popular G'schtack vidshow back home, dubbed into English and centered around a ship like this, and all the romances and dirty dealing that went on, week after week. Adding Humans to the Guild had just opened the plot lines up a little and added new markets for syndication.

He'd even had to watch a few episodes at one point, dating a woman who was totally engaged in the soap opera element of it.

Thankfully, Emmy liked to dance in her free time.

Greyson sat and sipped his whiskey, thinking dark and malevolent thoughts about the galaxy.

Didn't do any good. After a time, the stranger rose and walked closer, glass of something he took for their equivalent of wine in one hand. Round and stemmed, instead of square and bottom-heavy like his.

The place around them was relatively empty. He and Rachel made it a point to eat many meals together to talk case, but then separate so as to not get on each other's nerves.

That might have been a mistake tonight.

The Balo woman walked closer. Smiled at him. Used her face and posture to ask if she could sit at this table. Showed off her amazingly-long body and round curves to best presentation. Maybe stalking him. Maybe he'd just drawn the short straw today.

He shrugged and nodded. They were getting close to Beahrnz, but that just meant that he had a day or two before she might get off the vessel and go away. Greyson didn't think he'd be that lucky.

Better to deal with it now.

She sat, almost grace itself as she moved. Dancer, or whatever the Balo equivalent was.

Exuded the kinds of confidence that had drawn his eye to Denise or Emmy the first time, too.

Her skin wasn't quite the brightness of a marigold, but the lights were low in here. Romantic, he supposed was the intent.

"Greyson Leigh," he said, figuring he might as well just get it over with. And he spoke in G'schtack, just to make it easier for everyone. She probably spoke a couple of Earth languages, if she'd gone to this effort. "And you might be?"

"Lissa Jonez," she replied, accent not that bad. Maybe like a Quebecois being forced to speak to lowly Ottowans in English. "You looked like an interesting man, Greyson Leigh."

He fought not to let his native and trained paranoia overwhelm things. That might be an innocent comment, designed to play to the average guy's ego and vanity. Get them to talking. Guys did that when they got nervous, especially around a beautiful woman. You wanted to impress her that you had a brain and ended up doing all the talking instead of asking her questions.

Not that he'd ever learned the way to seduce a pretty girl by listening to them, or anything.

"Everybody is interesting," he countered. "The key is finding people whose hobbies and interests appeal enough to find common ground."

There, let her make of that what she would.

His own mother would have made a clucking sound with her tongue and described the woman as *forward*, using the ancient references from when *her* grandmother had been young.

Greyson didn't mind forward women. Preferred them, actually, because they tended to lead the most engrossing lives, not sitting around waiting for things to happen.

Like picking up strange alien men on starships.

"Oh?" she asked, one delicate eyebrow arching.

Except that they didn't have eyebrows. Or any hair beyond lashes. The flesh had a ridge there instead. Seemed to serve the same purpose, keeping sweat out of the eyes and communicating non-verbally.

"And what sorts of hobbies and *interests* do you pursue, Leigh?" she continued, her emphasis making the rest of the conversation all the more obvious.

"Earth stuff, mostly," he offered. "I was born before the sky opened, so all the options from beyond that are a little lost on me."

He wondered if she'd take that as a polite rejection. Her eyes glittered with a hint of excitement instead.

"And yet you are traveling at least as far as Beahrnz," she replied. "Something out in the wider galaxy must have drawn you."

The more he listened to her, the more it was like hearing a French girl talk. Something about the way her vowels slid around really worked, rendered in G'schtack. He wondered if she'd sound half as interesting in English.

"Going as far as Brees right now," he said. "Not sure after that."

The way her whole face lit up told him that she was also traveling at least that far.

He wondered just how far she might go.

"And what awaits you on Brees?" she asked, leaning forward just like a Human woman did in that way that brought all the cleavage to bear on a guy.

He paused to be impressed by it before returning to her eyes. Like her skin, they were yellowish, but more electric gold. Pretty.

"Criminals," Greyson smiled at her now. "I'm a cop, back home. A Hunter. My partner and I are pursuing a case."

Right about now, a civilian who might have secrets—deals under the table and the like—would clam right up. She did not.

"A hunter? Did I hear you right?" Lissa asked, cocking her head in that confused way that must have been universal. "What do you hunt?"

Greyson smiled. He had an out that would save him. Nobody liked Hunters, once they understood what he and Rachel really did. Doubly so in the Guild, where they didn't really do violence on the sorts of scales that Humans took for granted.

"Dangerous aliens that come to Earth to hurt people," he said. "The Hunter Bureau exists to stop them. To understand how to take them down hard and fast before more people get hurt."

He smiled at her now as her brain caught up with the fact that he killed aliens for a living. Like her.

Her whole being spasmed once, at least psychologically. Lissa's face fell completely slack for a long moment.

Greyson took another sip of his whiskey. In his head, he flipped a coin as to whether she would storm off right now, or become so aroused that she couldn't sit still. He'd seen both in his time. That described most of the women who'd ever really understood what he did.

"Take them down?" she asked in a slow cadence where each word grew more accented.

"Frequently, kill them," he said, matter-of-fact. "The most recent case involved at least one Phrenic who had killed a Human and was impersonating her."

Ah, the flinch. *Everybody* had nightmares about Phrenic. Slip in the window when you slept. Kill you. Steal your entire life and maybe live it better than you ever had.

Or something like that.

She was breathing faster now. Adrenaline spiking her system into fight-or-flight. Or arousal. Hard to tell with an alien. Even a beautiful woman.

"You are a killer?" she asked, sounding positively French now.

Greyson nodded and sipped his whiskey. He was getting low, so either he needed more, or they would be out of time shortly.

Or something like that.

"How about you, Lissa Jonez?" Greyson segued lightly across the entirety of civilized space in a single sentence. "What do you do?"

Educational, watching someone's mental processes break down and have to reboot. Like now. She held perfectly still for three seconds and then breathed out.

"I travel," she managed. "Eventually, my goal is to see all of the planets that make up the Guild."

"Fascinating hobby," Greyson nodded. And it was. Utterly bizarre, but still fascinating. "What made you choose that?"

Her eyes got shrewd, like he'd finally tangoed her back onto ground she understood. She reeked of wealth and breeding. Almost like an aristocratic scion with more money than they knew what to do with and no expectation that they ever had to do anything at all with their lives.

He couldn't imagine a more boring and banal form of existence, but the Army had taken a hollow, redneck gearhead, and pounded him into a weapon. Always moving, because stopping meant that someone could catch you. Find you. Kill you.

Unless you killed them first, then had to wait for their friends.

He'd been compared to a shark by people who understood the real him.

"One world seems to be much like the other, at least where I came from," Lissa offered now. "So I decided to see them all."

"How was Earth?" Greyson asked.

They'd just left. He would assume she'd spent some time down there.

"The Southern California Metroplex seemed to go on forever in brown," she said. "The Tokyo Metroplex seemed to be a brightly-lit museum. Or perhaps amusement park dedicated to a lost past they don't want forgotten."

Greyson had been to LA, back when it was a place. Before the Metroplex culture redefined the world. It did go on forever. And Japan was falling slowly into their dreams, turning inward rather than admitting that they were becoming irrelevant. Hell, even Beijing was sliding into senescence these days.

Only parts of Western Asia, South America, and most of Africa were really growing anymore. None of them had had any power or privilege to lose when the aliens decided that Human culture was all wrong and needed to be fixed.

Greyson nodded.

"Have you seen many places, Greyson Leigh?" she asked, again in an innocent tone.

"I traveled widely when I was younger," he said, leaving it at that.

Not where. Not what. Especially not why.

"But not now?" Lissa asked leadingly. "Aren't you going all the way to Brees?"

"At least," he nodded. "Maybe farther, if they run."

"Run?"

"Bad people, doing hideously terrible things to innocents," Greyson channeled his surliness now. "They need to be stopped. If they run, I just have to keep chasing them."

"And kill them?" she asked, sounding right on the edge of horrified.

"It is a short step from doing bad things to Humans, to doing them to G'schtack," he said. "Or Balo."

"You recognize my kind?" she sounded surprised.

Greyson wasn't. Most Humans barely recognized the difference between Chinese and Vietnamese, let alone being able to name any of the alien species beyond maybe the G'schtack. And even then they would often default to *Grays*.

"Indeed," Greyson nodded. "Perhaps the most like Humans of all the Guild species. At least physically."

"And otherwise?" she cocked her head at him again, back to playing games.

"People are people," Greyson replied. "They range the entire spectrum: intellectually, emotionally, or psychologically."

"I was right," Lissa smiled. "You are an interesting man, Greyson Leigh."

He shrugged. Beauty and beholders, he supposed. He saw himself as a simple man, with simple hobbies and interests. Sportsball conversations were more painful than watching mold grow. He solved crimes and listened to music. Danced when Emmy felt the need.

Not much more.

"And what are you doing to fill your days until you reach Brees?" Lissa asked.

"My partner and I are in a holding pattern," Greyson said, suggesting that there was more that she didn't know. "Mostly she's studying advanced criminal law and I'm teaching her more about the Guild."

He liked that little flinch when the woman understood

that his partner was female. Make of that what you will. Then confusion set in again.

"I thought you said you had not traveled, Leigh," she said.

"Call me Greyson," he replied. "I haven't. What I have done is spend many years understanding every alien that might be a threat to Humanity. Physically. Emotionally. Culturally."

"I see," she nodded. "And are Balo a threat, Greyson?"

"They can be, if they set their mind to it," he grinned. "You look like a dangerously-interesting woman, Lissa."

She smiled. Did something that drew his eyes down the front of her blouse again to appreciate her breasts. Leaned more towards him, Greyson supposed. They were nice breasts. Nothing under that blouse but skin.

"So if I wanted to proposition you for a few hours of sexual escapades, you might not object?" she asked.

He supposed it sounded better in Balo. Or English. Probably closer to *Come back to my place for a nightcap*. Or something. Her accent made it cute and charming.

On the other hand, Ofiyana had offered the same sort of thing, back on the Moon. Except she'd had other things in mind. Killing him and stealing his memories. He knew that because that's what he and Rachel had done to her instead. Him. Wailos.

It got complicated, separating a Phrenic from their latest victim, when trying to sort out a conversation.

I got your back, Ethen whispered in the back of Greyson's mind now, reminding him that he was actually a Phrenic who forgot that occasionally. She'd stepped right up and saved his life from Wailos. Taken that asshole down hard enough that Rachel could shoot the punk.

Greyson considered it. Couldn't find a reason to say no, beyond his natural surliness. And he had a lot of that, but this woman didn't deserve any of it. She looked like a spoiled, rich woman who wanted something to break up her endless monotony of traveling from place to place because she didn't have any bigger dreams than running from her past, most likely.

He'd known a few like her, though all Human. The Human mind needs something to do, or it rots. You do things, or you sit passively waiting to die one day.

He had a lot of other things to accomplish first. Apparently, it seemed, making love to a horny Balo woman who'd set out to pick up an alien stranger in a bar.

But then, Greyson Leigh had done weirder things.

He shot the last dribbles of whiskey and set the glass down softly, smiling at her.

"That sounds like fun," he said.

She smiled, so he rose and took her hand.

Brees was still a ways away. And it looked like he might have some interesting things to distract his brain from the case while he stalked his foe.

Nobody ever said that law enforcement had to be dull.

EIGHT

PROMISES

Rachel walked carefully past the table where Greyson was seated and made her way to the far side. Then she stopped, stepped back, and leaned down to sniff his shoulder.

Yeah, that was what she thought she'd smelled.

She grinned as the boy blushed, then plopped her happy ass down across from him. Rachel waved to the waitress for some coffee and studied her partner's face.

"You look relaxed," she observed innocently, just to watch his blush double.

Credit him that much. Badass, hardass Greyson Leigh just shrugged and sipped some more coffee.

"It was an interesting night," he offered blandly.

Rachel nodded. Sure. Whatever you want to call it. Found someone to take you off line so hard you didn't notice that she'd left her perfume on you this morning.

And it was a she. Guys wouldn't wear something that floral and sweet unless they were presenting as girls anyway. And Greyson was het, as far as she knew, killer alien babe inside notwithstanding. That would make any encounter a little weird, when you were fucking a mesomorph who could be anything with a little planning and some cold-blooded murder.

Rachel was far more flexible on those things, but she was a whole generation younger than the old man. Folks didn't care as much these days, once Greyson's grandparents finally all died off and took most of their stupid ideas with them.

"We want to walk around the concourse at Beahrnz this afternoon?" she asked.

"If the ship was going to be around long enough, I'd drop down to the surface, just to let you walk on an alien world, but we're only in for about eight hours of loading and unloading, so it's not really worth it."

She noticed that he was speaking in G'schtack instead of English. Might not even notice, so she'd been an alien babe, too. And she'd be a babe. It would take a complicated combination of things to get Greyson Leigh's attention. That was why Emmy and Metropolitan Upkins before that were who they were.

"So," Rachel changed the subject. "Kinda surprised you didn't end up having breakfast with her. Gonna see her again?"

"We have an understanding," Greyson shrugged, still jarred a shade off his usual self, so she must have been a tiger in bed. "I do breakfast with you. Then maybe I see her for another meal or maybe afternoon tea or something."

"Sounds serious," Rachel smiled. "I get to be the mom inspecting and making sure she's good enough for you?"

"Not really," he growled. "She's an heiress who doesn't want to handle the business. I expect to have some sort of fling with her until we reach Brees, then likely never see the woman again."

Rachel kept her snort of derision to herself. Poor boy didn't understand competence porn and the effect his awesomeness might have on a lonely woman. Especially one looking for a *fling* on a starship.

Privately, she made a bet with herself that the stranger might take an extended holiday on Brees for reasons not readily apparent to most bystanders.

Coffee got served. Breakfast got ordered. Life went on.

"So I gotta ask," Rachel broke the silence. "She's not a spy, right?"

"Nothing interesting is written down," Greyson countered. "It is all in our heads, for the most part. If she wants to try to fuck the information out of me, she'll be at it a while, not that I mind much."

"Just remember that you have to break her heart later," Rachel said.

It was a low blow, but Greyson Leigh was living on borrowed time and they both knew it. At any moment, someone might denounce him for what he really was, and then they would kill Ethen immediately. Or suspicions would grow and she'd have to tell her best friend in the galaxy that his time was done, after which one of several ugly scenarios might play out.

Personally, she liked the kidnapping and ransom one, as it let him go out a hero whose body was never found. Let Greyson Leigh be remembered for being the best Hunter that the Bureau had ever produced.

So far. Rachel wondered if she might be able to tell her own student the truth, one of these days. Or just end up being better than a guy like Greyson Leigh.

At least he nodded.

"Aware of that, Rachel," he grumbled. "Not the first time. Might not be the last time. Shit happens and nobody ever promised you tomorrow."

She nodded. Nobody promised you tomorrow.

"And I doubt she's a spy," he continued with a weary

smile. "I might have spent a lot of time around a certain class of people, about the time you were born. They did teach me a few things. She's just lonely and horny. I can help."

Rachel nodded. She'd considered doing something similar, but most men didn't like to deal with the fact that she was probably smarter than they were, and much tougher.

Human men, she amended herself. What alien guys might not have those kinds of wiring issues to overcome? And an alien meant that she wasn't going to get pregnant along the way.

Maybe she should find herself a chef or something. A professional artist who did his or her own competence porn and didn't end up competing with a killer cop.

Hell, they were kind of on vacation, at least until they started getting close to Brees. She hadn't really had time to goof off since…when? She'd been fourteen?

Even in high school, she'd set her sights on being a cop and eventually turning herself into a chief somewhere. Or a Captain of Detectives, like Rutherford Parsons back in Boston. Full-time job. Full-time night school, constantly reading books and writing papers, taking tests at her own pace because her school was all about remote learning for people with busy lives.

And she wasn't that far from done. Throw in an undergraduate degree and a whole bunch of new doors opened. Leigh could kick most of them down himself, but didn't want to. She could respect that. He was doing the thing he wanted to do most in life, and would continue, even if she got a job at Scotland Yard as a boss and opened a lateral slot for a man like him to come over.

And London would do that. Anybody would jump at the chance to get Greyson Leigh for their department.

Rachel smiled.

"Okay," she said. "Just as long as she doesn't break your heart, then."

He shrugged. She wasn't surprised at that. Greyson had always been an exquisitely private man. The new version of him had secrets that would get him killed.

Made a guy even lonelier than Rachel got.

He deserved a little happiness.

Rachel kept her sarcasm to herself for now.

NINE
STING

GREYSON HAD EXPLAINED himself to Lissa, at least as much as she needed to know. How much he didn't like crowds and noise. So instead of going to see a movie at the big cinema with all the pounding noise to give him a headache, they'd ended up in her cabin, turned sideways on the couch with her back against his chest and his hands enjoying her breasts as they watched a film.

There were far worse ways to go through life.

Credits rolled and she hopefully had a better understanding of Human culture now, having watched one of his favorite oldies. *The Sting.*

Lissa rolled over now and they ended up touching noses as the room fell to silence.

"Humans are weird," she said with the sort of earnestness that only an alien can manage with a straight face.

He kissed her.

"Yup."

"And Earth was like that just five generations ago?" she asked, turning a little to cuddle in on his lap.

"We were just starting to seriously explore our solar system with manned craft about the time you showed up," he said. "Hell, the first powered flight ever took place only a generation before that movie came out. And we landed a rocket on the moon about a generation later."

Balo lived for about two hundred and fifty years, converted. She might have been alive when Armstrong and Aldrin got there.

"Busy," she pronounced.

Greyson couldn't really argue that point with her. Many of the Guild species lived longer lives than Humans. He supposed that better health technology and overall living might change that in another hundred years. He'd be dead.

At least Greyson would. Phrenics could live much longer lives, since they had such perfect control of their biology.

Greyson kissed her on the cheek rather than comment on having the need to accomplish more when you had less time to do it. She'd already spent decades traveling the spaceways.

He felt a shiver take hold of the woman and wrapped his arms around her for warmth. Silence filled the room, but that was normal. Neither of them had to speak just because they found the silence oppressive.

"I have enjoyed this time," she said quietly. "We will be at Brees in a few days and I find myself already sad at missing you."

Greyson leaned down to kiss her on the top of her bald skull.

"I had never anticipated that something like this might occur," he said honestly. "And I am glad that it did."

"Truly?" she asked, turning again like a restless cat to look him in the eyes.

"You are a most interesting woman, Lissa," he told her. "In spite of the shell of mundanity you carry around yourself to hide behind."

"That sounds remarkably like someone else I know," she grinned.

He nodded. They both had secrets. Pains. Broken hearts.

She knew Greyson Leigh killed people. Not much beyond that, though she had looked up the case at Armstrong. None of the really good bits had come out before the ship had transitioned to hyperspace, so it was more supermarket tabloid crap. He'd told her a bit of the truth, just because he'd woken her up in the dead of night with his own nightmares.

Even unconscious, though, he was still Greyson Leigh, and not Ethen Boli.

At the same time, he knew she was an only child who had already inherited wealth almost on a planetary scale. She could have owned her own ship, but then would have been alone, so she just traveled, looking for something to keep her interested.

He wondered if his existence might have crossed that threshold.

She snuggled. They filled the couch because she was almost as tall as he was.

"Would the deadly, dangerous Greyson Leigh be offended if I also departed the ship at Brees?" she asked after a time. "We made no promises beyond the moment you arrived there, but I find myself greedy for more, even though you will be busy raising hell and disrupting the whole of the Merchant Guild with your investigations."

He hadn't said anything about what was really coming. At the same time, after a few weeks in close company, she seemed to have a pretty good hold on the kind of guy he was.

It had helped, that very first night when she'd watched him remove both a palmstunner and a nerve scrambler from holsters and put them on a shelf. He'd had to explain what they were.

That had brought it home to her. Then she'd demanded he fuck her utterly beyond silly. The first of many times, as a matter of fact.

"I can't make any promises about my free time," Greyson replied to both her questions. "The case will be complicated and ugly, because the kinds of prey I am stalking won't want to come quietly when I arrive to capture them. And there might be political ramifications."

"They cloned a Human to assassinate a Mooz," she said in a dread-filled voice. "At least that was what was being said at the time. And you haven't denied it. Can they do that?"

"Can they? Absolutely," he answered. "*Should* they is a much richer and more complicated conversation I want to have with someone. They might not appreciate it, though."

She shivered. Sheltered rich woman who had never been elbows deep in fresh blood, unlike the other half of the couch. Greyson had done a lot of things. Most of them were classified at a level that maybe only supremely-powerful aliens like the Engineering Master of Armstrong Base might know any shard of the truth.

"And I would not be offended, if you happened to be staying in the same hotel as Rachel and I," he continued, understanding that she was waiting for permission before doing something so silly as chasing after a man. Even a guy like him.

She looked up at him and he kissed her. Pulled her close enough to squish her against his chest. It took Lissa a moment to get involved, then she rolled off him and stood up.

"You should take me to bed immediately," she announced. "Like one of your characters in that silly movie."

He slid off the couch and rose. She'd gotten an education in the various oddities of Humans over the last month. He'd been prepared to say that they would always have Paris, and it might yet come to that. At least he got tonight.

Shortly, he'd be under green skies and two stars.

Hunting.

TEN

HUNTERS

Rachel had made sure the boy got his laundry completely done before they departed. Lissa was a lovely lady, but that perfume tended to stick to things. Better if Greyson kicked in a door somewhere smelling like sweat and gunpowder. Or something.

Captain Sheedo had come down from wherever to see them off. She hadn't been too big a pain in the ass, once she realized that she might have had a shot at Leigh and blown it. Weren't many ships that made the direct run to Earth from here, so there was a chance Greyson might be on her decks again.

And Lissa wasn't standing immediately close in the departure lounge as they finalized all the connections and stuff necessary to leave her ship and board the station at the heart of the Illymus Merchant Guild.

"It is exceptionally rare for people to board the station armed, Detectives," she said to them in a quiet voice.

Like Greyson was going to listen to her.

Greyson even smiled at the woman, but he'd gotten relaxed over the last month. Rachel wasn't sure she'd ever seen him this loose. Silly captain seemed to think that he'd gotten less dangerous as a result.

Wrong direction, lady.

"I can quote you all of the relevant stations, Captain," he said now. "Would you like me to?"

She supposed that he probably could. Old-timers had said that his memory was always phenomenal. Being who he was today had stepped it up another level.

"And nothing will dissuade you?" Sheedo asked instead.

"I am in pursuit of known felons, Captain." His smile turned cruel. "And intend to bring them to justice, however difficult they wish to make that chore."

Rachel liked that hard flinch that spasmed through the woman. Death himself, walking her decks, and she hadn't even gotten a chance to take him to bed to find out what that might be like.

Rachel had enjoyed a few one-nighters. The one Xaniea had been able to do amazing things to her with opposable, opposing thumbs. She just smiled at the Captain when the woman looked her way for help.

"So be it," Sheedo grumbled.

She turned and walked away. Greyson smiled at the galaxy. It was an unpleasant thing, but that was him thinking unpleasant thoughts.

"What's first?" she asked.

"We have reservations down on the surface, in Athund City," he said. "Lissa is staying downtown in Anic, but I wanted to be closer to the industrial district and the port. That's likely where things will be happening."

Rachel nodded. They'd been planning on approaching this somewhere a little better than tourists, but not much, so as to not give away just how much Greyson knew about the place. Instead, Lissa had stepped in and handled things, once Rachel and Greyson explained their needs.

She had to give the woman credit. Greyson had warned her that Lissa had way more brains than she showed. Defensive mechanism around money.

Rachel had never had money. Puerto Rican grandparents, before her parents relocated to Brooklyn, then she went to Boston as a grownup.

"Can we just pounce from orbit, then?" Rachel asked now, nodding and smiling over at Lissa, clear across the space like a stranger just happening to be going the same direction.

"Kind of," he replied. "I need a Guildlaw Judge first things first. That's when shit gets strange, because it will be the luck of the draw who we get. They might be honest. They might be so bent that they have to screw their pants on in the morning. I don't need a full grand jury at this point. All I need is a warrant sworn out and signed off on. Then yeah, boom time."

Rachel found herself getting a little excited at the prospect. Like Greyson, a month off. Less fooling around, but she'd also gotten so far ahead on her reading and exams that she might have taken a full semester off her degree. Like, spring graduation instead of fall.

Hello, Scotland Yard.

Ahead of them, the main hatch slowly opened, letting the mass of people and aliens spill out into another concourse, even better lit, where everyone had to go through the Guild equivalent of Customs. It would be even weirder for Humans who had never done it, but there was a G'schtack in uniform off to one side as she and her partner emerged. He even had a sign like they did at airports back home.

Leigh and Asher.

Huh.

Greyson didn't seem surprised. Rachel fell into his shadow.

"Leigh," he said simply, pulling out his badge.

She did the same.

"Captain Sheedo radioed ahead, Detectives," the man said, speaking G'schtack hesitantly, like he wasn't sure they could follow. "I am Investigator Arymo Moora. My understanding is that you need to be quickly and quietly transported to the surface, to Anic proper?"

"We are in hot pursuit, Investigator," Greyson told the man in flawless G'schtack. She'd even gotten pretty good over the last six weeks.

Rachel liked that little spark of excitement that came over the man. G'schtack law enforcement was positively dreary by comparison to what she did. Accountants with badges, ninety-nine percent of the time.

She wondered if the man ever had fantasies of car chases and gun fights.

"Right this way then, Detectives," Moora said. "I'm given to understand from Captain Sheedo that you are both currently armed?"

"That's right," Rachel said in a challenging voice, daring the G'schtack to do anything about it.

"Is it necessary?" he asked.

"Yes," she said bluntly. "Fortunately, we also have palmstunners, in case we don't need to kill someone along the way."

That spark turned into a shiver now. Human cops were prepared for a greater degree of casual violence than almost anybody in the Guild. And Hunters were even worse.

On the one hand, that meant that the rest of the galaxy was a more peaceful place, once those silly Human barbarians got over themselves.

On the other hand, the galaxy was likely not prepared for Humans, and cops from Earth like themselves would become even more necessary until the barbarians grew up. And somebody else stopped making assassins with perfect boobs.

Or was Scotland Yard just a case of dreaming too small? Should she be looking to carve herself out a gig on Brees or R'Onar? She had the background. And maybe some interesting new connections now, if Lissa Jonez was who Rachel thought she might be.

Greyson obviously hadn't looked too deeply. No such compunction stopped Rachel. There was a *Lissa Jonez, Balo*, who had her own entry in the Guild encyclopedia. No picture, and Rachel hadn't asked the woman's birthday.

Moora nodded and turned to his right, leading them to a secured door.

"Luggage?" he asked, eyeing Rachel's ubiquitous messenger bag and Greyson's utter lack of anything except their longcoats. Pockets, but not that many pockets.

"It is being transported to the surface by the hotel service," Greyson said in a voice with just a hint of snobbiness underneath. It had the effect of a whip cracked on Moora, so he got that part right.

"Very good." Moora hopped to and began to move, opening the door and leading them through.

Inside, it was a little drab. More police station than the gorgeous cruise line she'd just spent several weeks on.

Rachel supposed that she might have gotten a little spoiled.

Moora passed through to a lift tube, taking it first and dropping directly out of sight. Leigh went next.

She had to pause and look down. It was a form of freefall, contained in a special gravity field that held you safe and let you either drop to the bottom or step forward when you got to your floor. She'd heard about them but never seen one in action.

Didn't exist yet on Earth. Like a smart G'schtack would trust a Human to keep it tuned. She wasn't sure she would, and she knew her kind.

Still, she stepped out and plummeted. It didn't bother her, then she was on the lowest level of the station and the other two were standing off to one side where they'd been shunted.

Even dingier level, with maybe half the lights. Parking garage feel. She looked around and realized that she wasn't that far off, since some of those shapes looked like sky-to-ground transports.

Moora was in motion again. They followed.

Old, ugly, and battered. Too streamlined to be a panel truck, but it sure gave off those vibes. About fifty feet long. Kinda teardropped shape, but flat and wide instead of round. Steel gray oxidized to black in places. Probably from reentry.

"Time is utterly of the essence?" Moora asked as he stepped up next to it.

"Utterly," Greyson confirmed.

"Hop in, then."

Moora opened a hatch and they followed him in. Cramped, like a small truck. Moora went to the left and climbed into a pilot's seat. Leigh gestured for her to take the copilot.

Idly, as she buckled herself in, Rachel wondered if Leigh could fly this thing. She didn't even know what it was, but Leigh had a wealth of extra information available these days that he could tap. Over and above the hot green babe.

Moora frowned, but noted that she was doing it all correctly and had her hands off the controls. Leigh was taking a jumpseat. That couldn't be comfortable, but she wasn't going to argue.

Moora did his preflight and wrapped an earpiece and comm mic on his head.

"Inspector Moora to Anic Starport," he said simply.

The man fiddled a little, nodded, and brought the power on line. The truck lifted, oozed sideways just a little, then drifted into a tube ahead of them. Into the chute and boom, free flying in deep space.

Wow.

Rachel clamped her mouth shut and watched the stars as the planet rose up in the window ahead of her.

"Stand by for deorbital burn," Moora announced.

The whole truck shook. Shimmied. Writhed.

The edges of the glass got a little red, but that was friction as the arrow dove headlong into the atmosphere. Civilians were always safely back on a transport deck, where everything was through cameras and screens.

This felt like that car chase she wondered about earlier.

The edges of the sky had a green tinge, but she couldn't see either star that would be in the sky once she landed. Just another world. Maybe more green and gray than Earth, but she could see cities outlined on the night ground below them.

Next stop, Anic Starport.

ELEVEN

HOMECOMINGS?

G**REYSON** L**EIGH** **HAD** **NEVER** **WALKED** on the surface of
Brees. Never even left his home solar system. So he wasn't
about to explain how homesick the view out the front port
made him. It was all a dream anyway. Ethen hadn't really
liked Brees that much.

At the same time, it was a Guild world. And possibly the
last time she would walk on an alien planet before she
returned home to Earth to eventually die.

Greyson's dreams and nightmares the last week or so had
been utterly savage. Few of them in a good way, either.

Rachel was being the rookie seeing things. He could be
the jaded old fart in back, too cool to be impressed by any of
this shit.

He could still remember what the air in Anic City
smelled like. Every city on every planet had a different smell.
Brees was the single most cosmopolitan place in the known
galaxy. Everyone came here eventually, and like Rome, all
roads ended here.

Investigator Moora was doing a pretty good job of a what
a younger Greyson Leigh might have called an assault drop, if

they'd had rotors above them. Unknown and potentially hostile LZ down there. Bad people who might take exception to a skinny white boy with guns falling out of their sky.

It only takes once…

After a time, the ship broke through the clouds and things transitioned from space to flight. Countryside stretched out forever below them, more blue and gray from up here than flying over the middle of the US. Moora had maintained a running conversation, one-sided, with ground control somewhere.

From the feel, they were slipping out of the night to land at Anic not long after sunrise. About the time that most junior varsity criminals would be staggering off to bed. It was the professionals who kept banker's hours. Greyson rarely got to hunt folks that like, so lurking on someone's stoop as the sun wanted to rise felt normal.

Catch them distracted. Maybe drunk. Maybe thinking they'd gotten lucky and escaped instead of about to be arrested in front of whoever they'd talked into going home with them. Always an embarrassing outcome.

Moora was flying this run like he had an engine burning aft, but that was just hard, sharp maneuvers for combat insertions, rather than the soft turns that civilians could expect. Greyson had flown in worse, and Rachel was too stubborn to admit seasickness.

Cities started getting more complicated as they slowed down. Roads and clusters turned into something like a green version of LA. More parks and grass. Same amount of people.

Fewer, actually, but the same space consumed. Like Earth would be eventually.

"Stand by for transition to hover," Moora announced, grabbing the yoke he'd been flying and pressing buttons with his thumbs.

Greyson was holding on. Rachel got a bit of a spike. Below them, Anic Starport.

No place Greyson had ever been, but he recognized the layout of launch strips. Like runways, but most craft could take off straight up on repulselifters. You still needed corridors for flying in.

Moora did more things and from the sound and way the flight got choppier as the landing gear deployed. Like a jet heading in.

They dropped, slid sideways, then entered a bunker. Or something. Big space. Too underground to be a hangar, but it gave off the same feeling.

Moora had not asked a single personal question since they boarded. That changed now.

"Detectives, we have arrived," he said unnecessarily. "What's the first thing you need?"

Greyson flipped a coin in his head. This guy could be a good cop. He could be another Carlos Dominguez.

"I need a Guildlaw Judge in front of whom I can swear an Affidavit of Findings," Greyson said, watching the G'schtack cop's head rotate back like an owl. "From there, a Warrant for Entry and an Expected Arrest Warrant."

Perfect accent. Perfect legalisms.

Buddy, we're doing this by the kind of book that gets thrown at those fuckers.

Greyson smiled at the man. Affidavit of Findings was akin to swearing out a complaint, but had all manner of G'schtack and Guild overtones that Earth law didn't do. Sure got Moora's attention, though.

Greyson looked down instead of watching him and concentrated on unbuckling. This thing was meant to survive a crash and keep you safe. Bruised all to hell, maybe, but safe.

Greyson was up first, though he had to be careful not to stand up too straight, being about half a head taller than any

G'schtack he'd ever met. Way too easy to bash his skull on ceilings intended for shorter species.

"Who do you expect to arrest?" the G'schtack asked, lost now.

"Men and women who might be a threat to the safety and security of the entire Illymus Merchant Guild," Greyson smiled ominously, stepping now to the hatch and figuring out how to open it.

The other two followed him outside.

Moora led them to a slidewalk and Greyson made sure Rachel got on. It was moving pretty damned quick if you weren't paying attention.

Thing carried them in about sixty-yard chunks, with ten-yard gaps every so often for people to get on and off. The ride still took a while, because they didn't go through the terminal building where all the mass transit stuff was.

Instead, Moora went down a side corridor and they ended up in a garage. All the cars in here were identical. Greyson could see where the imitation Chandler Jouster back home was built on a similar frame, with different controls and less interesting body panels.

Four-door sedan. Seat six really friendly adult Humans. Comfortable for six G'schtack. Lifters front and rear, with wheels on the corners for driving if the rain and weather got ugly enough to stay low. Slate gray, with a light bar across the top and both bumpers.

Only so many ways to transport erect bipeds in relative comfort, after all.

"If you will join me, I will drive you there," Investigator Moora said, moving to the closest car.

"Are you assigned to the case while we are here?" Greyson asked in a voice right at the edge of rude.

"Given Human investigators, Hunters at that, it was determined that you might not be fully cognizant of

Guildlaw and thus need assistance," Moora replied, staring hard, black eyes at Greyson. "I suspect that someone may have underestimated you, Detectives."

Greyson let that one slide. He joined Moora in the front and let Rachel ride perp for now. He wanted to see the city. Plan steps.

"After we get to Guildhall, my partner and I will need to acquire communicators," Greyson said. "We have smart phones upgraded from Earth technology, but they are hardly going to be adequate for Anic."

Moora powered the vehicle up and rolled forward, out another garage door to a thing Greyson's brain kept wanting to call a helicopter pad. Except that the car lifted off instead.

"You are remarkably well prepared for Brees, Detective Leigh," Moora finally ventured when they got some altitude and he engaged the autopilot. "How is that?"

"We're Hunters," he replied simply. "The Hunter Bureau on Earth is one of the few law enforcement agencies trained and prepared to deal with aliens, in every sense of the word. I have a previous background in government work as well."

He ignored the mostly-suppressed snort from the back seat as Rachel listened to him spin his bullshit yarns. Moora didn't seem to catch it. Probably shocked to be talking in G'schtack with a Human.

If Greyson had to guess, they'd drawn the Investigator because he spoke enough English to get by. Not for any other reason.

Today was going to be a whole litany of surprises for a lot of folks. That bar was going to be so high around here that Rachel would have to work at it, next time she came out from Earth.

As it should be.

"My partner is completing a university degree in criminal justice, with expertise in a variety of legal systems, both on

Earth and beyond," he continued. "I have been working with her on conversational G'schtack as well, though others would be greatly appreciated, as I'm sure my accent is atrocious."

More lies. He spoke better G'schtack than most of the natives. Phrenic were born linguists. Maybe designed that way. And Ethen had taken a G'schtack at some point, imprinting the language permanently as the best way to pass.

But we don't talk about that in polite company.

Moora gave him a heavy dose of side-eye and remained silent.

High bar. Deal with Human Hunters at your own risk, anywhere in the galaxy, pal.

The flight went swimmingly. Nice morning sky. About the same time Rachel would swing by to pick him up at his place, if they needed a full day in the office before a long night of chasing people.

The autopilot put them down on the roof of a squarish, pixie tower that twisted one hundred and eighty degrees while climbing some one hundred and twenty floors. An elevator lowered the vehicle into the building almost immediately and Moora waited for the slab to shift them off to one side before they all exited.

"The temperature outside is extreme, but it will be back to comfortable shortly," Moora said.

Greyson nodded. He'd worn his longcoat today and made sure Rachel did the same. Weather in Anic could get a little iffy, at least this time of year. And the style would draw the eye.

He was taller than most of the folks he'd encounter, and Greyson intended to use that to its best advantage. It was a shame that hats had never really recovered from Kennedy. A brown Panama with his longcoat and he'd look like those old, private detectives from the 1930s and 40s.

The look would be lost on G'schtack, but it would put

him even more fully into a character he intended to run on these fools. Bogey had immortalized the shape of it, both as Spade as well as Marlowe. Maybe with a little Blaine thrown in for good measure.

Almost better than a gunslinger around these parts.

After a few minutes, Moora led them to a drop tube and programmed a stop. Greyson had never been in the building, so he just went along with it.

They exited about mid-tower. The tube would shunt you right out the front at the correct floor and you kept walking, so someone behind you had space.

Rachel stumbled exactly once and then was in line with them as they went through a side door into a large space with a desk and a hallway headed deeper. Bluish walls in a stone Greyson didn't recognize, but had the feel of polished marble.

A receptionist looked up as they approached. Antisaur, which was pretty rare anywhere, as they tended to stay much closer to their homeworld.

Greyson was pretty sure it was a she, since he seemed to remember they had two sexes, unlike some of the really weird Guild members. Blue scales covered the bits of skin not under a maroon tunic. Her headridge was also maroonish, with some black and yellow thrown in.

"May I assist you?" she asked Moora, ignoring Greyson and Rachel completely.

"We are in need of a Guildlaw Judge," Greyson replied, drawing her surprised eyes back to him. "Who is currently on duty to review an Affidavit of Findings?"

Never expected one of the newly-uplifted worlds to speak the lingo, did you, kid?

He smiled without teeth. Friendlier that way.

"Judge Rankev," she managed after a moment of stunned silence. "Let me call her Bailiff."

Greyson nodded and relaxed. Moora and Rachel stood with him as the woman lifted a handset and spoke quietly.

A few moments later, a beefy, male G'schtack appeared in the hallway. The man was almost Greyson's height, which made him tall for their kind. Probably weighed as much, too. Big fellow.

For a G'schtack.

"May I help you?" he asked now in a quiet baritone.

"Earth Detective/Hunter Greyson Leigh," he said, pulling out his badge and ID to show to the man. "My partner, Rachel Asher. Investigator Arymo Moora has been attached to the case to assist. I have documents for the judge to review, and need to swear out an Affidavit of Findings."

Again, the look that fell midway between puzzled and shocked. Most likely the first Human they'd ever met. Let alone one who was prepared for them.

Heh.

"This way," he said, blinking too rapidly, even for their kind.

Greyson took the lead following. Not that he had any clue what to expect, but because this really was his case once they left Earth. Rachel had most of the pieces, but only most. Investigator Moora almost none. Hell, Lissa probably knew more.

By design.

The Judge was an older G'schtack woman. Short and rotund. Shrewd eyes followed him as he entered her office, the woman seated behind her desk in light green robes, like they did here. Back home, it would be black, but the Grays had other ideas on many topics.

G'schtack were a shorter species. Everything they did always felt ninety-percent scale to Greyson.

"Your Honor," he said with a formal nod to the woman as he entered and moved all the way across to the back corner to make space for the others. The Bailiff had remained next to the Judge, on the side of the desk like someone might try to rush her.

She studied them for a long moment.

"Could you close the door, Investigator?" Greyson asked.

They were closed in, the five of them.

"I am Detective/Hunter Greyson Leigh, from Earth, Your Honor," he began. "In the course of investigating a case back home, we came across evidence of smuggling illegal goods to Earth that were of sufficient value and risk that the Engineering Master of Armstrong Base, one Virgar—"

"I know who Virgar Andell is, Detective/Hunter Leigh," she cut him off. "He transmitted a data packet to let me know that you would be calling as soon as you arrived. It came on the same ship and I received it last night, about the time you docked."

"How much information did it contain?" Greyson asked carefully, wondering if his case had already been blown up and the bad guys given a half-day's head start on him.

It would only be a head start. Not a getaway.

"Names and descriptions of you and Detective Asher," she said. "Extremely high-level synopsis of a case on your planet's main moon involving a Phrenic and various conspiracies and blackmail, resulting in several deaths, the apparent solution of which would lead you to Brees."

She was not smiling as she spoke. Quiet and hard, even for a G'schtack, who as a species generally tended to be compact emotionally.

"Oh, and that you were not someone to suffer fools and games when hunting, Detective," she added with a ghost of a grin underneath now.

Greyson nodded. All of it true, within limits.

"Rachel?" he turned and nodded.

She pulled the data chip out of her messenger bag and he

nodded for her to hand it to the Bailiff. From there, the Judge took possession of it.

That woman held it in one hand as if she could weigh the evidence it contained that way.

It was all in there. Everything he knew except the address of the place he wanted to raid with the help of a few Investigators and maybe a feral accountant or two.

"I have an address, Your Honor," he continued. "I would rather keep it secret until you have a chance to review the file, in order to give my prey the least possible warning that I'm coming, assuming they weren't already warned."

"You presume that my office leaks, Detective?" she asked hotly now.

"I'm dealing with Phrenic, Your Honor," he replied in a tone just shy of a snarl. "At least one so far, who managed to suborn the Legal Affairs Officer of Armstrong Base, and then allowed all manner of illegalities and smuggling to occur. Most of those problems can be handled by my people back home, and might have already been done, as it has taken us significant time to travel this far. How many more Phrenic might be running around?"

Greyson knew he was being a shit and still didn't care. Phrenic was the universal nightmare. A less civilized place than the Illumus Merchant Guild might have taken it upon themselves to wipe the species out entirely. Might still consider it one of these days, if they had the sense God gave a goose.

Instead, he was dealing with punks committing even-more-dangerous games. The ones where they could maybe create armies of killers like him. Or assassins like Anais. Or simply replace someone with what Humans always called a Manchurian Candidate, after the old movie with Laurence Harvey and Frank Sinatra.

What civilization could survive such things? Not many

Greyson was familiar with. Fortunately, most Phrenic were law-abiding folk. It was only the weak and the lazy that caused all the rest of the galaxy to have nightmares.

The Judge matched him scowl for scowl, which was fine. He already owed the Engineering Master a piece of his mind for sending any message. Probably thought he was being helpful.

The outcome of the next hour would determine that. If whoever it was got away, he'd eventually return to the moon to chat with the fellow. It might even turn out okay.

And pigs might fly.

She weighed that chip some more. Weighed his soul as well, no doubt.

"Everything else is on that chip, Your Honor," he said. "I'd like to go from here to absolutely ruin somebody's day, but I need your help. This has to be done precisely by the book, because I suspect that someone has high-level backing to have been able to commit the crimes they have."

"And you are certain that crimes have been committed, Detective?"

"Extremely high-value goods smuggled into the Earth system without paying the appropriate fees," he smiled, quoting a number in Guild currency. "That makes it just about as high a felony as you can get. The executive summary should take you about thirty minutes to read and digest. At that point, I'll be happy to answer subsequent questions."

He leaned forward now and put his weight on the back of the chair in front of him. He'd come this far. Made his case.

It either came together or fell apart, right here, right now.

"Very well," she replied. "Bailiff, see them settled in the lounge for now."

Greyson exchanged nods with the woman. High-stakes

poker and high-stakes power games followed remarkably similar rules and behavior.

He didn't do poker, because it was a game of random chance, despite the skill involved. Greyson preferred less chance when money was changing hands.

Better all the way around.

The Bailiff saw them out, down the hall, and into a comfortable space.

"Can I get you anything?" he asked.

"Human coffee if you somehow managed to have any," Greyson smiled at the fellow. "Otherwise, an herbal infusion safe for Humans would be fine. Hot or cold."

He ended up with a weak tea. Pinkish. Cool. Not all that sweet. Not particularly bitter.

Adequate to his needs. Today.

He could see needing to find something with caffeine in it at some point, just because he would need that jolt of angry bitterness, first thing in the morning, to get motivated.

The folks he was after weren't going to go down politely.

TWELVE

GREEN SKIES

RACHEL SAT in the lounge and considered reading more homework, but she was just too wound up. Instead, she stood and walked over to a window looking down on the city. The two men ignored her.

Green skies overhead. The first sun, Udoth, was up. Vaad would be along soon. The Hound and the Hunter. Kinda appropriate, but she didn't need to tell Leigh that. And Investigator Moora wouldn't get the joke.

Still, exactly like Greyson and Ethen had described it to her, sitting on the hood of the Chandler and eating Tommy's fries in the moonlight. Weird, but utterly glorious, even from here, hiding behind the glass and looking down at the tiny city below.

She'd gotten some juice to drink while they waited. Wet, sweet, non-fermented, non-poisonous to Humans.

When you barge in someplace without warning, you don't get to complain that they didn't hit the supermarket to pick you up any supplies. The hotel would be better equipped. Supposedly there was a Humantown out in Athund City and they were staying in or near it.

87

Like Chinatowns back home, she supposed. Small ghetto where a group of outsiders might congregate and organize little touches of the home left behind. Lots of Humans had left Earth over the last sixteen years. A group of them were here.

She'd meet them in a few hours.

Or tomorrow. Depended on the Judge and that woman's interpretations of all the crap she and Greyson had put into that file for today.

Should be an open and shut slam dunk. But if the Illymus Merchant Guild was infallible and honest, nobody would have been able to transport a killer named Anais Manel to Earth in the first place. And Humans wouldn't need folks like the Hunter Bureau doing things.

First sun outside and clock on the wall nearby both suggested they'd been in here about twenty minutes, translated from G'schtack into terms she used.

The Bailiff opened the door and nodded at them without breaking the silence, so everyone got organized and followed the guy back to the Judge's office.

She hadn't changed. Well, maybe her skin was a little more gray. Rachel had only Andell to compare things to, so she wasn't sure what the changes might suggest. A third chair had been added. Hopefully a good sign.

"Sit," Judge Rankev instructed them as they entered.

Rachel found herself in the middle, with Greyson on her left and Moora on her right. About what she figured. The door got closed again, this time more a promise of secrecy than anything.

Rankev positively glowered at Leigh. Losing battle, but Rachel wasn't here to offer suggestions on manners.

"If I had not been forewarned by the Engineering Master, I might have been tempted to dismiss all this as the most bizarrely fanciful load of shit I'd ever seen," she began.

"Imagine how we felt, living through it," Greyson fired right back at her, in that way he did to let you know that he wasn't taking any crap from anybody.

Captain Parsons had taken a few days to realize that when she became the new boss, back in Boston.

"Your conclusions on the possibility of what you describe as Manchurian Candidates in the appendix raises exceptional evidentiary standards, Leigh," the woman fired right back.

"They don't get to claim Executive Immunity until I accuse them of a crime," he said.

Instructional, watching the woman grimace. Rachel had helped write those sections of his report, copying and pasting straight out of a couple of law books in the process. Books she could lay hands on right now, because she'd seen the same set in paper back in the lounge.

Light reading, as it were.

"And you have specifically not gone that far, I note," she said, still talking to Leigh like they were the only two in here. "Why not?"

"Because I can get a conviction on the smuggling alone," he smiled at her. "Guild regulations mean I figure someone is facing thirty- to fifty- standard cycles in prison for that, minus time off for good behavior. Back home, we often pull folks like that aside and offer leniency. They plead guilty to a lesser charge then turn around to testify about folks above them in any criminal conspiracy, in return for a lighter sentence. At that point, I gain access to all of their records, including research, funding, and invoices for models already delivered. That's when I stop playing nice."

As if he was playing nice now…

"Do you understand that such accusations as you carefully do not level still implicate the highest ranks of the Guild, Detective?" Rankev grimaced.

"That's why I'm here personally, Your Honor," he said, in

his best hard-ass voice. "If anyone else had come, they might have been led astray. Or ordered to ignore certain evidence. Or to fall on their sword rather than follow the clues to the end."

"And you won't," she nodded. It hadn't been a question.

"I also happen to have an extremely rare set of skills and experiences at understanding those implications, Your Honor," Leigh said now. "And what might happen if things are left to fester."

Even Rachel found she could gasp. Boy was going to tell the judge what he used to do. The bad old days.

The assassin.

All eyes rotated to her now. Shit. She'd made a noise.

"You have something to add, Detective Asher?" Judge Rankev asked.

"A question for you, Judge Rankev," Rachel nodded.

"Go on."

"We've dealt with Phrenic infiltrators on a couple of cases now," Rachel said. "My first as his partner, as a matter of fact. Engineering Master Andell specifically asked for Leigh for this case because he thought they had another such creature. Except that when she killed herself after assassinating her target, she was still Human. Except that she wasn't. Human, that is."

"If not Human, what was the woman?" the Judge asked.

Rachel felt both the Bailiff and Investigator Moora lean towards her now. The Judge was already locked in. Leigh didn't give two shits. Nothing new there.

"If we're right about the various speculations, then she is a clone, Your Honor," Rachel said. "And not just any clone, as she was programmed to kill her target, then end herself before anyone could come to understand what she was or how she got there. If we hadn't gotten a full confession out of the one Phrenic, we wouldn't know this much."

"The file suggests that you, Detective Asher, executed the Phrenic, even after she confessed," Judge Rankev noted with barely-restrained hostility.

"A Phrenic on Earth without bio-restraints, in the form of a Human, is guilty of premeditated murder, Your Honor," Rachel countered. "Hunters are specifically empowered under Human law to destroy such creatures, if they do not believe that they can adequately restrain them."

"And you could not?"

"Your Honor," Leigh leaned forward and tapped his own angry finger on the desk between them. "A Phrenic could kill me in less than two seconds. With all my training and background."

"Yes, you were about to discuss those when we got distracted by Asher," the woman said. "What did you wish to tell me?"

"Earth years are roughly ninety percent of standard cycles, Your Honor," he nodded. "The current Earth year is listed as 2058 on our most common system. The Guild first contacted Earth in 2042, or sixteen years ago. Roughly fourteen standard cycles. Before that, from 2026 until 2046, I was a soldier in the military of one of the strongest national organizations on Earth, when we didn't know about anyone else. During most of that time, I worked for the Army as a professional assassin. My job was to kill people when it had to be done quietly, because they were either too well protected by their own armies, or they were politicians for opposing powers and my leaders had determined that removing them was for the best. I can't speak to the ethics of the thing, and have tried to make peace with it, but the legality and morality of the acts were pounded deep into my bones as an impressionable youngster."

Rachel liked the way Leigh had just about sucked all the air out of the room. Shit, back home, he had to worry about folks knocking on his door in the dead of night to maybe arrest him for saying such things to *anybody*. They'd bury him under the prison if they could.

Here, he was informing *another* Officer of the Court of it. Who would likely enter it into a record somewhere.

Did that boy have a death wish or something?

No. He was Greyson Leigh. Warning the entire Illymus Merchant Guild that he was coming, and nailing his resume to the bulletin board in case you thought it was a joke. Or that you could get away from him.

"So you've been a professional killer for…" she began.

"For about twenty-five standard cycles, Your Honor," he nodded.

"And the Hunter Bureau on Earth made you a Detective," she continued.

"There are some folks who think I might be the best in the business right now," he said coldly.

"Right now?"

She hated that little nod the boy gave in her direction. Hated more that he might not be wrong.

"Detective Asher will surpass me, one of these days," he informed the entire, freaking galaxy in that cold, deadly voice of his. "That's why we were paired up."

First off, that was a load of horseshit. He'd gotten her because Dominguez had gotten his neck snapped and they needed someone to work the case. And train her some more, so maybe.

Second off, did anybody really understand what Leigh was doing to her?

Rachel felt a moment of deathly chill descend on her like misty rain on a cold morning.

One person understood.

Rutherford Parsons. Captain of Detectives. Commander,

Eastern North America Division, Earth Police Special Missions.

Yeah, the boss knew what Leigh was up to, if not the why. Never the why.

Judge Rankev's head was on a near-constant swivel. She rotated those gun-turret eyes back to Rachel now. Fresh appraisal. Maybe understanding, after she'd dismissed the younger partner as a rookie tagging along with the old fart.

Rookies are still killers in this business.

The moment hung, pregnant with indecision and malice, like a particularly bad fart in a closed room.

Finally, the Judge leaned back. Next to her, Rachel heard Moora start breathing again. The Bailiff might have been carved from marble.

"And after all that, all you desire from me is a Warrant for Entry?" she asked now.

"I expect evidence of crimes in plain sight, Your Honor," Leigh replied. "Where I come from, what we would specifically call *High Crimes*. At that point, I get to arrest everyone. And sweat them."

Rachel shivered, in spite of herself and her knowledge of Detective/Hunter Greyson Leigh.

High Crimes and Misdemeanors was a very specific accusation, the way he was using it.

The Guild simply called it *treason*.

THIRTEEN

DOORKICKER

Looking around the open, green space at the people surrounding him now and waiting on his final words, Greyson had to keep scowling so he didn't smile and ruin his reputation as a complete hard-ass with Investigator Moora. And the others. Her Honor, the Honorable Murphely Rankev, had signed his warrant.

Such a little thing, and yet so much had hinged on that little act. A bent judge might have held everything up for a week investigating. And maybe made a phone call or three to some friends who would draw a liberal sum of ready cash to thank her for such consideration as they fled into the depths of space, one step ahead of the hunter on their heels.

A specist judge might have dismissed the silly monkey-folk from Earth out of hand, requiring him to find another judge and convince them. At the same time that the first judge was telling them to ignore the strangers.

He'd drawn the lucky card. Found a judge who believed in right and wrong from an ethical standpoint. The morality of cloning and genetic engineering on Humans was always going to be murky at best. The legality could easily be shifted around by reclassifying things. Or forgetting to fix certain paperwork when you should have. Like when a treaty was signed.

There was a reason he didn't trust such legalisms. Only ethics. The highest good for the most people, with the least pain to the rest. Always a balancing act. Humans were a rounding error in the overall population of the Guild. Earth, one planet in thousands.

He'd drawn the lucky card. Nothing more powerful in the universe than an honest cop and an honest judge.

And he'd been looking forward to this day for a bunch of weeks.

Greyson looked around now, coming out of himself and studying the city around him. Warehouse district. Wide roads with numerous parking and landing slabs. Squat buildings made of Guild concrete, usually three or four stories tall and frequently covering entire blocks.

With doors on all four sides, it was easier to just build huge then subdivide the interior, moving walls around as needed.

His particular target, viewed on a local 3D map, was such a monstrosity, down several blocks and around a corner. According to tax records he was now privy to with a warrant in hand, the corporation known as *Aeon Research Financial* filled roughly a sixth, instead of a quarter.

Incorporation records showed that the corporation went back hundreds of standard cycles, so they hadn't just spun up a new entity to work on Humans. Which suggested a monster-making facility with tentacles in other places as well.

Legal or not.

Around him, Rachel was standing close, but turned away, like a bodyguard getting ready to shoot someone. Investigator Moora had pulled some rank. Or triggered the fire alarm. Something. Parked nearby were more than a dozen vehicles that looked remarkably similar to how Greyson might have built repulsorlift assault transports, since you didn't need wheels or treads. Each big enough to hold a dozen folks.

He had commandeered a park for the afternoon, as folks had come from more than just one building to join him.

Greyson looked at a handful of the many faces and recognized the eyes, if not the people. Hard. He'd have said killers, but he and Rachel were the only two present with lethal firepower. Everyone else had stun weapons. The Guild was like that.

Ninety-eight percent of the time, rehabilitation was the better choice. The better outcome. Anywhere in the galaxy.

That last two percent were why folks like Greyson Leigh had a job. And a badge.

"I have no idea what the inside of the building looks like," Greyson told them now, sounding like a grizzled Master Sergeant he'd served under, once upon a yesterday. "Nor how many people we can expect to find when we arrive and storm the place. Each of you has been assigned a side, a door, or a field of fire. I expect you to capture and hold everyone emerging from that building for any reason. The innocent will go free once we sort them out. The guilty will go down."

"What about you, Detectives?" Moora asked now, his voice loud enough that everyone in the command circle heard it.

"Detective Asher and I have nerve scramblers," Greyson informed his team. "If there is a Phrenic involved, we'll take them down ourselves."

"Down," Moora echoed.

"In another form and without bio-restraints, they are already guilty of murder, Investigator," Rachel growled.

They'd had to say that to too many people. The whole

case hinged on what one such creature had been able to do. It only took a handful to make an entire species look bad.

Greyson Leigh was here to try and make the Humans species look good. Or at least dangerous enough not to fuck with. That reputation would go a long ways.

Greyson turned to a Mooz, standing directly across from him. Big woman. Largely covered with a fine, golden pelt under her uniform. Small jaw. Wide eyes. Ears that stuck out sideways like antennae.

"Team One will go in right behind me," Greyson said. "Detective Asher will cover the door with Team Two against anybody getting by me. Shoot to stun anybody that gives you any reason to doubt. Am I clear?"

She merely nodded, holding a long-barreled stun rifle that ought to be sufficient long ways down the block. The whole force was like that. Over-armed for something like raiding an illegal distillery.

Greyson had flashbacks to a similar warehouse in an equatorial city he wasn't at liberty to name, where they'd been refining all manner of illegal narcotics at enormous scales. Industrial brewery, just the wrong product.

They'd opened fire as soon as they realized that someone had come for them. Too bad for them that they'd stored all manner of volatile chemicals around the place. Especially when somebody put a wire-guided anti-tank missile into one stack of barrels. The first of several such weapons he'd used that day.

Here, most of the folks would get out alive, and probably get out of prison in five to fifteen.

Most.

"We are going to hit hard and fast," Greyson said. "Kick in the door and start arresting people. If we're lucky, nobody has to pull a trigger at all today."

"And if we're not?" the big Mooz woman asked.

"That's what you have Humans for," he replied.

Big. Violent. Crazy. It wasn't entirely true as a reputation. It wasn't entirely false, either.

And today would just reinforce that.

Nobody fuck with the Humans. Ever.

But as Rachel liked to tease him, there were worse things in the galaxy than having Greyson Leigh coming after you. They just weren't survivable, either.

"Questions?" he asked the half-dozen team leaders around him.

Shakes of head.

"Then let's do this thing," he ordered, walking towards the nearest of the transports with Moora close.

Rachel would ride in another one. The rest would take off from here, then box-drop on the warehouse, blocking all sides and disrupting three hopefully-honest businesses until everything was sorted out.

Inside, he was reminded more of a helicopter transport, minus the rotor noise. The smell was old grease, rank sweat, and the musk of the dozen or so troopers around him, heavy on Mooz and G'schtack.

He'd smelled worse in his time.

Automatically, Greyson drew his nerve scrambler and checked the charge before sliding it back into the holster. Then the spare powerpack, against the day he ever had to fire the thing enough times to actually deplete it. Hadn't happened yet in his career.

Yet.

Palmstunner was also ready, but he figured he might go the entire day without using it. Stun rifles let the cops around him be a little trigger-happy, because they hardly ever killed. Maybe one time in a thousand you triggered some underlying medical condition.

And he had medics with each team and ambulances on immediate call.

Just another military operation, in a place where they didn't have militaries. Not as Humans understood the term.

The old saying still held true, though.

There was a new Sheriff in town.

FOURTEEN

ARRIVAL

GREYSON HAD the documentation in one hand, copies signed, executed, and duly recorded downtown. Nerve scrambler and palmstunner tucked away.

Shit, he had an armed mob behind him, in case it came to that.

The pilot flew like the right kind of maniac. Nape-of-the-Earth at high speeds, risking sudden take-offs by others in his need to get there ludicrously fast.

The transport grounded harder than it was probably supposed to, but perfectly under control. Greyson thrust the hatch open like this was a hot landing zone and practically sprinted across the quad to the front door.

Behind him, slower troopers poured out of the first vehicle, with the others dropping all around him like the apocalypse had come.

Felt good.

Too many times, it had been Greyson going into a dark warehouse alone, knowing that there was somebody in there that didn't want to come peacefully. Having his own army for once along was nice.

The place was a warehouse with offices built out just inside a permanently-open garage door. All the other doors on this facing were closed, and all but two were marked as having been permanently shut, so they didn't get big deliveries of stuff all that often.

Or their product could walk out of their own volition and get into a cab. Never discount that.

Glass-fronted door. Opened outward. Just like home. Greyson pulled it open as he approached and centered his attention on the G'schtack woman that had a feel like a receptionist to her.

"May I help you?" she asked in a nervous titter.

Greyson smiled and walked close, holding out those innocent-looking papers for her. Having a dozen cops in armor and guns trailing in behind him was making her twitchy.

"I have papers for the person in charge," he said. "Could you stand up and step away from the desk, please?"

"I'm sorry?"

Greyson didn't want to be an asshole. At the same time, he didn't know if she had a panic button alarm under the desk that she might already be stomping on. He turned to the Mooz leader of Team One and nodded.

"Her," he said simply.

The woman shot the receptionist. Greyson watched her collapse like a sack of potatoes.

The rest of the space had a hallway to some offices down the left, and an obvious double-door entrance out to the warehouse on the right. Physics was physics. And architecture to serve intelligent, tool-using, erect bipeds could only move so many ways.

"Half of you cover that." Greyson pointed to the warehouse door on the right, even as he moved to the hallway.

Because he'd already ordered force, he drew the nerve scrambler. Greyson wouldn't call it his security blanket. At the same time, he wasn't about to lie and say it didn't make him feel better, holding death in his hand as he set down all the papers for later.

First door was open to a conference room. Currently empty. He pivoted across the way to what looked like a petite library. Old fashioned books with leather-looking bindings and lots and lots of map cabinets. Shallow vertically, but wide and deep. The kind of places you put blueprints when you didn't roll them up first.

Human blueprints?

Nobody in here. Good enough.

Down and to the left side again. Open door. Shadow approaching it from the inside. Probably someone who heard a sound and coming to investigate. Natural mistake. At least today.

Greyson got to the doorway at the same time as a G'schtack male in a nice suit. With his free hand, he grabbed cloth and jerked the man forward, turning and slinging him off his feet before rotating back and pointing his pistol into the now-empty office.

The only sound had been a squawk of surprise, a tumbling to the ground, and handcuffs clicking shut.

Last door on this side was shut. Simple interior door. Wood. Of an alien sort. Nothing durable. Keyhole in the handle, just to close it at night. Nothing to keep out a halfway-competent burglar.

Hell, if he wanted to, Greyson could probably pick the lock, just to show off. Mechanically, extremely similar to Human tools. Only so many ways to skin that cat.

Instead, he stepped into it and kicked just above the handle as hard as he could. And he could adjust his muscles when he needed to.

The locking mechanism and part of the door *shattered* under the assault with an ugly, tearing noise. Wood chips flew inward. The door bounced off a stop and started to close again, but Greyson was already standing there.

A G'schtack female sat behind a desk covered with papers.

And wood shards.

Executive. Middle-aged squishy around the middle. Slack skin at the neck. Expensive suit in burgundy shimmeriness.

She held a comm handset to one ear, but had stopped talking. Those eyes tracked him.

"Hang up," he ordered her, nerve scrambler centered on her nose. "Do not speak. Do not otherwise move. Or I will terminate you."

Hell of a weapon. Tiny bore on a nerve scrambler. Guild technology.

Still looked big enough to stick your dick in it when someone pointed one at you, in spite of being too small for even Rachel's pinky finger.

Great way to get someone's attention, especially if they knew what it was.

She complied with the sorts of care and deliberation the very old used when moving. Robotic, in this instance.

"Stand up," he continued. "Move around the desk. Do not make sudden moves. Do not resist arrest."

Other Hunters, including Rachel, had commented that he sounded like Death had a radio station when he was this wound up. This focused.

Here, it probably kept the woman alive, because she simply complied. The alternative was pretty fucking obvious.

Someone took charge of the woman and cuffed her. Greyson was already in motion with the Mooz team leader.

Back up the hallway. Into the waiting area. Nobody had scheduled any meetings today, obviously.

Greyson nodded to the half-dozen gunners watching that double door. Then he went right through it.

Warehouse. Freaking huge. Three- or four-story roof overhead. Necessary, because there was a bank of…*equipment* down one side. And enormous tanks like he'd expect at a brewery on the other.

Greyson was pretty certain that none of them held beer.

"Hey, what do you think you're…"

The G'schtack male's voice trailed off when Greyson had rotated in place and centered the pistol on him. Thirty yards. Most cops didn't train at that range. Greyson still held a variety of expert marksman ratings with the Bureau.

Maybe good enough to shoot the fellow's eyes out from there.

Greyson ignored the rest of the space and stalked towards what felt like a foreman. In his head, he kept expecting submachine guns to suddenly appear and start chattering, but that was an Earth thing. A Human thing. React to an invasion like this with gunfire. Even around dangerous chemicals.

"I have a warrant to investigate the premises," he said as he got close enough to not be yelling.

And working to keep the adrenaline under control so he wasn't screaming in the fellow's face.

Anything else was interrupted as somebody opened fire with a beam weapon.

Greyson exploded into motion, grabbing the G'schtack by the shirt front and using him as cover. His automatic instinct was always to kill someone, but he didn't need to today.

Today.

Team One cut loose with rifles instead. Hopefully, nothing in here would react poorly to stun weaponry. He kept tracking those enormous tanks of liquid and hoping they didn't explode.

The G'schtack started to resist, so Greyson chopped him on the side of the skull. Nothing intended to be lethal. Painful box if he had external ears, but the Grays only had a little ridge of flesh and a hole.

Still, it stung, as intended. Greyson grabbed him again, never letting the nerve scrambler move from his face.

Looking around, Team One had successfully suppressed someone, as all fire stopped as quickly as it had started. Greyson got a chance to study the wall of equipment in front of him.

But only briefly, as somebody else opened fire. It was too exposed here, so he dragged his new best friend over behind a four-wheeled cart like you used to move boxes around. Not a forklift, but in the same family. Distant, kissing cousins, as it were.

Solid enough to keep things like bullets from getting to him if he stayed low.

Across from him, a Human-scaled door next to the garage doors opened, letting light in. Probably somebody making a break for the fire escape thinking they could get outside and vanish.

Like the US Army hadn't taught him how to deploy a multi-layered ambush or something. Whoever didn't get far. Then another team of his people poured into the facility through that same door, introducing crossfire.

There were no sides of this entire warehouse without a full team of folks covering, including three teams that had dropped onto the roof, just in case someone wanted to fly away.

Not fucking around today.

For several seconds, the sound of beams escalated, then

just as suddenly fell to utter silence. Greyson had been listening, but watching his new buddy grow uncomfortable. As he should.

"You're under arrest," Greyson finally got a chance to explain to the G'schtack in a friendly-enough voice. "I have the place surrounded. How many people showed up to work today?"

Took a couple of seconds to get through to the fellow. He had a look on his face like they should have expected a discreet phone call announcing a planned raid of a speakeasy, so folks could hide all the evidence.

There was no way to hide the wall of equipment over there. Only to skip town one step ahead of an arrest warrant.

Nobody had called.

Greyson rattled him with the hand holding cloth.

"How many people?"

"Six in the warehouse," he finally said.

"Including you?"

The man nodded.

"Team One, five out there to account for!" Greyson yelled. "Count noses!"

He turned his attention back to the G'schtack.

"Hopefully, you haven't lied to me," he warned the man in a calm, deadly voice.

The G'schtack foreman shivered. Nobody liked someone to drop combat teams on them from out of the blue.

"All accounted for, Detective," the Mooz woman called back now.

"Excellent," Greyson smiled.

He stood and dragged the smaller man to his feet.

"Team One, contact all outside teams and get some more folks in here to sweep for bodies!" he yelled. "Do not touch anything, because it might explode!"

Probably wouldn't, but fear of booms would keep the juvenile delinquency to a minimum.

"And keep the perimeter in place!" he continued, starting to walk back to where he already had a few other friends.

One of the cops took charge of the foreman, and Greyson happily let the fellow go. Rachel appeared from where she'd been. Investigator Moora joined them.

Everybody else around here held the functional equivalent rank of Sergeant of the uniformed division. Good cops, but not detectives. Not ready for the political side of the can of worms Greyson had just opened.

He walked silently towards the wall of equipment, getting close enough now for details to become clearer.

Rachel was cursing in five languages right now. Moora might understand the English. That would be about it, unless he'd had reason to study Spanish at some point. Or Russian.

Greyson stepped close and *studied* things.

Wall of metal parts like you got in a factory. Robotic, as it was wires and waldoes, rather than handles and pedals. He couldn't identify most of it. Didn't need to.

He found a staircase that took him to a second story catwalk across the front. Almost a mezzanine.

What he'd seen from below was a series of glass test tubes, scaled up to huge proportions. Big enough that each one could hold a figure. A being. A person, once he got close enough to gaze at them.

The first half-dozen were G'schtack. Nude, Four female. Two male. Nobody he recognized. Greyson worked his way down the line. Dyarnan. Mooz. Minbe. Osleen. Xaniea. Nese. Antisaur. Balo.

And Human.

He didn't recognize the male on the end, but the first one in from this direction was a female. Busty natural blond, floating naked in a greenish liquid. Her eyes were closed, and her hair was contained in a net, but he recognized her.

Perfection. Utter perfection. If her eyes had been open, she'd have the prettiest blues you might ever manage to encounter. Perfect breasts. Flat stomach. Flawless skin. Golden ratio hips.

A work of art. A Masterpiece.

He wondered if this was the original they made copies from, or if someone just kept a spare copy grown. Maybe because they took so long to mature?

He had a lot of questions. None of them would be pleasant for someone, because all of this would go into evidence, and he'd be utterly damned if anybody, anywhere, thought that they would sweep all this under a rug to keep him from blowing shit up.

"Part of me always thought that you'd overreacted," Rachel said quietly, standing next to him and speaking English now in a tiny voice, like a child that had had a bad dream and needed comforting. "That maybe you'd let your paranoia get the better of you. I don't mind that you were right. I wish we lived in a place where you didn't have to be right all the time."

He nodded. Same, kiddo.

Investigator Moora had followed, though he hadn't just spent weeks with this case. With pictures of this woman. The one Rachel called Little Miss Perfect Boobs.

Because she was. Perfect. A perfect clone of someone. Probably an improved model, as he'd never, ever met a woman like that. Or heard of one.

"Who is that?" Moora asked.

"We called her Anais Manel," Greyson replied. "That was the name on the papers, when she arrived in the Earth system. Before she triggered this entire case."

"A clone?" Moora asked.

"An assassin," Greyson replied.

"And the rest?"

"That's why we're here," Greyson nodded.

Who were the rest of these people?

What were they?

FIFTEEN

BODIES

RACHEL REACHED DEEP INSIDE and found that same fount of rage that seemed to fuel Leigh on any given day. She'd always wanted to be a cop. Only after they'd started working with her had other folks come along and offered her a *more interesting* fate.

As he'd said more than once, you can't teach *Killer*. Beat cops didn't need that sort of psychology, though way too many of them still had that bully thing going. That just made them assholes.

Rachel had the ability to execute a Phrenic infiltrator for no other reason than they were on Earth, in disguise, having killed someone to steal their life.

Until recently, that had been the single worst thing she'd thought that people could do to each other.

Turned out, she'd been dreaming too small.

Manchurian Candidate.

Greyson had made her watch the original version of the movie. And the remakes. Read the book upon which the whole thing had been based, back when that had been a science fiction horror story.

Before you could just program someone like Little Miss Perfect Boobs here.

She turned to the guy in the next tube. Shivered.

Anyone studying Humans from the outside would have assumed that women wanted a beefcake stud with broad shoulders and an eight pack. Possibly with a beard and pelt, depending which year it was in romance covers.

This guy was anything but. Long and lean, like a surfer. Well-defined, because he was constantly out on the water, working hard, and not overeating. Felt about six feet tall, but hard to tell since he was floating above her.

Dirty blond hair, feathered back and past the collar. Sharp cheekbones. Large eyes like a Japanese anime might do them. Amazing cheekbones. Rich, full lips. Slender jaw, instead of a lantern.

Tan. And all of his was visible. Uncircumcised. Looked like he'd be nicely hung, but not painful.

"Jan Michael Vincent," she muttered under her breath, flashing back to Greyson and all his old movies he liked to watch.

Actor big in the late 1970s and early 80s, before he blew up his life. He always had that Southern California Dude thing going, in ways that most women would find utterly hot. Beefcake was for guys buying comic books. And romance covers. Most women really wanted a guy much closer to *bishonen* from an anime cartoon or manga comic book. A man who could cook, paint, and hold an intellectual conversation, as well as going down on you and making sure you had the first orgasm and then held you while you recovered.

Someone who understood Human women had built the shell in front of her. If they'd nailed Anais psychologically, she suspected that they might have the perfect man as well.

Shit.

"Kinda looks like him, doesn't it?" Greyson replied.

Not her type, exactly. She'd want more meat. Maybe some hair on his chest to run her hands through. But it was like she could see the programming inside, and just knew that he'd fix her an amazing dinner before going down on her. And it would be astounding.

Right up until the moment his secondary programming kicked in and he pulled out a nerve scrambler. Like the bitch hanging next to him.

Rachel growled and put away her own nerve scrambler before she decided to see how insulated the cloning chamber in front of her was.

Or went for a hammer.

Moora had moved down to the G'schtack end of the row. She joined him there. Felt Leigh lurk behind her, just close enough that she could smell him, but never hear a thing.

He was out on the edge right now as well. Probably back south of the border somewhere, doing bad things to worse people.

"Recognize any of them?" Rachel asked, gesturing to the half-dozen.

For all that people said all the Grays looked alike, they really did have individuality. The lack of hair just threw a lot of people off. And she didn't know more than a handful of G'schtack on sight, anyway.

"No, Detective, but there is something…" he said, voice trailing off.

"Utter physical perfection?" Rachel supplied.

She couldn't see it, but the Human models had it. No reason to expect someone to cut corners on the G'schtack.

"Yes," he said heavily. "That's it. And the Human woman was a copy of your killer on Earth?"

"The same," she replied. "Little Miss Perfect Boobs,

because a Human woman's chest starts great and then sags with age."

Rachel studied the four nude G'schtack women. They were built like Humans externally. Mammals with two breasts for feeding young. Then tended to be built like her, short and without a lot of hips. Butts and thighs instead.

Even here, though, they stood out.

She turned to Greyson.

"We're back to the old question," she noted, flashing back to another of those late-night conversations that ranged over all manner of *Hunting*. "*What is perfection?*"

"Symmetry," he replied. "Draw a line exactly down the center, top to bottom, and look for mismatches, like a broken nose or a smile that only pulls to one side."

Rachel studied the women. Caught what he was saying.

"Exactly matching breasts," she said.

No Human woman could say the same. At least with the ones they'd been born with. One was always more something than the other, regardless of size and shape.

These four looked like the Gray equivalent of the ancient Barbie dolls. Perfection in plastic in that case, but rendered in flesh here, because you could program the machines just so, decant a perfect model, and she wouldn't be around long enough to develop asymmetry.

"Skin tone is another cue," Greyson continued. "Hardly any freckles, because those are often a reaction to solar radiation. Skin is smooth and silky like the creams many women buy to achieve. And the hue is a critical non-verbal cue of fertility. Varying with the era, there is always a perfect tint to skin that all women strive to achieve in cultures where men hold an inordinate amount of power and wealth."

"Breeding cues," Rachel growled.

Didn't help that most Human men were only hot for her body until they found out what she did for a living, then they tended to leave cartoon-like cutout holes through her door, running away as fast as they could.

Occasionally, she just told them she was an accountant. That served her immediate needs when she got horny.

But nobody would be able to compete with Anais. Or any of the G'schtack women.

Shit.

"What?" Greyson asked as she turned and shoved him out of the way.

Rachel ignored the two men and made her way back down the stack. Whatever, whatever, whatever.

Here.

Okay, good.

Balo woman. NOT Lissa Jonez, but Rachel could see how close to perfection that woman had been born, just by comparing her to the utter perfection someone had on display here. Smaller chest, but perkier. A bit less curves through the hips. Narrower shoulders.

Rachel wondered if Lissa might be what this creature eventually turned into, if she were decanted then left to age for twenty or thirty years with perfect genes. Mellowing like a good wine.

Greyson was right behind her.

"Shit," he muttered.

She turned and looked up at the man.

"I need to know exactly how long these things are programmed to survive," she said, including Investigator Moora in the comment. "When we tear this place apart, I will *require* an entire team of geneticists assigned to that exact question."

"Is there a problem, Detective?" Moora asked, lost.

But then, he'd never met Lissa Jonez. Never understood just how beautiful and amazingly sexy Greyson's playmate on the trip was.

Or how she might have been the source material from which this thing in the test tube behind Rachel was drawn.

Assuming that she hadn't come out of a tube herself, once upon a time.

That was going to be an interesting conversation.

Rachel focused her entire being on Moora now. Not ignoring Leigh, but understanding that he'd been compromised. Maybe only a little, and all personally, but if Jonez turned out to be a clone, every one of his decisions could be called into question if they put him on the stand.

Assuming the case turned out that way.

"There is a device," Rachel scowled at the G'schtack who'd drawn the short straw this week. "A medical scanner. I don't know how to describe the model, but they had one back home on Earth's Moon, at Armstrong Base, because the doctor doing the autopsies had one. The one I need specifically does bloodwork to extract genetic information. If it's portable, I need one immediately. If not, then I need to know that immediately, and then I need to know where the closest one is, and how soon I can borrow it for a few minutes to scan someone. Am I clear?"

She hadn't once explained *Why?* to the man. He didn't need to know. Nobody needed to know.

Not until she was sure that Lissa Jonez was a real person. And not another clone, maybe sent to kill Greyson Leigh.

SIXTEEN

BALO

GREYSON HAD FELT the world falling out from under him. Nothing but air below. Not like the drop tubes. Those held you in a little cocoon of power and air as you descended.

No, this was HALO jumping out of an aircraft in the dead of night. *High Altitude, Low Opening.* Nothing but planet below you and not too long to recover if your first chute went wrong.

Fortunately, Rachel was here to save him. He could already see her taking charge of the case. He turned back to look at the Balo equivalent of perfection, assuming that the folks building these creatures were after another Anais Manel.

Moora had left to communicate with his superiors. Greyson needed to interrogate his prisoners.

Right now, he took a long, hard look at the Balo woman in the cloning chamber. The species were the closest to Humans externally, once you got past the skin tone and lack of body hair. The rest all generally fell into the same pattern.

Rachel was the only one within earshot.

"Thoughts?" he asked, with the first trepidation he'd felt

in…*yeah*. And spoke English, so maybe Moora was the only one who could listen in.

"Three deadly options," she replied quietly. "First not so bad. Deadly Option One, she's the original and they took her DNA-equivalent and tweaked it a little, but not really that much, though I've never seen Lissa nude."

"Not that much different," he agreed. "Ten pounds heavier, spread out in all the right places. Hips, thighs, chest, muscles."

"Right," she nodded as he glanced over. "Deadly Option Two, they have been doing this for a very long time, and decanted a version who has been out of the tube long enough to put on the weight, as well as those other signals that put her closer to forty than twenty. Still a clone, though."

"And Three?"

"They assumed a Human cop," Rachel said. "Someone smarter than Dominguez. Maybe they knew that you'd likely get the call when they sent Anais to Earth in the first place."

"They might have done me in on the flight, then," Greyson said.

"Or they were just trolling for hits," she countered. "Leave her out there like bait, and check out every Human male coming from Earth that wasn't previously known. Not that many, as I remember, since most of the guys that wanted to hit on me had wives back home and affairs on the road."

"Do we round her up and take her in for questioning?" he asked now.

"Good way to burn the relationship permanently," Rachel shrugged. "Sure you wanna go down that path?"

He thought about it. Pulled out his phone and started taking pictures. Anais and Jan. Both Balo. Everybody. Evidence techs would come along and do a professional job of it later, but he wanted personal proof to show the woman when they had their next confrontation.

Next? That suggested another one after that? Had he already assumed that she was safe? Bad. Very bad.

Greyson would need Rachel and her med scanner for that scene. On the Moon, that doctor had been able to show that Anais appeared to be six years old, instead of twenty-something. The same model here would have to be pointed at Lissa.

"As you noted, several options," Greyson said when he was done. "You missed the possible fourth or fifth."

"Oh?"

"They built these to look like the most beautiful Balo woman they knew, which might have been her," Greyson said. "I know she's kinda rich and famous, just from things she said."

"Oh, buddy, you have no idea, do you?" Rachel laughed.

He turned to fully face her, tearing his eyes away from the creature in front of him to do it.

"What?"

"America has a terrible fascination with English aristocracy," Rachel laughed again. "Weird, because lots of other places also have them from the old days, but only England holds their attention."

"Goes back to Lady Diana in the 1980s," he said automatically.

"So imagine instead your friend was Korean, Greyson," she said.

He nodded, a little confused.

"Lissa's father owns one of the largest corporate conglomerates on her homeworld," Rachel said. "*Owns*. Not runs, though he is involved. Thing is so big that there are cousins and relatives running divisions, plus the man put pros in charge. Richest guy on Earth right now *might* be allowed to belong to the same country club, if they made an exception for third-tier wealth."

"Oh?" he asked.

She had money. He knew that. Wasn't a predator like Emmy, but had a brain in there.

"Yeah," Rachel assured him. "What's number five?"

"There is an expression of perfection for each species," Greyson replied. "Convergent evolution meant that these people tweaked their design to get close. Maybe Lissa did the same thing. As you noted, she apparently has the cash."

"Huh," Rachel considered. "And a sixth."

"What?"

"She's a Phrenic," the woman said, and he felt the bottom fall out again. "Adjusted a few things somehow during transformation to make herself the perfect honey trap?"

Would he be able to tell?

Not if they're good enough actors, Ethen whispered in his ear.

He filed that for now. Too many open-ended questions and no easy way to answer them.

"Let's go," he said instead, drawing Rachel after him and heading to the front of the warehouse.

Through the double doors, he could see more vehicles arriving outside. Forensics of all kinds, from physical to financial, because he'd rattled a few cages in the process of gathering everything and everyone for a snap raid.

Outside, he saw a perimeter fence being unrolled. The kind of thing folks did for a traffic wreck, but they had enough rolls of the stuff to surround the entire building. Everybody in the other three sections would be sent home early, once they got verified against their ID and local records of employment.

Greyson Leigh wasn't in the mood for halfway measures. And the Judge had agreed.

He found his four main victims handcuffed and lined up in the reception area with too many stun rifles casually pointed in their direction. Cops, being cops. Wanted to show how tough they were.

Greyson decided to give everybody a masterclass in tough today. Helped that Rachel was utterly freaked out right now. That would communicate a manic pixie energy that would be misinterpreted as *carnivorous* if you didn't know Humans. And few folks in here would.

He didn't bother with names. Just titles.

The Receptionist was in this because she had to know too much, just because the stuff in back was out in the open. The Foreman was the same way. He might not know *why*, but he certainly could answer all sort of questions about *what*. The male G'schtack in the nice suit was the Lawyer.

That left the Executive. The woman whose door he had kicked in. Who had been on the comm, but probably hadn't had time to react to the noise and call for help.

There was too much noise outside to just sweep this one under the rug later. He might have done that on purpose. Harder to make it go away when so many people were going to be whispering about it, leaking stories, and asking questions.

Just to establish some pack dominance, Greyson walked right up to loom over the sitting group. Helped that Humans tended to be so much bigger than G'schtack anyway.

He smiled. It was not a pleasant thing. He wasn't feeling pleasant.

Greyson turned to the Mooz woman guarding the room and leading Team One. They exchanged the kind of non-verbal nod that spoke volumes, then he grabbed the Executive by her elbow and stood her up politely.

"Investigator Moora, could you join us please?" he said as he pulled the unresisting woman in the direction of the conference room that had been empty before.

All the other rooms had evidence that needed to be

tagged and inventoried. Probably here, too, but nothing that looked important, as far as clues or convictions went.

The four of them were quickly alone. He left the door open, just so she couldn't claim they'd beaten her later.

Physically. What he had in mind emotionally and psychologically transcended far beyond what a couple of Human treaties around war generally allowed.

He already had all of these people dead to rights. Hell, he'd been expecting to raid the place and capture all their shipping records showing smuggling on a second set of books. That would have gotten a conviction.

This was even better.

Greyson smiled at the woman after he seated her at the head of the table. Rachel was standing by the door, like she generally did in these scenes. Moora took a seat. Greyson sat a hip on the edge of the table itself, again looming over her.

Moora was going to Good Cop this. Suspects have rights. Big, bad, Human cops can't just come in and torture confessions out of people. Et cetera. Whatever.

He didn't need torture. Not how Moora saw it. The Illymus Merchant Guild were junior varsity when it came to interrogations, anyway. Greyson had been through far worse when he'd been a soldier.

So he sat. Watched her with an ugly smile. No words.

She had to be uncomfortable, with her hands behind her in a chair with a back. Discomfort was the goal. Folks want to escape discomfort. They'll talk, in order to break a heavy, pregnant silence.

Greyson just sat there. Moora fidgeted, but he didn't understand how to stand next to a game trail with a crossbow because a rifle made too much noise that might attract the wrong kind of attention.

The Executive began to fidget after a time. He'd have said

Human nature, but the two folks seated weren't Human. G'schtack had enough of the same mental wiring.

"As you no doubt know, you can remain perfectly silent," he suddenly broke his. "Never utter another word from now until you are convicted of everything I can make stick to you and your friends. I walked in here planning to find evidence of smuggling without the appropriate tax stamps. You've already made my case infinitely easier, because we've moved on to illegal genetic engineering of intelligent species. That's probably good enough to put you in prison forever."

He stopped talking and smiled nicer. At her. At Moora. At Rachel.

Executive-lady didn't respond. He didn't expect her to. Not yet. The day was far from over.

He turned back to her.

"And now the fun part," he said. "I brought forensic accountants with me today. You know, smuggling and all that. Got a small mob of them outside, just itching to take your books apart and find out everyone who ever bought your products. And anyone who ever invested in your little company."

G'schtack had larger eyes than Humans, though not as emotive. Maybe the species was not as close to the animals they'd evolved from as Humans were. He still watched the first seed of fear take root in her eyes. Black pools that were suddenly contemplating dread.

"You'll obviously remain silent through the whole affair, no doubt protecting the people who gave you money under the table in exchange for…whatever purpose they might want to buy a programmed clone for. Whatever itch they needed to…*scratch*."

He smiled at her some more, rather enjoying himself at this point. All the shit a guy had to wade through chasing criminals got paid off when you had them so bloody dead to rights.

He especially liked the little flinches passing through her frame. She had rights. He wasn't violating any of them. All he was doing was talking. Investigator Moora could be put on the stand and swear to that. Plus, both he and Rachel were audio recording all this. Standard procedure.

Cover your ass against people lying later.

"The best part is that I don't even need your cooperation," Greyson sighed happily now. "I might have, until five minutes ago. Then we discovered a Human woman in one of your little doodads out in the warehouse. She's a spitting image of another woman we encountered on a case back on Earth. That woman's name was Anais Manel, at least on her paperwork. She looked Human, but wasn't, so I brought a complete copy of her DNA readout with me. I can compare it with the woman in the warehouse. And with your computer files. I wonder what interesting things I'll find."

More twitches. Chinese water torture was illegal under all the Geneva conventions. And other places. That was why he wasn't using water. Just words. Random drops spanging off your forehead to drive you crazy enough to react. To speak.

To do anything to *make it stop*.

The woman wasn't there yet in her mind, but that first light of madness was also taking root, next to the fear.

Forever in a prison cell is a long time. Particularly for a woman wearing an expensive suit.

"Oh, and Anais Manel, the one on Earth?" he continued, just because he was angry and had a victim who wasn't a victim. "She was programmed by someone to be an assassin. I'm certain we can find out how and prove that with your records, too. I wonder whose signature we'll find on the order to twist a Human clone around like that? To make her a murderer."

Even Moora was twitching now, out of the corner of Greyson's eye. Executive-lady was shivering.

Obviously, never had to deal with the outcomes of her little operation.

Never had *consequences*.

Never met an angry Human in person.

Greyson's smile turned feral. It was all an act. At the same time, it wasn't.

Free will was about the only thing God ever promised any of us. If you take that away from a person, you've taken everything.

He did NOT growl at her. It was only in his eyes. And his hands. And her twitches.

"So now I'm going to turn you over to the fancy folks who will cart you off and enter you into the system as an arrestee," he said blithely, downshifting gears headed into a sharp curve. "They'll take that nice suit and swap you for prisoner blue. Put you in a holding cell until I can get around to having you arraigned. We already have enough to hold you for a while. More than long enough for superseding indictments to be filed when I hear from the accountants. Long enough for *forever*."

He stood up and paced now, that extra span of time being just another drop of water.

Greyson reached the far end of the table and kicked the chair out of his way so he could put both hands flat and lean into it. The whole table separated them, so he wasn't looming over her. Wasn't threatening her.

Physically.

"At some point, you might want to consider that leniency for a murder conviction is going to hinge on you providing information that is actually worth letting you out of prison this side of death," he said simply. "Or maybe one of the others outside will want to talk. To roll over on you so that you can take the blame for everything. Silence, and all that, as you'll be protecting bigger fish. They're small fish. They can buy a shorter sentence by convicting you. By sending you away *forever*. And I'll have your entire corporate existence to enter as evidence when we get that far."

He watched her from a table-length away. Watched the twitches. The water drops. The horror dawning. Not a single threat. Not anything. Just him calmly explaining his position to a person in his custody.

Greyson had gotten pretty good at this over the years. The decades.

The lives.

He turned and headed to the open door. Stuck his head out.

"Team One," he said, getting the Mooz woman's head turned his way. "Your prisoner."

Again, the silent communication. She'd have made an excellent leader of any heavy response team he ever had to call in on a case, if she wanted to get a job on Earth. Hard, committed, sharp.

She moved his direction quickly, drawing one of her dozen people with her.

Both entered. Greyson gestured to the Executive.

"Keep all four of them isolated from each other and other prisoners," he instructed the woman. "Haul them downtown in separate vehicles, at separate times, just to be sure. We've got the arrest warrants. They just need names filled in. Or fingerprints at this point. I'll let you and Investigator Moora handle that side of things, because we want every step of this written down with such careful precision that no lawyer can find a hole to exploit later. Questions?"

"Negative, sir," the woman nodded.

Greyson smiled at her. Smiled at Executive-lady. Smiled at Moora. Dismissed everyone.

Thirty seconds later, he and Rachel were alone in here. He sat at the low end of the table, watching the space his prisoner had just vacated. Outside, forensic techs and other detectives were starting the process of cataloging things.

Greyson felt like he was riding a log that was floating and spinning at the same time. Except that it was a gator. And there were other gators in the water, just waiting for him to slip.

But what else was new?

SEVENTEEN

RANKEV

Rachel heard someone getting directions to the conference room from one of the cops outside. Someone out in the reception area looking for her and Greyson.

Partly, she was so keyed up for violence right now that time seemed to be moving slow. They had been alone for all of about three minutes. Just long enough that she'd heard the four main prisoners all get shuffled out and hauled off to jail.

Footsteps announced the approach, but most people wouldn't hear them. Greyson was almost as hyped as she was, so they both turned to the door as a shadow appeared.

Judge Rankev was not quite the last persons she expected to appear, but close. The woman had changed out of her robes into a simple suit like you might see on the streets of Boston. Slacks and a blazer-like top, both in dark green.

She even smiled at them as she entered, a sardonic grin. Leigh even stood up as she walked to the head of the table and sat in a chair that might still be warm.

"I watched your friends being hauled off," she began. "And heard some of the rumors and gossip."

"How long have you been here?" Rachel managed, when Greyson remained silent.

"I arrived with the first wave of officers and Investigators," she grinned.

"That's not normal," Rachel pointed out.

She'd been diving that deep into the law books lately, building up several cases against need.

"True," Rankev nodded. "But this is not a normal case."

Rachel would give the woman that one. And in Guildlaw, judges were a little more like prosecutors. More Napoleonic Code, sort of, if you squinted just right. The American model made better justice, because the judges weren't involved in the prosecution, so they tended to be more neutral and make you really prove your case.

"Would you like to see what you made possible?" Greyson asked now.

Rachel was a bit surprised, but maybe he saw the Judge as an ally. She obviously hadn't tipped anyone off to the coming raid after signing the paperwork. She'd had more than four hours when something could have leaked.

"What I made possible, Detective?" she asked curiously, centering her gaze on the man.

"You could have told me to piss off, Your Honor," he smiled, still standing. "Could have stretched this whole affair out so long that someone, somewhere, would have leaked it and we might have arrived here to discover the facility emptied out, or burned to the ground. Instead, we caught them with their hands in the cookie jar."

"Did we now?" She rose and Rachel escorted both of them back into the warehouse, dodging evidence techs and Investigators going about a rousing business in something. She wasn't sure she could call it justice, but maybe close.

As Leigh liked to say, someone was getting theirs, hard

and painful. That was really what usually mattered in law enforcement.

Out in the warehouse, two Mooz cops were arguing with a G'schtack male in dirty coveralls and his hands cuffed in front of him.

"Because you can't just leave this on autopilot, that's why!" the man was yelling as Rachel headed that way.

The man was getting worked up. Rachel made her way close. He looked at her and nearly jumped out of his skin.

"Problems?" she asked in a soothing voice that included all three of the people.

"They don't understand, Investigator," the man said, gesturing to the two cops. "The machines will hold baseline pretty well, but they aren't fully automated. Somebody has to keep watch on stuff or we start going off center. Too far off and you get terminal failures in any of a variety of ways. Or mold gets into the intakes and you have to dismantle the whole thing and steam it clean with ammonia before you can start it up again."

"And you were volunteering to put your reputation on the line to run the machines until techs can be brought in and trained?" Rachel asked. "At some point, the whole thing will be dismantled. This operation is about as illegal as it gets. If something were to happen to my evidence, that person is in for a ration of shit from me."

He grimaced. Clenched his jaws shut. Positively glowered at her.

"Somebody's gotta watch it," he muttered.

"They are just clones," Leigh said from behind her.

That got a sharp rise out of the man that was almost enough for one of the cops to stun him. Or for Rachel to punch him in the jaw. He controlled himself short of getting cold-cocked.

"I am not an educated man, Investigators," he retorted.

"But it isn't right to just grow them up and then dump them and kill them. Any one of them folks could step out of the chamber right now and just be a person, you know?"

"Unprogrammed?" Rachel asked, getting right up into his face.

Helped that he was hardly any taller than she was.

Again, the grimace. And a flinch. He knew what she meant, even if nobody else in here but Greyson and maybe Judge Rankev did.

"Far as I know," he muttered quietly. "Base models. Don't remember any special orders come in lately for nothing."

"How custom is all this equipment?" Rachel asked, gesturing to the wall of machinery and the many tubes holding…people.

"Maybe half," the guy shrugged. "And three-quarters of the programming that keeps stuff balanced. Hard part is understanding what a sensor is telling you so you can tweak the right valve elsewhere. They never automated that part all that well."

"But you can keep it running for a week or so?" Greyson asked, leaning down on the guy in that way he did.

"Sure."

"Your Honor, would we consider that a valuable contribution to the case, were he to keep all this evidence intact against the risk that police techs might accidentally damage something?" Greyson asked.

Rachel smiled at the prisoner. He'd thought the woman was a cop. Not a Judge.

"I can see it contributing to mitigation later, Detective," Rankev said in a stage voice kind of way.

Playing for the galleries, like Leigh always did.

"I'll make you a deal," Greyson turned back to the prisoner. "You keep all this running right and I'll go to bat for you with the prosecutors and the judges. You're guilty, just because you work here, but that doesn't mean I have to throw the book at you. Or put you in jail forever. Look at this as a head start on your rehabilitation and we'll try to convince them to mark today as part of your overall sentence, when some of those folks won't go before a judge for months. Or maybe years."

"I can do that," the man nodded. "Gonna need some techs to train, though. This place normally runs around the clock, though it is not that hard of a job. Just sharp when things start to wobble."

Rachel turned to the two cops. Picked the shorter one because she was shorter.

"You and your prisoner accompany us," she instructed the man, before turning to his taller partner. "You go find some techs who can ask this guy esoteric questions and understand his answers, so we know who to bring in."

That cop nodded and Rachel led her new mob to the stairway up to that catwalk. To all those bodies, floating in liquid.

"Oh, fuck," Judge Rankev muttered when she got to the top and realized what she was looking at.

Rachel had specifically chosen the end with Little Miss Perfect Boobs and Jan Michael. Just for the impact.

"That's the woman from your murder at Armstrong Base," she said as they came to rest.

"Perfect copy of a perfect woman, yes," Rachel agreed. "Leigh thinks that just having her here means that this case is about to freaking explode all over the place."

"And he might be right, Detective Asher," the woman agreed.

"Then you'll want to see this end," Rachel replied, leading her little tour group to the G'schtack end, where Judge Rankev taught her a whole new litany of G'schtack profanities she'd never encountered before.

"Recognize any of them?" Rachel asked.

"No, but I'm not on any sort of social circuit, either," Rankev replied.

Rachel liked the way the woman rounded on their prisoner now.

"You will keep them all alive, and all healthy," Her Honor Judge Rankev the Suddenly Bloodthirsty commanded. "As of now, all appear to be citizens with rights. That would make this roughly thirty-odd cases of First-Degree Murder if something happened to them before a Court ruled. Am I clear?"

Hell, even Rachel wanted to gulp at that tone, and she'd only caught the fringes of it. Bright boy over there nodded like his head was coming off.

"Just so you understand your position as a zookeeper, citizen," the Judge layered another level of threat on top of that like frosting, in a manner that maybe only Leigh could have managed.

Rachel found that she needed to learn a few tricks from this woman, too. Educational day, all in all.

Rankev stepped back until her butt was up against the catwalk railing. Couldn't really see more, but it let her take in both ends, sort of. Rachel joined her, thinking that she was going for a wider perspective on things.

Forest, instead of trees.

Maybe she and Greyson had been spending too much time as lumberjacks on this case, but that was necessary sometimes, when you were trying to cross an impossible jungle and all you had was a machete.

Bodies in test tubes, like some horror flick late at night on one of the weirder networks. She remembered a couple like it, made way back in the 1970s or something. When technology got to the point that people could see *how* to do it. If not when.

Someone had once said that horror as a literary genre was when things that routinely happened to non-whites suddenly started happening to white people, too. Fast forward that from Humans like her, Puerto Rican in that old saying and not white folk, and now it might be happening to the G'schtack.

And everybody else, just in case you missed the powerful symbolism of what the fuckers who owned this place had been up to.

Rachel turned to the Judge.

"So everything I know comes out of textbooks and videos," she was willing to admit, in front of someone that Greyson seemed to want to treat as an ally. "Moora can share with you what Leigh did to the woman running this facility, in the way of a non-interrogation. We're going to actually ask questions next time, but we need someone expert at what we can say and do without jeopardizing our case."

"Non-interrogation, Asher?" Rankev asked.

"He occasionally plays hardball with suspects," Rachel grinned. "Didn't ask a single question of the woman. Didn't threaten her. Just laid out a series of observations that are likely to cause her to either roll over on whoever owns her, or open her up for ninjas."

"Ninjas?"

"Assassins," Greyson stepped close. "A specialized subset from Earth history with powerful sociological overtones. Killers who can penetrate any facility and get to anyone, regardless of the security around them."

"What did you do to the woman, Leigh?" Rankev asked.

"Explained to her what her options were," he said in that off-hand way that he'd either been born with, or practiced on a daily basis when nobody was looking.

"And she has options?"

"Until someone else decides to turn State's Evidence and

tell me anything she would have," he smiled. "Then I don't need her cooperation and she can go to prison forever."

Rachel liked that tone. Leigh was feeling his oats right now, having been proven *beyond right* with this raid. Instead of accountants finding him the next link in the chain, he'd gotten so much evidence that heads were going to roll everywhere.

Hopefully, before the two of them—three if Rankev stayed around—burned the Illymus Merchant Guild itself to the ground.

Rankev nodded and turned to Rachel now.

"You need a trained interrogator?" she asked.

"I need a trained lawyer who can draw us bright enough lines that we don't mess things up and let someone walk on a technicality," Rachel replied. "We can ask all the questions. Leigh never once threatened the woman, but she looked close to pissing herself when he sent her off to be put in jail."

"And Investigator Moora?"

"He drew the short straw when two Humans from out of town happened to need a guide to Brees," Greyson stepped in. "Good enough cop, but I've known him six hours longer than you, Your Honor, so I don't know if he's right for when the reporters get hold of this. Or when my suspects suddenly have high-powered lawyers show up to advise them."

"And you expect something like that?" Rankev asked.

Greyson gestured to the wall of machinery.

"This was not assembled over the weekend," he snarled at the universe. "Someone put out a lot of cash to build and run it. That means that they had a lot of cash coming in for...*services rendered*. That means someone with money. Usually, either they have power, or connections to power. Tomorrow, this case gets even uglier. My goal is to make sure nobody can just sweep it all under the rug, pat me on the head and send me home, while everyone else walks away free and they start over somewhere else."

Rachel moved to draw Rankev's eyes now.

"Last spring, we found ourselves in possession of the complete blackmail files that a former police official had accumulated," she said. "Enough to pretty much destroy all the top players in Eastern North America, which is one of the biggest and most important regions back home."

"I see," Rankev replied as a placeholder.

"He used it to get a full confession out of the man," Rachel said in a quieter voice. "Then we burned everything. Literally, in a dumpster with chemical propellants. It was the only way to keep from bringing down the whole government. Some of the guilty got to remain in place, but they were no longer being blackmailed, and the man responsible is *never* getting out of prison. We don't have to shatter the Guild, despite what a hard-ass my partner might be."

Rankev studied both of them. The cop and the other prisoner were standing nearby, both with jaws just about as dropped open as physiology would allow. Rachel turned to them.

"And you'll be quiet, or I'll come for you personally," she told both men.

They nodded. Small fish in the presence of big, hungry sharks.

Long, calculating silence.

Rankev turned to Leigh.

"How far did your original writ take you, Detective?" she asked.

"It ran out about ten minutes ago, Your Honor," he nodded. "Come to Brees. Get a warrant. Come to this address with folks who could capture it with all the records intact."

"That's all you had?" she asked, surprised.

"My information came from a now-dead Phrenic," he growled. "They only knew that they could contact this operation with specific details to get a Human assassin programmed and sent to Earth's moon, where a Mooz businessman was murdered, before the clone ended itself. That's when Andell brought us in."

"So are you returning to Earth in the short term?" Rankev asked.

"I have funding from Armstrong Base that will run for a time, but not forever," he nodded. "Nobody knew what we'd find, or how it would turn out. Andell never imagined this. Nobody did."

"You are both Officers of the Court?" she confirmed, going back to that thing that spanned species and planets.

Cops, all sworn to uphold the greater Guildlaw, while dealing with local stuff too.

"That's right," Rachel spoke up.

"Then let me talk to some people about getting you transferred to the Anic Metroplex, at least for the time being," she nodded now. "That will help get you temporary housing and access to funds to live on."

"Might not be all that temporary," Rachel said firmly.

"Oh?"

Rachel gestured to the whole warehouse now, both hands out.

"We've uncovered something bigger than we thought," she said. "That's a knot that's going to take some time to unravel."

"Yes, you're probably right," Rankev said. "All the more reason to send a message home to let them know you might be a while."

Rachel nodded. They had once called it the Gordian Knot. Something so messed up that it was impossible to untangle, until somebody—Alexander the Great?—just took a sword and hacked it apart.

She could see Leigh standing over the bisected corpse of a corrupt Guild, bloody sword in one hand.

Hopefully, it would never come to that.

EIGHTEEN
IMPLICATIONS

Greyson had found a taste of home. A joint that would deliver Chinese takeout and hot coffee. Neither were all that impressive, but he didn't feel safe leaving the scene of the crime until everything had gotten organized. And the food was good enough.

He and Rachel were out in the waiting area, eating. Team One had ordered delivery from other places more suited to their biology. Computer techs had ripped out all the hardware in the office space, while others were in back getting trained by their new friend, the G'schtack male Irelyn Woldt, on how to maintain everything. That poor unfortunate would end up living here for an indeterminate time, but Rankev had assured him that cooperation now would go a long ways later when it came time to sentence him.

As in, if everything worked out, Woldt might spend a whole weekend in jail, just for the symbolism. The others were going away forever, as far as Greyson and Rankev were concerned.

A vehicle landed out in the parking lot, inside the area

cordoned off. The facility would be as empty as it could get in another few hours, then locked up tight and run by Woldt and his trainees for however long it took a judge to sort out custody issues.

How the hell do you handle clones who might be one of several copies of someone running around? Especially if the rest have all been *programmed* to some task? Like murder.

Greyson figured that the rest were all more likely to exist in some sort of high-end, private brothel, if they weren't stalking someone.

Greyson stopped eating and watched the transport. It had sleeker lines that the brute he'd ridden in earlier. Power, wealth, importance.

He was no stranger to politicians showing up once everything was safe. Raid like this was a great way to get yourself on the evening news, Boston or Anic. Some things spanned species.

A man emerged from the back. Tall for a G'schtack, though no broader. Lanky, like Greyson. Nice suit in the parking lot lights, sort of a steel blue with glittery, electric threads woven. Pretty, unlike the man himself. He looked to be built out of vitriol and barbed wire from the scowl on his face.

A woman emerged, but she wasn't a date. Also G'schtack. Much older. Almost elderly, though she moved with grace and kept up with the taller man as they crossed the parking lot at a good clip.

Several others moved in a circle around them. Bodyguards. A variety species represented, but all had that hard edge of contained violence that he recognized.

Greyson nodded to Rachel and stood. Murphely Rankev had left a while ago, saying she was going to return to her office and make some calls.

Greyson assumed that this was the result. Hopefully, it

would be a good one. He'd eaten, and had some coffee to give him a growlier edge. Might be weeks before this case didn't require that from him.

Team One started to stand, but he waved them back to eating and moved off to intercept the newcomers on the sidewalk outside, Rachel on his flank like a wing in a dogfight.

Closer, the G'schtack male was almost his height, so a giant among their kind. The woman was even smaller than Rachel, but that just meant short for a G'schtack.

Greyson went formal and pulled out his badge. The two approaching had that feel about them.

"Detective/Hunter Greyson Leigh, Eastern North America Division, Earth Police Special Missions," he introduced himself. "My partner, Rachel Asher."

Technically still a Patrolman/Hunter, only because she hadn't been around long enough to take the exam. Everyone treated her like his equal, and were right to do so. If they wanted to get fussy later, he'd deal with it then.

The two came to rest at a comfortable distance.

"This is Metropolitan Tine Ricia," the man gestured politely to the woman. "Metropolitan of the Anic Metroplex."

And thus, even more important and powerful than Denise Upkins, back home. Anic was to the Illymus Merchant Guild as New York City had once been to Earth. Back in the day. Or London. Or Hong Kong. Big players far outsized for what they were. Power and money.

"Pleasure to meet you, Your Honor," Greyson said.

He bowed his head to the woman. Denise would have shown up for something like this, but she would have brought along Edgar Redhawk, who was the exact opposite of the man across from him.

Redhawk was quiet. Subtle. Greyson had never been able

to accurately judge the man's age, other than he got jokes and references from Greyson's youth when others didn't.

The G'schtack man was much louder physically.

"I am Yaran Ikoshi," the man introduced himself now. "Captain of Detectives, Anic Metroplex."

"Sir," Greyson nodded to him as well.

Maybe the next step up the ladder from Captain Rutherford Parsons, depending on how you cut things. Outside of Earth, the Hunter Bureau wasn't as needed. More mature civilizations and technologies. Better scanners supposedly able to pick out a Phrenic moving around in disguise. Less violent crime.

Greyson just hoped that they wouldn't ever see him for what he was. Dave's hardware back home was supposedly state of the art, but nobody could explain what he and Ethen had turned into. Phrenic who lost control of their projection supposedly turned into Deathwalkers. If there was a stage beyond that, nobody had ever seen it in person to understand. To know that a projection like Greyson Leigh could somehow take charge of the combined body and run it well enough to fool everyone. And their medical machines.

As Rachel had muttered a time or two: *Anybody but Greyson Leigh…*

"I have been in touch with Judge Rankev," Captain Ikoshi said now. "She's brought me up to speed and explained why you didn't file all your formal paperwork with the Division before gathering up however many cops you could lay your hands on and executing a search warrant. I won't say I appreciate it, but given the scope of things, I will also not argue with your logic at this time, Leigh. You will provide a full debriefing later."

It wasn't a threat. Not exactly. More a promise. And exactly why he'd found a place that did Earth coffee, however badly scorched the roast had been. Caffeine and bile. Kinda what he'd expected he would need when this moment arrived.

"Looking forward to it, Captain," Greyson lied with a pretty smile.

Right up there with getting a root canal on a day a sadist dentist was out of drugs to numb his jaw ahead of time.

"Is the facility fully secured?" Captain Ikoshi asked.

"For now," Greyson gestured around them. "At some point, we'll need to make decisions about the organic contents of the building. Until then, Judge Rankev ordered one of the suspects to cooperate with police techs to maintain things in a holding pattern. The facility will need to be occupied constantly, so Woldt, our suspect, has volunteered to live here for now and train people."

"Organic contents?" Metropolitan Ricia said with a twinkle in her eyes. "What an interesting choice of words."

"As far as my partner and I have been able to tell, given relevant statute and case law, those beings are clones that have been illegally manufactured, Metropolitan," Greyson said. "I honestly don't know if they are fully sentient, which would bring with it all the commensurate rights of citizenship."

"As opposed to?" the woman asked sharply.

"My case started when a clone from this facility was brought to Earth to assassinate an unsuspecting victim, before destroying itself," he smiled down at the woman, happy to explain, yet again, just how twisted and weird this thing had been from day one. It had only gotten worse since then. "She had been programmed to self-terminate after completing her mission. I would argue that such programming made her a tool, and not a person. Woldt seems to think that the clones inside are blank slates at present. What he couldn't tell me was if they had been impressed with any personality at all, or were just biological containers that would need to be turned into people later. Lacking that assessment, are they people or are they empty bottles?"

She positively glowered up at him. Obviously didn't like being lectured by what these fine folk might consider a caveman from the back of beyond. Especially one fluent in G'schtack and competent at their laws and culture.

"Show me," she ordered in a grim voice.

Probably not the evening she had planned.

He began to walk, flashing back to the night Fred Jansen had nearly gotten run over by a semi while running away for his life from Greyson and Rachel. Captain Parsons had shown up in the dress she'd obviously worn to the opera, looking nothing like her usual self.

Metropolitan Ricia had more the look of a woman who'd been working late in the office. Or maybe had been back in her office all day just getting briefed by folks like Investigator Moora when he showed up with interesting prisoners to process. And watching news reporters sitting outside the safe zone with telephoto lenses trying to identify key players and formulate a coherent storyline from fragments they overheard.

It would all leak eventually, but he'd gotten here first, and had all the evidence in hand before it could be burned.

Well, it still could be, but now you had to burn it in an evidence room. Which meant a bent cop and someone probably leaving fingerprints in the database when they tried to do something stupid for a couple of bills under the table.

Like that had never happened in Boston.

They passed inside and Greyson watched Woldt already training a team of evidence techs how to maintain things. He'd been frightened into compliance, and then given the opportunity to get out of this way easier than anybody else.

Still a criminal, but Greyson could see him being fully

rehabilitated first of everybody involved. Man seemed committed to doing the right thing. Just had a screwy take on right and wrong.

They went up onto that catwalk. He was starting to feel like a docent in a museum, or a tour guide in a wilderness park. But these two needed to see this. To internalize that the crimes went far beyond just experimenting on the silly monkeys from Earth.

All the species of the Guild were at risk.

He supposed that someone had just boiled the frog exceptionally slowly, to the point that nobody had really understood where such things might take you.

Of course, nobody else in this building used to kill random strangers for a living, not counting all his friends in test tubes, dreaming whatever dreams a clone did before they turned into real boys and girls.

As before, they started at the Human end.

"This woman is a perfect copy of a suspect that murdered a Mooz businessman in the Earth system," Greyson explained, yet again, tapping on the test tube and hoping she didn't open her eyes right now. That would utterly freak his shit completely out, no questions about it. "My informant got a cloned killer from the folks who operate this place, shipped it, and only got caught when the G'schtack Engineering Master of Armstrong Base specifically requested that I be put on the case."

"Why you, Leigh?" Ikoshi asked in a sharp tone. Cop. Doing his job.

"Virgar Andell knew she wasn't Human after looking at her medical readouts," he replied. "Turned out that he also had a Phrenic inside his administration causing issues. We killed that creature after she confessed to everything and then pursued the case to Brees."

Both G'schtack shuddered. Humans were violent.

Phrenic running around in somebody else's life had it coming.

"Phrenic?" Metropolitan Ricia asked.

"That's right," he said, noting that Rachel was being quiet and demure right now. Not setting him up but setting these two up for later.

"Do you expect more Phrenic here?" she asked.

"Investigator Moora already took my four main prisoners in and got them scanned, but I doubt they were," Greyson replied. "Mostly just being safe. The connection to Aeon Research Financial was purely a business connection the Phrenic had made after they'd killed an Osleen here on Brees several years ago."

"So where does this case go next, Leigh?" Ikoshi asked.

Greyson smiled and started down the line. They made interested noises as they started encountering species they knew better.

Then he got to the six G'schtack in their tubes.

"I don't recognize anybody here," Greyson said in a deadpan sort of way to set up the best jokes. "Are you familiar with any of them?"

Ricia's hiss of surprise was interesting. Ikoshi was just angry.

Shoe was suddenly on the other foot, wasn't it? Young, beautiful, perfect.

Oh, and programmable. What did you want your robot clone to do? And who did you want it done to?

"I asked Judge Rankev for some help, because we're new to Guildspace, and especially Brees," he lied delightfully. "This case has grand political ramifications that go far beyond my pay grade. Extremely far beyond. Obviously, we impressed that upon her, so she contacted the big hitters and asked you two to get involved. I'd like your assistance in making sure that nobody escapes justice on this case."

Always play to a politician's ego. And a Captain of Detectives was a political job. That's why Greyson threatened anybody who ever offered to promote him even to Lieutenant/Hunter. Fuck that noise.

The Metropolitan of Anic was possibly in the top half dozen most powerful beings in this solar system, at the end of the day. Or wider. At least from the standpoint of a bully pulpit from which to make noise.

"Clones," Ricia said, drawling the word out a ways.

"As far as we know," Greyson said. "I'm now given to understand that you can take an existing being and program their biology, adjusting and improving things as you go, in addition to what you can put into their heads. Until a tech discovers records or someone talks, I have no idea what these things are. Do they have rights? Should they be destroyed immediately? The ethical implications range far beyond the legal and the moral here."

"You mentioned justice," she said, turning her whole body to face him now.

The G'schtack translation of the term wasn't a perfect match to English. It had ramifications that went beyond the *quality of being fair and reasonable in the administration of law* as Human code saw it. It flowed over into the sorts of places Greyson liked to reside.

Delivering to someone what they really *deserved.*

"That's right," he said simply, showing no emotion on his face now.

High-stakes poker with big-shot players.

"You are impressively fluent in our language," she noted dryly.

"Hunters need to be able to communicate with as many people as possible," Rachel spoke up, nailing the accentlessness perfectly. "The Guild speaks G'schtack, so it was critical that we be conversational. Again, part of the reason we were selected for this case."

She'd been sandbagging, of course. Both Ricia and Ikoshi nearly jumped out of their skins when she spoke. Possibly thought she was ignorant of the language and unable to follow things when she was really a trapdoor spider, lurking in her web.

Greyson wondered if Scotland Yard would utterly pale by comparison to the real big leagues, after all this was done. Would she aim for a gig working for the Guild directly?

Would he follow?

It might mean giving up Emmy as anything but an occasional fling. Assuming she didn't turn around and decide to conquer the businessfolk of the Guild like she had the Humans back home.

It might open up options like Lissa Jonez. Assuming she wasn't another trapdoor spider even now getting updated instructions from someone who held the keys to her programming.

Metropolitan Ricia tore her eyes away from Rachel and studied him now.

"Justice, Investigator Leigh?" she asked.

Who's getting his?

"Someone is creating clones," he said. "That's illegal. Period. Rachel and I have discussed that it might have started out innocently enough as a medical research program before Humans were admitted to the Guild itself."

"Research?" Ricia probed.

"Understanding the newest species so diseases can be accounted for and stopped before they mutated and jumped across species boundaries, for instance," he said. "Being able to treat a Human in any hospital because they had already cataloged us, thus allowing a doctor to make informed decisions, instead of bringing in a veterinarian."

"A what?"

"On Earth, veterinarians are trained to handle an incredibly wide range of possible patients, all of whom are non-Human," Rachel offered brightly. "Both family pets as well as food animals, depending on their specialty. It would be the best starting point for dealing with an unknown alien, if one had crashed on Earth in the old days, because a medical doctor would be a specialist in Human physiology, and thus more likely to make terminal mistakes."

Greyson kept the shit-eating grin inside. She was treating this like a job interview. As she should.

He just wanted to nail somebody's hide to a wall as a trophy. Different outlook.

Different outcome.

"Oh," Ricia deflated a little.

Dangerous barbarians, and all that. Who spoke conversational G'schtack while accurately quoting legal statutes.

"However, on the date that the Articles of Acceptance were signed, Humans became an intelligent species under Guildlaw," Greyson continued. "Medical research would continue be acceptable, but only under tighter ethical standards. Cloning us like sheep, less so."

"Right up there with making programmable copies of G'schtack," Rachel noted helpfully.

Boom. BIG boom. The best kind. Blow this whole thing big and wide, and you can't just order everyone to forget everything they saw.

Not without asshole cops like Greyson Leigh asking even more questions.

"Recommendations, Leigh and Asher?" Ikoshi asked now, including Rachel as a full partner in this bullshit enterprise.

"We need resources, Captain. Metropolitan," he said.

"People to guard this facility. People to help maintain it while lawyers argue about what to do with these test tubes and their contents. Ethicists to advise on all those thorny questions. Judge Rankev signed the original Warrant for Entry and Expected Arrest Warrants, so she will be contacting the appropriate office of prosecuting attorneys. They'll need additional staff to handle all this quickly, as well as Special Masters to advise the Court when it comes time to indict."

"Why quickly, Leigh?" the Metropolitan asked.

He waved at the wall. Tapped on a perfect G'schtack woman's glass home with his knuckles.

"This place was not built overnight," he said. "This enterprise represents a lot of money invested over a long stretch of time. Humans joined the Guild fourteen standard cycles ago, so maybe—maybe—those two at the far end were legal before that, but should have been shut down. Why wasn't it? Who authorized it to continue? Who didn't order it dismantled? And then you have the other thirty tubes, all of whom have been flatly illegal for centuries now. These are questions for your Investigators to undertake, possibly investigating the Metroplex government of Anic itself. I am not the cop to handle that portion of things. Not unless you want a bull in a china shop."

They might. Bulls, standing in the ruins of a lot of fragile pretty things that had been stomped into shards. He was good at that.

"Where are you intending to go next, Leigh?" Ikoshi asked.

Five minutes, and the Captain already knew what he was dealing with. At least at certain levels. But a Captain of Detectives had to understand all the oddball folks who were good at this sort of thing.

"How many other killers are out there right now?"

Greyson asked the man. He reached back and tapped. "How many of these folks are walking the streets of Anic or Athund City or some other planet like R'Onar? What is the risk to the Guild itself, if one of your top politicians was secretly removed and replaced with a clone somebody had grown and *programmed*? I honestly don't trust anybody, until such time as they undergo the kinds of bloodwork tests that our doctor back at Armstrong Base did when he studied the copy of the Human creature down at the other end of this balcony to study."

"What did he find?" the man asked sharply.

"The apparent age, based on various tests configured for Humans, showed my perpetrator as being roughly five standard cycles old, instead of the eighteen or so one would expect as a young adult Human," Greyson said. "When you grow them in a tube, they are not a perfect replacement that way. I assume that from his notes, which are in the case files Judge Rankev has, that your doctors can prove everyone is what they present as. Until the full historical files of this facility are dismantled, we don't know who they might have replaced, or what they might have done along the way."

The Metropolitan had gasped about halfway through that speech. Greyson wondered if she had somebody on staff that had suddenly started acting differently one day.

He remembered explaining it to Andell. A Phrenic inherited the memories but not the laziness or excuses, so they tended to be highly productive for a long burst, compared to the person they replaced. The same might happen if you suddenly dropped a clone in. Doubly so if you left most of their programming alone, but *just changed* a few things.

Like loyalty to the state being shifted to loyalty to a few individuals. Or implanting orders that would make them double agents inside an enemy compound later.

He'd known a few of those over the years. Exploited them. Hunted them as well.

Greyson studied the woman now. He asked a question with the set of his face, but either she didn't get Human body language, or didn't want to admit to anything before suddenly subjecting someone to a forced physical exam.

Greyson could see a lot of those happening in the next few days. He wondered if he might flush out a couple of Phrenic that had just been hiding, like he was. Not all of them were assassins. Some were just career criminals who might have found a gig so great that they wanted to retire for a while.

Or save the galaxy.

NINETEEN
MIDNIGHT, AND THEN SOME

Rachel, Greyson, and Moora were out on the front sidewalk, under weird stars and safe from the breeze by the bulk of the building itself.

She had joined her partner in drinking coffee that made Carl's nasty shit, back on Boston Commons, taste palatable. If Greyson thought he needed to be up and sharp all night, she'd be pacing the boy until he fell over from exhaustion.

It was amazing what his sort of anger might manage.

Midnight local had passed. The clock was different, but noon and midnight were concepts, not just points in time. Way past middle of the freaking night, and they were still going like hell.

Metropolitan Ricia and Captain Ikoshi had finally left. Most of the facility was shut up tight. Woldt and his new team were busy learning. Uniformed officers were keeping the parking lot and building secure in rotating shifts.

Investigator Moora had returned from downtown, looking like a man pulled backwards through a knothole. About like she felt.

Rachel paused and counted, realizing that she'd been

going for something like thirty-six hours at this point, napping on the shuttle down and drinking bad coffee.

She was going to fall over eventually.

They were all three standing just outside the front doors of the place. The night air was cool enough that she'd hooked some of her longcoat closed, just to keep the biting wind out.

"In my entire career, I don't think I've even heard of a case this big," Moora said. "Let alone been involved in it. What's next?"

"Did you get my gadget?" Rachel growled at the man.

She was kinda past friendly and polite at this point.

Moora blinked and flinched a little under her tone, but hey, he'd only known her for a day. And it hadn't even been a one-night-stand kind of thing.

"I did, Detective Asher," he nodded a little too enthusiastically.

"Show me," she ordered.

And then followed the man back to his transport, which looked more like her Chandler Jouster than the big ones they'd ridden in earlier. Not manufactured along Earth lines, but she could see where they could have taken this beast and swapped out body panels in Detroit or somewhere.

He pulled out a lunchbox-sized device done in some extremely lightweight alloy. A gray so faint as to be almost blue in this light.

"How does it work?" she asked, still a little grumbly.

Moora opened it. Greyson was lurking nearby, perfectly silent at this point because this was her part of the case. Especially if Lissa turned out to be some sort of artificial lifeform.

Inside, it had a thing like one of those defibrillator paddles you saw in vids and shows from the late Twentieth or early Twenty-First, when doctors or paramedics needed to zap someone's heart to save their life.

"You hold it like this," he demonstrated, pulling it out by an obvious handle across the back.

A cord connected it to the machinery inside, and a screen came live as he removed the pad, holding the rest in his other hand.

"Do me," she said, just as he was about to ask Leigh to volunteer.

Bad idea. For a lot of reasons. Leigh flinched anyway.

She held out a hand and felt the cool kiss of the metal touch her skin. Moora thumb-pressed a button and the machine beeped politely. Rachel didn't feel anything, but the screen lit up a few seconds later, looking a lot like the stuff that Doctor Zarna, that Pakistani dude at Armstrong Base, had.

Heart rate. Blood oxygenation. It had even immediately identified her as Human and shifted to a Human screen.

Which was why they weren't about to point it at Greyson Leigh. Let sleeping dogs be.

She moved him to the hood of the Skycruiser and had him put the box down. Rachel started flipping screens from memory until she got to the one she wanted.

"There," she said, pointing. "Apparent age eighteen standard cycles. Not bad for a *chika* in pretty good shape, eh?"

"And your original suspect showed an age of five standard cycles?" Moora asked with a tone of near-disbelief. "A grown Human woman?"

"A manufactured clone," Leigh growled, but she'd figured he was getting to the edge of his own patience. And energy.

The guy got surlier as he went. She'd been around him enough to know that the crash was coming.

At this point, about all either of them had the energy for was just going back to the hotel to sleep.

"Is there anything else we need here at this point?" She looked up at the man.

Bags under his eyes that weren't just exhaustion. Stress. The thought that he'd been sleeping with another Anais Manel on the flight here, and not even known it. He'd probably be really paranoid about where he stuck his dick for a long while.

Gods knew she might handle her own issues herself for a while. Medscanning someone, while smart, kinda killed the mood. Unless they were into that kind of scene.

She'd burn that bridge when she got there.

"I don't think so," Greyson mused. "All the useful stuff has been hauled off, and Murphely is going to sic the right folks on it immediately, while ordering our four held as extreme flight risks."

Murphely? As in Judge Rankev? Boy was more tired than she'd thought. Or he'd developed a personal attachment to the one person who could have made or broken this case yesterday.

Yesterday? Shit. She needed sleep.

She turned back to Moora.

"We need transport to the hotel where we're staying, and neither of us are fit to drive at this point."

"Understood," he nodded. "Hop in and I'll let the machine fly us over."

They did, her in front and Greyson leaning back with his eyes closed behind them. It flew like a Jouster, too, so she was prepared for that blip as it went from flying straight up to horizontal. Something about the repulsors changing alignment, same as in every Jouster she'd ever ridden in.

Athund City was an industrial suburb kind of place. Lots of warehouses that gave way to hotels and retail *Genericas* as you got closer to the Anic city limits. Humantown was right on that line, which made sense. If you were hauling goods, you put them in Athund City while dealing with bankers and industrialists in Anic.

Medium-sized tower covering a full city block with several landing bays, about every ten stories of the sixty-story rise. The Jouster put them down in the front drive anyway.

"I wasn't sure if you were fully checked in or not," Moora apologized.

"This is good," Rachel said. "We are, but it was done remote, so I'm not even sure which rooms we're in, so we need to check with the front desk."

"How soon should we look for the next pieces?" Moora asked as Rachel opened her door.

"I would like to say we're going to sleep in, but that might be all of local dawn," she said. "And it will take us both a few days to acclimate to a new planet. The lighter gravity will help."

"Lighter, Detective?" Moora asked, a bit surprised.

"Earth is about ten percent heavier surface gravity than Brees, Investigator," she said.

"Call me Arymo," he replied. "I've been assigned to this case long-term by Judge Rankev, so I'll be working closely with you while you are here."

"Arymo," she nodded. "I'm used to heavier everything, so sleeping might be easier. I'd like to sleep in, but we're still going to be up early."

"Right," he said. "Oh, I forgot something."

She watched him open the glove compartment and pull out a pair of comms. Same rough size and shape as a Human smartphone. Pretty much the same functionally, though light-years more sophisticated. He handed her both, as Leigh was already out and standing a little back.

"Thank you," she said.

"All the numbers I could think of are already programmed for you," he said. "Just call when you need anything, or the hotel can also arrange to drop you off downtown."

"Excellent," Rachel smiled. "See you in the morning."

And he was gone.

She had the lunch box slung on her hip by a strap, feeling like one of those scientists in that ancient science fiction show. *Have tricorder, will travel.*

Leigh didn't smile, but he wasn't about to. At least until they sorted a lot of things out.

Lissa Jonez was just the next one on the list.

Inside, the front desk was cheery and prepared. Probably had been watching the news because they knew her and Leigh on sight.

Being Human helped. Weren't that many around here.

Oh, and the television was on in the background. She even saw herself moving around and talking to folks as she stood there.

The hotel used palmprints instead of keys. She supposed that it was one fewer thing to lose, though winter would complicate her life. Assuming they were still here when snow season rolled around.

"All of your luggage was delivered earlier, Detectives," the helpful Mooz woman behind the counter said with a cheery smile. "Six-twenty-one and six-twenty-three, Base-10."

"Thank you," Rachel said, steering Leigh off for the lifts.

Base-10 was always necessary when giving numbers. Most common of the four counting systems around here, from eight to fourteen. Thankfully, G'schtack had the same number of fingers and toes.

These lifts were much more subdued and careful. Civilian models for folks not prepared for some things.

Still, six was a quick hop and they stopped in front of twenty-three. His room.

Rachel wasn't feeling entirely benevolent, so she drew her nerve scrambler and held it down by her side.

"Is that really necessary?" Greyson asked.

"It is not yet unnecessary," she countered.

He glowered at her for a long second and then shrugged, putting his hand on the sensor until the locks shot open with a thump.

Rachel hip-checked him out of the way and went in first, like she was clearing a training sim. A real situation and she'd have had the palmstunner in her hand, firing at anything and everything as fast as she could pull the trigger. Always useful in tight rooms.

Leigh probably would have chucked a couple of stun grenades in and pulled the door shut. *Probably* stun grenades. He didn't do things halfway.

Nobody was there. She checked the closet and bathroom, just in case. She even looked under the bed. His stuff was sitting in a corner, waiting. Presumably hers was next door.

She'd clear it exactly the same way. This medscanner was going to be closer to her than anything but a nerve scrambler for a while.

"Put a chair under the lock," she smiled as Greyson walked to the bed and sat.

"Very funny," he scowled.

"You need to crash for a while," she said. "Since she's not here, that confrontation can occur when you're sharper, because you should not be handling open flames or sharp objects, right this moment."

"Not arguing with you," he nodded. "Trying to decide if I just lay down like this, or actually get ready for bed and all that jazz."

"Just secure the door, okay?" she asked.

"Yes, Mother," he nodded, rising again.

"Greyson, for what it's worth, I hope she's normal," Rachel said.

"You and me both, kid," he said as she moved to open the door and stepped out. "You and me both."

She waited until she heard him set the locks inside, then moved down to confront her own space. Odds spoke against Lissa being in her room, but that wasn't about to cause Rachel to let her guard down. Door lock. Nerve scrambler. Hip it open, reading to fire on movement.

Nobody.

Good. Last thing she needed tonight was to shoot some stupid punk and then have to be up until daybreak doing paperwork. Not that it would stay her hand, or anything.

She set her own locks after sweeping everything. Like Greyson, she considered just collapsing on the bed, but needed to wind it down.

In the end, she took a hot shower and let the water rinse some of the stupid off her back.

Tomorrow would be there in a few hours. She wouldn't be ready, but she'd at least be prepared.

TWENTY

BALO, CONTINUED

GREYSON HAD SLEPT. Some. Maybe enough for now.

Still felt like eight kilometers of bad gravel road with a dead-end sign that some lark had painted *April Fool* on.

Not trusting anything else, he'd left a call for *way too freaking early*. That was his usual mode at home, but he needed a few days in order to achieve zen with this planet, and didn't figure he'd get them anytime soon.

So he was downstairs when the breakfast bar finally opened. Real eggs, so he presumed someone had brought chickens to Brees. Maybe just for Humans, but Greyson didn't figure that a lot of species would have much biochemical problems with them. Eating meat was still an issue with about half the Guild.

More power to them. He was having three eggs, English-style sausage links, and a Danish close enough to get away with calling it that.

Maybe a pre-jellied sweetbread with icing. Whatever. Enough.

The coffee here was burned. Everybody always over-roasted it for transport. Kept longer on a shelf once you'd turned it to asphalt.

Greyson could see making a fortune by investing in a coffee roaster someplace like Brees. Financial capital of the known galaxy, and all that. Find a spot on the planet that could grow coffee directly, then only roast it through first crack. Maybe second. Not burned beyond recognition. Yuck.

Idly, he wondered if the gods were telling him to just start taking caffeine pills instead of drinking yucky asphalt sqwamph like this. They could be like that.

Then she entered the space.

Back home, Greyson would have called it a sundress. Single piece of a jersey-like fabric that clung in all the right places to show off her amazing curves. Dove gray, thick enough to not be translucent, but still light enough to give you hope, staring at her.

Elbow-length tight sleeves. Knee-length with a second piece of cloth stitched around the bottom to provide weight and texture, but done in the same color.

He felt like a shit, because the first thing that crossed his mind was double-checking how hard it would be for her to have a weapon hidden in there. Between the thighs, maybe. Or down the front in a bra, except that she wasn't wearing one.

He stared hard enough at her chest to confirm that.

Lissa smiled as she stepped closer. He ratcheted his paranoia back down to only a little crazy and smiled back at her.

"Good morning," she said brightly as she approached. "You were on the news last night."

"Occupational hazard," he rumbled back at her with as much of a smile as he could manage.

Lissa nodded and turned to the breakfast bar and the cook.

He allowed himself a long minute of appreciating her bottom as she spoke to the Human woman tending things. Presumably figuring out what she could eat safely.

Greyson already knew she could handle most Human food. She'd often joined him in Human-designated spaces, back on the ship.

She moved delicately now. Getting some fruit, some toast, and several sausages to go with a glass of apple juice. Just watching her move brightened his morning.

The creature in the test tube would be lucky to age into a body that nice, were she to live outside long enough.

Lissa approached and he rose. She sat with a grin and he joined her. Old manners pounded into him a long time ago. Not worth trying to overcome them now.

"How did last night go?" she asked as she ate daintily.

"They never saw us coming," he replied quietly.

She flinched, but that was a Guild member reacting to the sorts of casual violence that a Human Hunter took for granted. Most Humans weren't emotionally prepared for that sort of thing, either. He was in favor of a galaxy that didn't need Hunters at all.

He just needed to take down enough bad people to get there.

And pigs might fly.

"So what happens now?" she asked around a sausage.

Greyson had to keep perfectly still so he didn't flinch when she spoke. It wasn't her. It was what she might turn into because someone had programmed her to be a spy. A replacement.

A killer.

Like him.

"Today, I have a number of meetings already scheduled," he shrugged as innocently as he could. "Indictments will be handed down after I go before a few grand juries to testify as to the parts of the case that gave us a reason to raid Aeon Research Financial in the first place, but that's mostly *pro forma* at this point. We found enough inside to ruin lives, assuming that nobody can manage to get the evidence suppressed or thrown out."

Her brow muscles furrowed.

"They can do that?" she asked.

It took him a moment, then Greyson remembered that G'schtack video preferences didn't have legal thriller shows like Humans did. No cop-tv, as it were, either. Most citizens might not understand the intricacies of law enforcement in the ways that the average Human absorbed, one hour at a time from their nightly entertainment.

Though Hollywood never got the Hunter Bureau even remotely close to accurate. He'd considered offering to advise a few times, when he'd been retired.

Maybe if he survived to a second retirement.

"They can," he answered. "Everybody goes before a judge and lays out what they know. Prosecutors make a case for why someone should be tried. Defense tries to pick apart things by suggesting that evidence was illegally obtained. Things like that."

"Can they succeed?" she asked as she kept eating, almost as rapt as a student in a college class.

"They can try," he offered. "Rachel and I spent an inordinate amount of time organizing and researching things before we got here, exactly so our paperwork was bulletproof."

"Bulletproof?"

He cursed himself. Some terms didn't translate culturally.

"Watertight," he offered instead. "Everything done perfectly right. Even then, Judge Rankev might not have immediately signed off on the paperwork we'd prepared, needing to check things herself. But she did, so I could slip into the nearest precinct and recruit an enormous strike team quietly. Then drop them on the bad guys. Worked, too."

"The news suggested that you found all sorts of evil inside that warehouse," she said. "Anything you can talk about?"

"Not yet," he said, dangling the promise that he might later.

If she was perfectly innocent, he didn't necessarily want her getting away.

If she was guilty, she was never getting away, either.

It was a tightrope in high wind.

His breakfast was gone. Hers was going quickly. Rachel showed up before he tried to talk himself into persuading Lissa into going back up to his room for a chat. Or whatever.

His partner didn't have her medscanner on her hip, but he wondered how long until it became like a purse she took everywhere she went. And what that said about life in general.

Rachel made eye contact from the doorway, where Lissa couldn't see her. Greyson nodded. They could have entire conversations without words at this point.

Lissa noticed. She turned back and looked.

"Should I leave you two alone so you can get to work?" she asked.

"Not yet," Greyson replied. "There are a few things that came up that you might actually be able to help us with."

"Me?"

Right about now, he could get latency off the woman. Things unseen but there, like that case back in the spring where he'd had to deal with a whole other class of assassins coming for him.

If Lissa Jonez was a programmed clone, she might know it, and flinch right about now that her cover was blown. Didn't help that Rachel hadn't moved from her spot, other than to shift a little so she could get into her jacket easier.

Greyson would go for hand-to-hand combat across the table, since Lissa didn't have any obvious weapons visible. Hopefully, they hadn't upgraded her muscles to something he couldn't handle in his base form.

Turning into a Phrenic right now would blow the case to smithereens and ruin Rachel's career, too.

On the flip side, if Lissa had been programmed by an expert, she might not flinch now. Or the necessary code might not trigger, so she would present as innocent.

Hell, she might even be innocent, but he'd already had to deal with one of his own kind on this case, plus all the even-crazier shit.

"You," Greyson said. "Rachel and I are outsiders to the Guild, so as much as we might study, there are probably things we'll miss."

"Oh," Lissa brightened. "How can I help?"

He nodded Rachel closer and waited.

"You finish eating," he said. "We had a couple of quick questions, but not anything to discuss in front of people. I'd like to take you back up to my room, just so we can talk privately without worrying about anyone overhearing and drawing the wrong conclusions."

Or the right ones, but he wasn't about to say that. Not now. Especially not with others around.

Rachel slipped in and sat.

"Should we wait for you to eat?" Lissa asked her.

She'd been close enough to hear the bullshit yarn he'd been spinning, so Rachel just shrugged.

"As he said, five minutes," she replied. "Then we can figure out where we need to go next."

"But you might not eat?" Lissa asked, a little surprised.

"Serves me right for sleeping until dawn," Rachel laughed. "He's always up that early."

"Always?" Lissa asked.

"Assuming we haven't been out all night chasing folks, I normally picked him up at his place about the time the rest of Boston was thinking about waking up," Rachel smiled. "Then breakfast somewhere to discuss current cases, or anything else interesting. We'd get into the office about when the rest of the folks did. Or all the office drones in the blocks around us."

"Sounds like a job that would grind you down eventually," Lissa noted, spearing her last sausage and chewing now.

"It might," Greyson offered. "But still easier than all the things I'd been doing before."

Lissa knew he had been in the Army. After he'd explained to her what an army was. And what it did. And why you had one.

Greyson had been intentionally vague as to his actual duties. Like he was with most people.

"And you, Rachel?" she asked. "Will you still be doing this in ten or fifteen cycles?"

"My goal is to become management," Rachel grinned. "We have a captain back home who is a pretty good role model there."

Greyson suppressed his chuckle. Rutherford Parsons was tall, blonde, fashion-model-gorgeous, and Ukrainian. Just about the opposite of Rachel on any axis except drive or deadliness. Then she was only a distant third behind him and his partner.

Lissa finished eating and looked at the two of them. His coffee was gone. Good riddance. As was his food.

"Let's head upstairs," he said, sliding out of his chair.

Lissa nodded, but he didn't think she caught how both

he and Rachel kept her in front of them all the way to the lifts.

This thing just kept getting deeper and hairier.

What would he do if Lissa Jonez was another clone?

Or rather, whose life would he set out to destroy next?

TWENTY-ONE
UPSTAIRS

RACHEL TOOK the first lift up, just kinda accidentally boxing in their latest suspect in ways she might not even grasp immediately.

Up on six, they started down the hall.

"Hey," she said innocently to the woman walking beside her. "I have something I need in my room. Why don't we just go there?"

Rachel knew Greyson was keyed up for violence on a wholesale level, but Lissa just nodded and followed.

A palm keyed the door open and Rachel went in, still ready to attack anything that moved, assuming that Greyson would kill whoever had made that sort of mistake. She grabbed her tricorder thing and got back to Greyson's room quickly.

She wouldn't say she liked living inside his head, but Rachel understood the paranoia now. He'd lived with it for more than thirty years. Never knowing when a room you entered was about to become a firefight zone.

Or someone might turn out to be an impostor.

In the old days, he'd just had to deal with double agents.

Lissa Jonez, like Anais Manel, might take his rampant paranoia two or three new levels above that.

"You sit here," Rachel pulled out the chair from the table as she went by.

Lissa did. Greyson was covering the door. Rachel looked at him and he nodded for her to continue the interrogation. Rachel figured she might as well just rip the bandage off clear the first time, rather than dinking around.

"So Lissa, we have an interesting concern that came up yesterday," Rachel said, forcing the woman's eyes on her, so the Balo *chika* might not realize how close Greyson was to drawing his nerve scrambler right now.

"Yes?"

Rachel shifted to put her hand on the medscanner/tricorder thing.

"The facility we raided yesterday had a machine," Rachel continued. "A monstrous, freaking thing as big as a bus. It was where they grew clones."

"Clones?" Lissa's eyes bugged out a little.

Made her look even more Human, once you got past the utterly bald part. And the yellow-green skin.

"Artificial life forms," Rachel continued. "Greyson has mentioned some of the details from Armstrong Base. This kind of builds on those."

"Okay," Lissa nodded now. "How can I help?"

"The clone known as Anais Manel showed up with some really strange values when subjected to a medscan," Rachel said as her hand wrapped around the carry handle. "Like, completely insane numbers. I'd like to scan you right now, just to confirm some things."

In her heart, Rachel was prepared to bash Lissa as hard as she could with the device, assuming that it was either rated for that sort of drop, or that she could replace it if she managed to break this one.

At least Lissa didn't come off the chair. Just kind of stared at her in a confused way. The way a dog might cock their head at you when you've done something utterly stupid.

"Okay?" Lissa asked. "Why?"

"Scan first, then I'll explain everything," Rachel said, mentally crossing her fingers because *everything* wasn't about to be remotely close to the truth. *Enough* might be more accurate, once everyone knew.

She watched. Lissa nodded, a little off-center now, but in a confused way. Unlike the poised deadliness standing by the door.

"Hold up your hand," Rachel continued.

Lissa did. Pretty skin. Wrong color, but utterly flawless. Just enough muscles to turn on a guy like Greyson. It was like they'd gone into his psyche to build the perfect woman for him.

Even more perfect than Emmy, which was saying an awful lot.

Rachel opened the case and pulled out the shock paddle, powering the device on. She rested it on Lissa's forearm, watching for any twitch that might necessitate strangling her with the cord.

Scan. Beep. Results.

Rachel stepped back before she looked down.

Balo. Adult female. Flip, flip, flip. Relative age thirty-one standard cycles. Roughly thirty-five years old, give or take. Exactly what she looked like. Past the physical perfection of late twenties, grown into her sexuality and confidence enough to take a Human lover on a starliner, and maybe follow him when he got off, because Greyson Leigh was about as good as most women were ever going to find.

Not Rachel's type physically, but she'd forever be comparing any guy to Greyson for brains and personality.

Rachel let out a sigh and nodded to Greyson. Let him explain it, if he wanted.

Instead, the son of a bitch nodded right back to her. Because he was probably standing on a mental ledge, looking at the cold water below and wondering what monsters might be swimming in it.

Probably better if she did this, then.

Rachel closed the case and sat down on the bed now, facing Lissa from close enough to make this personal, rather than an interrogation.

"I'm sorry this was necessary," Rachel began, watching that first hint of dread fill the woman's eyes.

"What?" Lissa's voice had gone up a third.

"This is part of the case that must remain a secret for now, Lissa," Rachel said, waiting for the woman to nod before she continued. "We saw actual clones in the facility. Like people asleep, floating upright in test tubes filled with a murky fluid that kept them alive."

"Okay?" Lissa said/asked, looking like the heroine in a horror vid now, as the *thing* was closing relentlessly in.

Not the most inaccurate way to describe Greyson, but he wasn't after Lissa. Not now, anyways.

Rachel pulled out her phone and flipped to the camera folder, cycling until she found the one she wanted. She turned it for Lissa to see and heard the woman's gasp.

"She's beautiful," Lissa whispered.

"She is," Rachel agreed. "Perfect in all the ways visually that either Greyson or I could identify. That's part of the problem here."

"What?" Lissa squinted at her in confusion.

"She looked like your younger sister, Lissa," Rachel said, just damning the torpedoes now and full steam aheading. Or however it went.

Not a section of history she'd focused much on.

Lissa gasped again and studied the picture closer. Pulled the phone out of Rachel's hands to zoom and pan, making strangled noises as she did.

Then Lissa Jonez looked up and Rachel almost went for her own nerve scrambler. Had to force herself not to draw and cover this Balo woman across from her, even as Greyson shifted his weight just enough to let Rachel know he was doing the same thing.

"What?" Rachel demanded in a voice like soft steel.

All killing edge, as it were.

Lissa seemed to shrink in on herself, though, instead of getting poised for violence.

Expecting it, maybe?

The Balo woman took a breath, possibly to prepare herself. Then another. Finally sat up a little, mostly by leaning back into the chair.

The room had taken on a deadly stillness. Rachel felt like a woman standing beside a game trail with a crossbow holding poisoned bolts. One of Greyson's favorite images when hunting.

Let them come to you, then kill them silently before they knew what had happened.

"It's possible," Lissa finally said.

"What is?" Rachel replied.

"Sister," the Balo suspect admitted. "Well, not sister, but something."

"Something?" Rachel prompted, back into interrogator mode, though she already felt like Bad Cop.

Greyson Leigh could always be Worse Cop. Whatever *worse* was. He was good at that.

Another quick breath as the woman seemed to be looking for the right words.

"I did something stupid when I was younger," Lissa finally admitted. "Rebellion phase and all that foolishness."

"Talk to me," Rachel ordered her.

"I come from money," Lissa said. "A lot of money."

"I suspected," Rachel admitted now. "I don't think Greyson looked you up, but I did. Cop, protecting her partner."

Lissa flinched. What person wants all their dirty laundry out on the table, even in a private hotel suite?

"When is your birthday, Lissa?" Rachel asked.

The woman told her. The date matched the entry in the Guild encyclopedia. Kind of a Who's Who section of important folk. Like her father who owned stupid amounts of factories, companies, and industry.

"So I know who you are, at least on a superficial level," Rachel said. "Greyson does not, but you two probably should have that conversation at some point, depending on how the rest of this one goes."

Lissa nodded, almost hangdog.

"Teenage rebellion," the Balo woman said. "I was offered a lot of money, which I really didn't need, because I already had more than I could ever spend. The people who contacted me offered something else."

"A kind of immortality," Rachel guessed.

"Yes," Lissa said. "You understand? I'll never be hungry. Never lonely, as long as I could afford friends and parties. But I was going to grow old eventually. Stop being one of the most beautiful people around."

Rachel had to give her that. Approaching the end of young-adult now and moving on towards middle-aged soon, and still utterly stunning. And smart.

"They offered to create an even more perfect version of me," Lissa said. "At the time, there was even talk of being able to transfer my mind and memories to the younger body when the research advanced far enough, though I don't think they ever actually went anywhere. Or if it did, they haven't said anything to me."

"When was this?" Greyson suddenly spoke, Zeus-like from across the room, about the time you might have forgotten he was in the room.

Rachel watched Lissa flinch under that hard, angry tone. Woman had only ever seen the nice side of Greyson. The Human side, as it were, and not the Hunter.

Lissa's eyes lost focus as she thought back. Assuming the body language was the same, the next words would be honest ones, too, rather than a fabrication.

"Eleven cycles?" Lissa said. "No, closer to twelve, now. I could get you the exact date, because they deposited in my bank account what was probably a mind-boggling amount of money to them. My annual clothing budget in those days was greater."

"In those days?" Rachel had to ask.

"Teenage rebellion and soul-searching, Rachel," the woman replied, turning both serious and rueful. "Not all of us are born with the luck to fall into the perfect job. I'm not even sure there is such a thing for me. Maybe because I never had the kinds of hunger for anything that you and Greyson faced as children. I just kind of float through life and the galaxy. The biggest thing I've ever stuck to was trying to visit every single world in the Guild. I'm past the halfway mark now, but live a much quieter life. All those parties grew smooth and pale eventually."

Rachel nodded. She didn't get it, but she could see it from a purely intellectual standpoint. Like the woman had said, Greyson had been raised by redneck gearheads in Oregon. She was Puerto Rican descent via Long Island, with blue collar parents who had helped her get to the point where she could be a cop.

Hunter came later.

"Have they been in touch with you since?" Greyson asked now, not thundering because he was modulating his voice and body language, but Rachel could see how close to the surface it was.

Lissa cringed a little, and Rachel saw the empathic side of the woman emerge a bit more. The introvert who didn't want to do all those parties, but had done so anyway because that was what you did. The people you hung out with.

Until you decided to go do something so long-scale and dreary that all the party hounds would peel off eventually, leaving you alone to relax and recover.

Rachel could see where she might have made similar choices, once she'd gotten over herself. And Lissa Jonez had grown up.

"They have," Lissa admitted now, voice tiny and compressed. "Every cycle or so I get a message, then a courier shows up and takes a vial of blood. Are they growing more of them? Of me?"

"I doubt it," Rachel interjected. "More likely identifying how your genes will age, so they know what diseases and tendencies to adjust for. You as a mature adult are probably already too much for most people. All those brains in a teen hardbody would be an irresistible threat to the galaxy."

Lissa chuckled in a pained way.

"That was why I did it," she admitted. "If they could put me in a younger body…"

Rachel could see the draw. All the shit you knew now, in the body of a younger version. Maybe a never-growing-old version. She could only imagine what a Greyson Leigh her age might have been like.

Impossible now, for all the reasons nobody but her knew, but wow.

Would Rachel Lupita Asher want to live forever?

Dumb question, bucko.

"So how much trouble am I in?" Lissa asked now.

Damned good question, chika.

Rachel didn't know. She turned to Greyson.

"Are you willing to become a witness, Lissa?" he asked, voice soft with all the ragged edges magically gone.

She could see him falling for a woman like her.

Rachel figured she'd let the lovers have their time. She'd have to break somebody's heart eventually.

Shit.

She must have said it out loud, because the other two were staring at her.

Rachel waved her hands.

"I need to process this thought before trying to explain it."

They took that at face value. For now, anyway. Leigh would want to know more later.

How fucking insane would it be, though, if they really could grow a Human clone of Greyson Leigh, and put his mind inside it?

Could Rachel Asher stand in a room with both Greyson Leigh and Ethen Boli at the same time?

Talk about the ultimate incentive. And the ultimate risk.

Greyson let it go and turned back to Lissa.

"Witness?" the woman asked.

"I need to go testify about a lot of things we found," he said. "Criminal proceedings. Potentially ongoing, Guild-spanning criminal conspiracies, if they'd been working with you for that many cycles. If your DNA, or whatever Balo use, is a close enough match for the woman in the tube, that's just another nail in their coffin, because now I have another avenue to pursue and a lot of hungry accountants to feed."

Double shit. Could they really find the people responsible and hit them in the pocketbook? Like, next week?

She'd been expecting to chase the fuckers across the galaxy.

"She needs to vanish," Rachel said to her partner. "Immediately."

"Agreed," he said, then turned to Lissa. "So I might be ruining whatever plans you had, but you are entirely at risk right now, and we might not have even realized it. The people you've been dealing with are killers."

Rachel watched her complexion fade as all the blood drained out of her skull. Her hands came up to her mouth in the most Human way. She gasped.

"You thought I was another clone," she finally realized.

"That's right," Rachel admitted, wondering at the odds that had this woman crossing paths with her and Greyson in a manner that ended up here. Strange shit, but she'd seen worse. "Anais Manel was a killer. Might not have even known it at the time. We had to be sure."

Then a thought struck her and Rachel turned to Greyson.

"There's a base-model Anais Manel running around somewhere, isn't there?" she asked. "And Jan Michael, because they probably only got recruited into the system in the last decade or so."

He paused to consider it.

"If we were home, I'd reach out to one of the computer forensics teams and ask them to do a partial face matching," he replied. "We got so wound up in this case that we never thought they might have just tweaked an existing woman, rather than building one from scratch."

"What is it you always say about lazy criminals?"

"Busy cutting corners," he agreed. "But I question if they did all that work on Earth."

"How so?" Rachel asked.

Between them, Lissa went back and forth like a tennis match.

"Let's look for lazy immediately," he grinned. "There can't be that many Humans in the Guild records, as they have not, to the best of my knowledge, cataloged all Humans on Earth. Too much work. Doubly so for criminals."

"Beautiful people," Lissa said now, interrupting both of them. "Do you have a picture of her?"

She was still holding the phone, so Rachel flipped back to the Anais-model clone in her own tube, not that far from the one they might call Lissa's sister.

Lissa studied her for a time. Squinted and scowled as she concentrated on the image.

Then she looked up at Rachel.

"I might know her sister…"

Greyson had brought a nicer outfit, assuming he was going to have to stand in front of a judge and courtroom at some point, swearing an oath and trying to look nice.

Still wasn't wearing a tie for anybody but Emmy. Owned exactly one, and as she hadn't come, neither had it.

Nice chocolate-brown slacks that had never had blood or alien gore splattered on them. Nicer white shirt that Emmy had gotten for him from a real tailor. You dealt with the armored boots, but he'd gone so far as to have the machine in the hotel lobby polish and seal them again. Darker brown blazer, really almost bronze with flecks of paint in the threads, completed the ensemble.

He'd gotten his hair cut on the ship right before they landed, just so it would look professional when he needed to.

Rachel's outfit was close enough to his as they entered the courtroom. Investigator Arymo Moora had taken Lissa into protective custody today, just so she wasn't alone, both for her peace of mind as well as Greyson's.

This place reminded him more of a Star Chamber from

English history than an American courtroom. Five judges sitting up on a dais that was wide and just curved enough that everyone could see each other without having to lean out.

All wore robes that matched Murphely Rankev, seated today in the middle. Three of them were G'schtack, including her, with a Mooz and a Nese rounding it out.

The space before the judges had a single table centered, rather than paired. The gallery was closed, with forty or so empty seats visible as Greyson and Rachel walked up the central aisle and took their spaces behind the chair.

Behind them, a Bailiff closed and locked the door.

What did it say that not even the Captain of Detectives or the Metropolitan were here? He wasn't that sharp on Guildlaw, but they might be legally excluded, as this was a grand jury and not a proper trial. That silliness would come later, assuming everyone got taken alive.

Greyson smiled to himself. He wasn't willing to make that bet, at the end of the day.

He was still a Hunter, subject to Human jurisdiction because he was still pursuing the original case of Zentra Izelth's assassination by a creature not known to be Human, externalities notwithstanding.

"Be seated," Rankev began, nodding to them.

Rachel and Greyson sat and watched the men and women up there. And how they watched him.

"Two days ago, you arrived on the surface of Brees, Detectives Leigh and Asher," Rankev continued. "Bearing with you a rather extensive and well-researched case file accusing a local corporation of a variety of illegal activities, beginning with but not limited to smuggling contraband materials to a proscribed world."

Very few things were allowed to be imported to Earth right now, while the global economy tried to recover from an end to organized warfare and all the folks who had gotten rich from it. That ended up being a significant proportion of all industry on the planet, once you stripped away certain things.

Almost everything was cheaper to manufacture off-world, so they could have flooded Earth with stuff and destroyed what was left.

Thus, the prohibitions.

Plus, smuggling was right up there with treason and first-degree murder, in the eyes of the Illymus Merchant Guild. Weird people, but making money honestly was etched into law with a sledgehammer, and woe unto the fool cutting corners and not paying taxes on things.

Rankev had paused. Greyson nodded, as she hadn't asked anything. Mostly just making sure he and Rachel were following. On a sailing ship, the horizontal post that held a sail onto the mast was called a boom, if he remembered right, which was where the phrase 'dropping a boom on someone' came from. Or something like that.

Walloped upside the head with an irresistible force. The only question was if you just went down, or went overboard, instead.

"Having arrived and making accusations found to be viable in front of the Court, you presented an Affidavit of Findings and asked for a Warrant for Entry and an Expected Arrest Warrant with names to be determined after arriving at the facility listed. Is this correct?"

Greyson rose. He figured it would be more polite to stand.

"Your Honor, it is," he said simply.

"What did you find at the facility when you arrived, having taken the time to recruit sufficient local forces to contain the situation?" she asked.

He smiled. Sufficient forces for a small war, had they

been Human soldiers, but he didn't go there. Seventy-odd cops plus support forces probably did look like an army to the G'schtack.

They didn't understand that sometimes dropping an overwhelming force—a boom—on bad guys made it easier for everyone.

Greyson Leigh had been prepared to follow his nerve scrambler into the warehouse and let it establish boundaries on folks. Also not something you talked about in polite company.

"Your Honor, and Members of this Court, we located a facility that appears, on the surface, to be dedicated to the illegal manufacture of intelligent life forms," Greyson said.

As far as he knew, only Rankev had been fully briefed yesterday, after he'd gotten some sleep, and had his confrontation with Lissa.

Hopefully, he could make it up to her eventually.

The other four Judges ranged from skeptical to outraged, from the reactions he could see. About what he expected, when he'd possibly toppled centuries of polite behavior.

Ya flipped the light on and watched the cockroaches scramble madly for cover. Same as back home.

Just another reason he lived in a concrete building.

"Intelligent, Detective Leigh?" the Mooz woman asked.

"Affirmative, Your Honor," he nodded. "Artificial Humans were the reason we came to Brees. At the facility, we found several species currently represented by the Guild, including six G'schtack. Two male and four female."

Gods, but he loved dropping booms on people. Especially stuffy judges.

Murphely had to actually pick up her gavel and slam it into a marble stone on her side of the desk to get the other four to shut up.

"And you have submitted all of this?" Rankev asked now.

"Your Honor, everything we have been able to identify and unscramble, as of half a day ago, was submitted under seal." He nodded to each of them individually. "With the understanding that the local police authorities have assigned a significant number of officers, detectives, and specialists to go through everything. Subsequent filings will come as they succeed, but I am given to understand that it might take years for all of the information to be decoded. After consulting with the local Captain of Detectives, Captain Yaran Ikoshi, it was determined that hot pursuit would continue to be invoked, allowing myself and my partner to turn much of the case over to local forces that have a much better understanding of case law and precedent, while we went after certain individuals who appear to be implicated, before they can flee from justice or destroy evidence of crimes."

More stir up there. They were all politicians, like Ikoshi or Metropolitan Ricia. They didn't understand a guy who didn't want the limelight of fame. Greyson Leigh wasn't about to run for any sort of elected office, or need to build up his name to the point that he got selected as a Judge somewhere.

Fuck that.

He had bad guys to hunt down and capture. Maybe capture.

Again, Rankev had to gavel to get everyone to shut up. Probably the first time in her career she'd had to use it twice in one day, given how staid and predictable these things were supposed to go.

"To confirm, you are not planning to remain central to the prosecution of this case?" Rankev asked.

Somewhere, it was all being recorded for later. She was playing for the same galleries he was intently avoiding.

"I have solved my original case, the assassination of

Zentra Izelth by an artificial life form that appeared externally to be Human," he said. "Evidence led me to Brees, to locate and capture the facility that was responsible for her manufacture. Assuming that it is the only one at this point, one can presume that no more Human assassins will be manufactured. Nor Human armies intended to conquer all of Guildspace and create some sort of alien tyranny."

More boom. Third gavel banging.

Greyson wondered what the absolute record was, and if he should aim to break it. The day was young.

"Human armies, Detective Leigh?" the lone male G'schtack judge asked.

"If you can grow one killer with absolutely no qualms about murdering someone, you can grow a hundred," he replied deadpan. "Or ten thousand. Or ten million. At some point, you establish a preponderance of force and can begin capturing others, either physically or under threat of annihilation. That was the real reason we had to come to Brees in the first place. Someone was playing with fire and might threaten to conquer or destroy the entire Guild."

"Impossible!" the man scoffed.

"Normal Humans can kill, Your Honor," he replied. "Trained ones can be quite good at it. Manufactured ones can do it without any hindrance whatsoever."

"And you would know this how, Detective Leigh?" the man asked.

"Because I was a trained killer for one of the local governments on Earth for a Human generation," he said. "Before I became a cop. And the Hunter Bureau is an agency intended to handle non-Human criminals that have come to Earth to prey on less culturally or technologically advanced folks."

"How many people have you killed?" the man gasped.

Greyson couldn't help the ragged chuckle that emerged, like cutting warm ice with a rusty saw blade.

"I am not at liberty to discuss those numbers with most civilians," he answered, locking eyes with the man. "Yourselves included. I do not believe that the number rises to five digits, Base-10."

He was pretty sure it was less than ten thousand. Probably. Collateral damage on certain scales tended to wound far broader than it killed, assuming any modicum of medical facilities nearby.

Fourth gavel. Possibly going for high score after all.

Eventual silence, once all the muttering died away.

"And has there been any evidence of Phrenic shapeshifters on this case, Detective Leigh?" Murphely asked now.

"Only the impostor who brought the assassin to Earth in the first place," he answered. "My partner killed her after she confessed to most of what we built our case on coming here."

All eyes tracked now to Rachel Lupita Asher, possibly seeing her for the first time.

He'd have liked to tell them right now that she'd end up maybe in Ikoshi's spot one of these days, assuming nobody talked her into becoming a judge instead. Less pay. Better perks. Fewer people trying to kill you.

She just bristled at them. Like she did. He did smile at that.

"I would suggest, however, that you haul in a lot of the folks around this case and test to make sure they aren't Phrenic, just in case," he added, mostly throwing gasoline on the fire at this point.

The sooner they were done with him, the sooner he could get back to nailing hides to the wall as trophies. Obviously, the folks of the Illymus Merchant Guild weren't sufficiently frightened of Humans to treat them with respect.

Yet.

He'd have to do something about that before he went home.

Boom. Fifth gavel. Utter, freaking chaos.

The best kind, because he really didn't give two shits what they did, but someone would leak this tape, just to make someone else look bad.

Nobody could touch him, because he didn't care. Greyson Leigh was just here to identify the ethical solution to a legal conundrum. Or a moral quagmire.

High score couldn't be all that far away, if he felt like reaching for it.

"Detective Leigh, if you are passing off most of the prosecution of the case to others, based on better experience and relevant skills, what do you anticipate happening next for you and your partner?" Murphely asked in a leading way.

"We have recently come into contact with a potential witness who can tie others into this case, beyond the names you will find in the various files as they get itemized," he said.

"A new witness?" Murphely asked.

She knew the truth. The other four did not, as far as he knew. Murphely Rankev was setting them up.

Or going for high score herself. Hard to tell. She had a wicked smile in her eyes right now.

"That's right, Your Honor," he nodded politely. "As the thirty or so beings in the test tubes are all indistinguishable from normal people, we were lucky to find one that might have been the source for one of the creatures."

"Creatures, Detective Leigh?" the other female G'schtack judge asked.

He hadn't bothered learning any names beyond Murphely, as they were just here to put evidence in front of five officials who could issue more warrants for various things. Right now, they just had to sign off on everything he'd found at Aeon Research Financial. He was pretty much done with that part.

Forensic accountants and other carnivores would take it from there. Probably laughing maniacally, if the G'schtack version of that monster was anything like the Human one.

"If they are copies of existing citizens, what are their legal rights, Your Honor?" he fired back. "And if they were manufactured illegally, do they have any rights? Are they fully sentient, if they have been programmed to commit certain crimes or activities that their source material would find objectionable? These are not questions a detective such as myself should be answering. These probably require professors of ethics and philosophy, and I never went past high school back home. Ergo, I should turn a lot of this over to better qualified folks. I hunt people and drag them to justice for folks like you to sort out."

"I see," Murphely said now, interrupting before anyone else could get involved. "Will you have recommendations?"

"Not until someone figures out their programming," he said. "And only if someone asks me. In the meantime, I'm talking to various folks, trying to see how many other models might exist, and if they might have been put to other illegal uses. Rather than explain myself again, I will refer everyone to the section of the case file marked Manchurian Candidate, and I have also made a copy of the original film and book available for you."

He sat. Seemed like a good way to end the conversation, as they'd need time to digest that someone they knew might be a replacement being, programmed and all that in manners and behavior that would be rather a lot like a Phrenic.

"At this point, we shall adjourn to review the updated file," Murphely announced with yet another bang.

"Detectives Leigh and Asher, you will let us know before departing the planet, in case we have questions."

"We will, Your Honors," Rachel said.

He just smiled.

Now, the really fun part started.

TWENTY-THREE
LISSA

Turned out, Greyson really had set a new high score, for what it was worth. There would be several Judges who remembered Humans next time, though he doubted that any of them would make as much boom as he had.

Unless it was Rachel and she was feeling feisty. That put a bigger smile on his face.

They were downstairs now, in offices that Captain Ikoshi had assigned him, Rachel, and Arymo Moora. Another semi-squalid detective bullpen that never got cleaned enough and had too many desks and people crammed in. Didn't help when you added all the interesting scents of the various species in here.

Not bad, just a weird mix, like having Italian takeout, a Cantonese place, and a Kimchi joint side-by-side on a food court.

Greyson checked the local time on his phone. Close enough to lunch that he had an excuse if any of the Judges decided that they needed him for something. He just wanted to be out under green skies and two stars.

How often would he see something like this again, anyway?

He stood. Rachel looked up from her paperwork.

"Lunch?" she asked, her stomach no doubt on the same schedule as his by now.

"Lunch," he agreed, turning to Arymo.

The Investigator rose and joined them as Greyson went for the lift, down, and out the front door.

"Is there a reason we're walking?" Arymo asked as they emerged.

Vaad was high in the green sky. Udoth was tapering off. Cool breeze ran down the canyons of the tall buildings around them.

"Wanna walk," Greyson said, turning left at random.

Rachel ended up on his left, Arymo on his right.

"So any questions about what I did to the grand jury this morning?" he asked as they went.

Somewhere, there would be the G'schtack equivalent of a coffee shop. A random burger joint like Tommy's was asking too much. Hell, that would be too much anywhere else but Los Angeles. Those folks took their burgers seriously.

"You really don't mind if I end up getting a bunch of whatever glory rolls past the Captain?" Arymo asked.

"Kid, I prefer it that way," Greyson laughed. "The folks who need to know will. The rest will underestimate whatever Human Hunters come back next time."

He could call the Investigator a kid. Arymo was about ten standard cycles younger. A bit more senior as a cop, more or less, though the ranks didn't line up exactly.

However, like most folks in the business, especially on Brees, Arymo was more a bureaucrat than a gunslinger. Back home, that was why they needed Hunters.

"So what happens with Lissa Jonez?" Arymo asked.

"After lunch, assuming no emergencies, we're going to go

to the safehouse where she's hidden," Greyson said. "I want to debrief her. How soon until we know that it was her source material that made the clone?"

"We have a first approximation match now," Arymo said. "That was why Ikoshi and the others were so willing to move quickly when I asked. Your friend seems to be what they started with, before tweaking a few things."

"They tweaked more than a few," Rachel snapped across the way. "It just won't show up until you decant one and start doing psych evals."

"What do you expect to find, Rachel?" Arymo asked.

"Anais was, at the end of the day, a sex object," she growled as they walked. "A Pleasure Model, to use an old Human term that the Guild should have known better than to pursue. I have no reason to believe that a perfected version of Lissa was set up as a lawyer or a doctor, if you get my drift?"

"Brothel worker?" Arymo asked, surprised. "But that sort of thing is legal, Detective."

"Legal, sure," Rachel scoffed. "Now, ratchet that up a level so you have a woman who will happily indulge in any bizarre kink or fetish you can possibly think of, Arymo. Who has no sense of self-preservation if you want to really push the envelope into dangerous and ugly territory. Back home, there is a thing called a snuff film. People get off watching others be murdered in cold blood. Now, imagine the victim is a beautiful woman who will load the gun for you and smile as she hands it to you, because she's had those parts of her personality removed. That's what Anais did to Zentra, back home. Orgasmed after he did. Pulled out a nerve scrambler. Shot him dead. Turned the weapon on herself."

Greyson watched the shudder pass through the man.

Sure, Humans might be barbarians, as far as a lot of the Guild was concerned, but that just meant that they had a much greater understanding of such things as might be too *genteel* for such august folks as the G'schtack.

"The thing about sex workers is bad enough," Greyson cut in. "Armies of killer Humans, all identical, is worse, because of what they could do. Programming a perfect clone and shifting them is the worst, because nobody will know the truth. Possibly ever. Personally, I can think of no worse horror story to encounter."

"Phrenic," Arymo nodded.

Everyone had that nightmare. Greyson's was just more realistic.

He'd have thought that the example of the Phrenic would be the sort of cautionary tale needed to not create clones, but Greyson supposed that it had turned out to be the exact opposite.

After all, the clones couldn't suddenly turn into someone else when you weren't looking. Couldn't steal a face and a life to escape afterwards, if they needed to.

"Hey," Greyson turned to Arymo. "Where's a good place we can eat around here? The afternoon feels filled with ugliness, so we need to refuel now."

"Is something happening?" the Investigator asked.

"No, just a bad feeling," Greyson said.

In his time, he'd learned to accept such things and run with them.

Usually his subconscious warning him that all hell was about to break loose.

Now would have been the time he checked a pocket for spare magazines.

And maybe a stun grenade.

TWENTY-FOUR

SAFE

RACHEL LOOKED AROUND THE SPACE. Like many things, the Guild didn't really get espionage, so their idea of a safe house wasn't all that impressive. Mostly just rented a cottage in a residential district of Anic and put a couple of plainclothes cops around the place to protect Lissa.

In her time, Rachel had had to hide witnesses from retribution. This place was too open, had too many approach points that couldn't be easily covered, and was not all that far from a retail district that would let watchers hide. Or escape.

Still, as far as she knew, nobody even understood that Lissa was involved just yet. They might not understand that the firewalls separating themselves from Aeon Research Financial had been breached in a back corner by the weirdest luck in the galaxy.

They were all in the kitchen. Both assigned cops had made themselves scarce, with one just outside on the back porch, watching the postage stamp yard. Hell, there weren't even fences. Just pathways connecting all the cottages together.

And you didn't park close, because the pads were all over

there, meaning you had to walk through rain or snow to get to your ride on a bad day.

Nice retirement community, she supposed. Folks who didn't necessarily get out much or go anywhere. Not like Rachel's grandma, who went down to play bridge or help out in a niece's restaurant by adding grandma magic to the food.

Like Leigh, a damned good example for life later on.

Rachel stood with her butt against the wall by the refrigerator thing. Arymo was by the stove. Greyson sat at the table with Lissa. He was just finishing up what they had learned in the last day.

Lissa was paler than she'd been five minutes ago.

She laughed now, but it was brittle. She turned and located Rachel.

"So much for immortality," she said weakly.

Rachel nodded. What woman didn't want to be young and beautiful forever? Men were just as bad. Most of them, anyway, but they wanted to be big, burly beefcakes and rarely wanted to put in the work.

Lissa just had to remain beautiful as she aged.

"Now what?" Lissa asked.

"Arymo here has already added a team into tracing your annual payments for the blood work," Greyson said, nodding to the Investigator. "Because we have a long pattern, those will be easy enough to track back. Fools never think about money transfers."

"How do Humans handle that?" she asked.

Rachel chuckled. That caused everyone to look at her. Greyson nodded for her to explain.

"In the way old days, even before this crotchety bastard came around, folks would carry around literal suitcases full of money," Rachel laughed. "One-hundred-dollar bills, when that was a lot of money. Maybe a couple million cash that way. Then the European Union started using the five-hundred-euro bill. Criminals didn't use banks, except after they could launder cash."

"Launder?"

"Governments eventually got smart," Rachel nodded. "Deposits above a certain level had to be reported to revenue agents, who are just as mean on Earth as they are here. So you found a business that tended to be handled in cash, and either bought it or used the owner. Your cash got slowly legitimized and could be moved around in bigger numbers. Or you just carried around briefcases full of money, all the way up to pallets so big you needed a forklift to move them around. Lots of folks got into gold for that reason. Way more compact value for the mass involved."

"So the people sending me money regularly will be easy to trace?" Lissa asked, eyes going from face to face.

"Given the speed with which Judge Rankev is responding to requests for expansions of the investigation, there might be folks already on their way somewhere to serve warrants and possibly make arrests."

"But you don't know?" Lissa asked.

"I solved my case," Greyson replied. "Now, all of this has turned into a political crisis, because I guarantee you that the folks behind it all have official friends who were in positions to overlook things, or call off investigations before they got too close. A genteel kind of corruption, if you will. Subtle things between friends, not to be reported in the evening news."

"Because they didn't count on you," Lissa nodded.

"Babe," Rachel laughed. "Nobody ever counts on Leigh. If they did, there'd be a lot less crime in the galaxy. Might yet be, depending on how this one shakes out, because the two of us are happy to keep pushing when others might start to flag off."

"Even if it brings down the Guild?" Lissa gasped.

So did Arymo, but he'd only been part of this mess for days. Rachel had been living with it since she first laid eyes on Little Miss Perfect Boobs, cold on a medical slab.

"If something can be destroyed by the truth, it deserves to be," Leigh replied on a hard voice, quoting the old nameless street prophets. "I realize that the Guild swooped in because us Humans had messed up our planet and our global economy so bad that we might have collapsed all the way back down to barbarism if they hadn't, but they also showed us a better future."

"The Phrenic Dilemma," Rachel nodded.

Again, everyone looked at her. She figured it would be easier for her, since this case was already doing strange things to Greyson.

"When a Phrenic takes somebody, they see the bright, shiny, exciting bits," Rachel explained, going back to Leigh's stories. "Not the bad or lazy parts. They come along and really get things moving. To an outsider, there is sudden rejuvenation. And you can't go back, because that past is literally dead and gone. Humans coming into Guildspace means that the locals have to react to bright-eyed youngsters asking why they aren't living up to their own laws and ethical codes. Those cause uncomfortable conversations."

Nods, all the way around. She and Greyson were true outsiders, because Guild folk, for all their urbane galacticness, were still a fairly insular culture. Born on a planet. Live there your whole life. Die there.

Lissa was traveling, but probably only seeing the expensive tourist spots on any planet, and Rachel was willing to bet that those all started to look alike after a while.

Hitchhiking across the Indian subcontinent or down the Chinese coast was an utterly different way to approach life. Not Rachel's but other folks'.

Greyson's comm chirped right then, a weird warbling

sound that probably made sense to G'schtack, but left her cold and slimy inside.

He put it to his ear as she watched.

"Leigh," the man grunted, like always.

Not many people had this number to contact him in the first place.

"That's right," he continued, nodding absently. "Sure. Ten minutes? That's perfect."

He hung up and turned around to find her, ignoring the rest.

"That was Ikoshi," he said simply. "There's been a development."

TWENTY-FIVE
CAPTAIN OF DETECTIVES

GREYSON HAD LEFT the rest of the gang inside with Lissa, as Captain Ikoshi had asked. Walked out the back down and down the path a bit to meet the man on the stone walkway from where he'd apparently parked his skimmer, down in the restaurant district a few blocks over.

The two of them were alone in what amounted to several backyards that all kind of bled over into one another. The day was nice enough that back windows would be open. Folks would be able to hear whatever conversation went on, but the tall G'schtack didn't want Rachel hearing it.

Or, more likely, Investigator Moora. Arymo would still be around when Greyson and Rachel went home. Assuming that happened in another month or three.

There were still folks on Earth who needed a reckoning. Of course, there would always be those people. Same as Guildspace.

Greyson wasn't entirely keyed up for violence, but images of him and Ofiyana Ovich—alone in Greyson's room before she turned back into Wailos Gritchkan—filled his mind in uncomfortable ways. Didn't help that Yaran Ikoshi was the

G'schtack equivalent of a basketball player, being as tall as Greyson was.

The man stopped closer to Greyson than was normal for their culture. Barely two feet away. Close enough to lean into a punch, though Greyson was pretty sure his reflexes would see it and block it before it connected.

What that same training would do to the man afterwards remained to be seen.

"Detective," Ikoshi said in a quiet, pained voice, far less gruff and angry than the first time they'd met.

"Captain," Greyson nodded, equally quiet. Electronic surveillance wouldn't be bothered, but little, old G'schtack grandparents would probably miss things from the distance. "I understand that there have been developments in the case? Cases?"

"That's right," the man nodded.

He seemed distracted. Eyes looked over Greyson's shoulder at where the safe house back door should be closed. Rachel might be inside watching, but she'd do that anyway, since Ikoshi didn't want her present for whatever was about to happen.

Greyson was still better at violence than anybody alive that he knew.

"Your presence on Brees has unsettled things, Leigh," Captain Ikoshi said in an offhand way.

Greyson nodded. Small pond. Big rock. Mud everywhere.

"As Captain of Detectives for Anic, my hands probably haven't been as clean as they should be," the man continued.

Greyson was watching those hands now, gauging the distance to kick the fool right in the balls. Worked just as well on a G'schtack as it did a Human.

"Go on," Greyson prodded when the man lapsed into silence.

"Seeing those women in the cloning machine…" Ikoshi started to say. He paused, grimaced, and his eyes zeroed back in on Greyson now. "I recognized two of them, Leigh."

Greyson let himself blink in surprise. Power corrupts. A theory as old as power itself.

The whole reason you needed laws was to constrain Human behavior.

And, apparently, G'schtack.

"Worse," Ikoshi continued while Greyson just watched him for tells and signs of impending violence. "I've been intimate with one of them."

"Intimate," Greyson repeated the word in three distinct syllables, just to make sure he'd heard it correctly.

"That's right," Ikoshi nodded, blushing now in that way that gray skin turned almost black when flushed with blood. "As you have suggested, a brothel of such women. Sex objects, as you classed them in the paperwork, rather than sex workers, because they might not have ever been given a choice in the matter. Might not even have the free will to understand that there were other choices."

Greyson nodded. Rape wasn't always physical penetration. You could do all sorts of evil, just to someone's mind.

"Here on Brees?" Greyson asked now. "In Anic?"

"Close," Ikoshi grimaced. "Out in Chenta, at a—I suppose you might call it a lodge. Out in the country club part of the hills, south of town. A private facility. It was a private party for a certain class of politicians."

"Politicians?" Greyson confirmed.

G'schtack were like Humans that way, too. Political power often caused them to cut corners. Overlook things. Have *expectations*.

"Not the Metropolitan," Ikoshi said sharply. "As far as I know, Tine Ricia is about as honest as they come, and demands that her staff have white hands. The rest of the administration…"

He shrugged. Greyson nodded. Long-term civil servants. The folks that would never get rich on their government salary, but who had access to things that they could parlay into money and favors from rich people.

Like sex parties with enthusiastic whores of all flavors and colors.

Greyson refrained from cold-cocking the man in the jaw with a fist angry enough to possibly break it.

Barely.

In his mind, the tall fellow in front of him had just shrunk half a foot, put on a beer belly, and sounded a lot like Olek Zielinski, former Captain/Hunter back in Boston, currently doing life plus *forever* in a maximum security cell in Tennessee, may God have mercy on his soul, because Greyson had none.

"They have Pleasure Models there?" Greyson ground out the words like flour coming out of a stone mill.

"As I said, I recognized two of them from the tanks," Ikoshi nodded hesitantly, like he could smell the violence coming off Greyson's being right now. "There were other women, but they might have just been sex workers. That, or there is more than one such facility. Or perhaps they have more clones in their databanks than the thirty-two we encountered at Aeon."

Greyson had considered that. Wondered if the fools in charge would stop at the ones visible, or if those had just been the most popular, the *current lineup*, as it were, so they were kept ready to be decanted.

As far as he knew, they were still in the tanks, but it had only been three days. No government moves that fast, in anything less than a natural disaster.

Or political revolutions.

"What happens when this news gets out?" Greyson asked.

There was no question of covering this up. Not if some of the senior officials he would need to work with could be blackmailed over it. And Greyson was an expert in handling blackmail cases after Zielinski.

"I don't know," Captain Ikoshi said after a moment. "Depending on a number of things, the fallout could be anything."

"What happens to a Captain of Detectives?" Greyson asked. "How does his career handle reporters starting to poke into other aspects of things? Old rumors. That stuff."

Another grimace. A pause. No hint of violence about the man. Nothing confrontational.

If anything, perhaps relief. Having to admit what he'd done and confront it in the light of day would be painful, but possibly only in the short term. As Arymo had said, sex work itself was legal. Greyson didn't know if the Captain was married, or how such a spouse might react, but that was a private affair.

It was when the sex workers were slaves that you had a problem. If the Captain had confronted that just in the last few days, and was willing to assist the case, rather than impede it…

"I might get a slap on the wrist," Ikoshi replied finally. "I might be forced to retire but I have a pension. And it might be that my mistakes are far less than those of other folks around here, and I kind of get lost in the shuffle."

"Why are you here, Captain?" Greyson asked.

That was really the answer he wanted. The man could have covered things up. Or at least tried. He was facing Greyson Leigh and Rachel Asher across the battlefield.

Maybe he'd come to realize what a suicidal move that was.

"I've watched you work for several days, Leigh," Ikoshi replied, straightening finally from where he had been a bit hunched over. Like he'd been expecting a body blow that hadn't come. Yet. "You came in here like a storm front. Blasted in, stirred everything up, and demanded justice be done. On your terms, which just happened to be Guildlaw terms."

Greyson nodded. Only way to handle something this big had been to blow the top off it on Day One and then ride the ensuing tidal wave until it petered out well inland.

Not like he'd never done that before.

"When I saw the G'schtack woman in the tube, I recognized her," Ikoshi said. "Fucked her, not to put too fine of a point on it, though it was a different version of the woman. The body was the same. As was the face. You found a sex object assassin that had been sent to Earth. How many more of them are out there?"

"We don't know yet," Greyson said.

"That's right," Ikoshi said. "We don't know. We can't know, until we drag it all out into the twin suns. The Hound and The Hunter."

He paused there, and Greyson finally understood. A G'schtack wouldn't understand a Road to Damascus reference, but that seemed to describe the cop in front of him. A man who didn't run up and down the stairs, everywhere he went. Who didn't seek out the mom-and-pop diner, settling instead for the big corporate chain that was closer and convenient.

Settling.

It could be seductive. Greyson had seen it, though that sort of laziness had been pounded out of him a long time ago by a drill instructor who probably had the most responsibility for what Greyson Leigh had turned into.

The only fear you will admit is failure.

Yes, Sergeant!

"How many others am I likely to splash mud on?" Greyson asked now. "Are there judges I should worry about?"

"You got lucky with Murphely Rankev," Ikoshi chuckled. "I'm not sure I know a more honest person. Even the Metropolitan only comes in second. I don't know about judges, but she might. Or I can call in a few favors. Offer leniency on prosecutions, if some folks are willing to come in from the dark, like I am."

"I can't offer you anything, Captain," Greyson growled. "I'm just a Detective/Hunter. A lowly street cop who has opened a can of worms that the rest of you are going to be years sorting out."

"They're politicians, Leigh," the man replied, staring at him hard now. "They rarely understand what we go through in keeping the peace. In keeping people safe. I had forgotten, until you came along and reminded me. All I ask from you is that you understand what I say when I mean that I did things I'm not proud of right now, and need to find a way to make it all better later. If that means I retire, so be it, but I think that I'm not all that compromised and can help at least bring this to completion. Afterwards, maybe I do need to depart, but I'll have left things better than I would have a week ago. Does that make sense?"

"It does," Greyson replied, amazed that their voices had never risen above a murmur for all the emotion involved.

Sometimes cops forgot why they wanted the job. They cut corners. They flash a badge and demand free coffee and maybe a free dinner, with the implicit threat of trouble for a failure to comply.

All of Yaran Ikoshi's life was likely to become public fodder when all this came out. And Greyson would make sure that it did.

Sunlight was the best disinfectant, and Brees had two suns shining down.

"What do you need from me right now?" Greyson asked.

Ikoshi slipped a hand into his blazer pocket, which was good because if he'd gone for a breast pocket, there'd be a nerve scrambler touching one of his eyeballs before he realized it. The Captain pulled out a piece of paper.

"I've made arrangements for you to talk to the Metropolitan, later today," he said. "You and Asher. I honestly don't know if Moora is safe to include in these conversations, at least not without asking the kinds of questions that would give it all away. This is the location of the place, along with notes on what I remember from the few times I've been there."

Greyson took it and Captain Ikoshi turned and walked away without another word. Just squared his shoulders once, pulled his head up, and walked back down the path he'd arrived by, like nothing had happened.

Greyson let him go. The man might have found a way through his own crisis of conscience. Time would tell.

Road to Damascus.

Greyson turned and went back to the safe house door. Rachel was watching through the glass, nerve scrambler in one hand, but the other two people weren't visible. Nor was the plainclothes officer that had been watching the back.

Rachel opened the door as he got close, but Greyson didn't speak until he was inside with the door closed again.

"Moora?" he half-yelled to the front of the small space.

"Here," the Investigator answered from the front room.

"You, Rachel, and I are going back downtown," Greyson said. "Let the others know to keep the place secure."

"Where are we headed?" Rachel asked.

"Got a very interesting break in the case," Greyson said.

"Need to dump a ton of bricks on them before they realize someone's coming for them."

"Again," she nodded.

"Always," Greyson said.

Justice was a fleeting thing, forever chased.

But he had the spoor now.

TWENTY-SIX
METROPOLITAN

Rachel had met Metropolitan Upkins, the boss of the Eastern Metroplex that ran from the old US/Canada border all the way down the East Coast, touching the Metroplexes of Toronto, Chicago, and Houston on its western borders. Didn't know her hardly at all, but the woman had dated Greyson back in the way old, and still had a soft spot in her heart for him.

That much was obvious the few times Rachel had been around her.

Tine Ricia, Metropolitan for Anic and a good chunk of this part of the planet, was hardly anything like Upkins. Short and slender for a G'schtack in a way best described as petite. Until those eyes opened up and locked on you. Then she was a predator spying lunch.

Or competition, since it was Greyson Leigh across the desk from her. Match made in hell, if you would.

The office was huge. Like forty feet wide and nearly eighty long, arranged into three distinct sections.

You entered at the low end, into something of an inner reception room, having just come from an outer area guarded by people and secretaries. That part had two comfortable-looking couches and a wet bar, so folks could enjoy some tea or coffee-like substance while chatting.

Past that, a thing like a drafter's table, but ten feet wide and twenty long. Too tall for a conference table, but just perfect to lay maps on if you were planning the invasion of Guatemala or something, like those old movies.

Finally, you got to the top section. Again, enormous desk, like eight feet wide by four deep. Shorter though, to fit a small woman. A few trinkets and a pen stand right out of an old movie, presumably for signing laws that the legislature had sent over.

Captain Ikoshi had said something interesting to the Metropolitan's staff, because it was her, the three of them, and a Dyarnan woman who reminded Rachel of nobody so much as Edgar Redhawk, Upkins's aide and killer who even impressed Greyson.

They'd all been welcomed. Had tea outside while waiting for a trade delegation of some sort to be sent on their way. Were settled in three chairs on this side of that giant wooden battlefield from the other two.

Small talk had been handled. The Metropolitan was locked on Greyson now.

"Yaran Ikoshi was adamant that I meet with you this afternoon, Detective Leigh," she announced. "Without explaining. Why is that?"

"He had come into possession of new information on the case, Your Honor," Greyson said calmly. Quietly. Almost negligently. "It has…*implications.*"

Rachel liked the way the Dyarnan woman perked up at that. If she was anything like Redhawk, her job was to destroy people quietly, like Machiavelli had insisted upon when talking about a corrupt Pope and his dilettante asshole son.

"What kind of *implications?*" Ricia asked now, apparently willing to play the straight man in this vaudeville routine.

"You remember the clones in their chambers," Greyson said leadingly, pausing until he got a nod to proceed. "Captain Ikoshi is aware of a place where we might find similar models. In the wild, as it were."

Oh, yeah, both of them perked up right now. *We've just gone from theoretical to practical, haven't we?*

Rachel watched both of the strangers, as well as Moora. Greyson had said he might be safe.

And he might not.

"So why haven't you gone before Judge Rankev with a new Affidavit of Findings?" the Metropolitan asked.

"Ikoshi suggested that such a raid will uncover connections to your administration," Greyson said with a smile in his voice now. "Not you, personally, or even your immediate staff, but those folks who came with the office. Long-term civil servants who might not be seen in their best light, when this next bit of news comes out."

"And what do you expect me to do about it?" she demanded politely.

"Be prepared," Greyson said. "Ikoshi suggested that a lot of folks were going to be so compromised that they might need to be fired and possibly prosecuted. He did not exclude himself from that list."

Rachel watched both of the women across the desk absorb that knowledge, like taking a punch to the stomach. Politicians never had to deal with shit like that. At most, they grinned through a scandal until everyone forgot it, or resigned to spend more time with their families.

Until people forgot.

Ikoshi was willing to fall on his sword, if it came to that.

Rachel wouldn't have expected that of the man, but Greyson could have that effect on people, even when he wasn't trying. Just look at her. She'd considered taking some of that chicken fried steak money. Nobody would have ever known except her, and she could have had a guaranteed-easy retirement.

But she'd have known. And had left it alone as a result.

Honest cop was a hazard, hanging around Leigh. Seemed to be catching.

The women recovered pretty quick.

"He thinks he might be out of a job when it comes to light?" Ricia asked.

"It will paint him in a bad way," Greyson replied. "Maybe compromise him too much to continue in his current job."

"Then why did he do it?" she asked.

"Because it was the right thing to do," Leigh replied in that hard, heavy voice he used when you asked a stupidly annoying question.

Greyson Leigh was all about doing the right thing, so much so that even Ethen Boli had succumbed to it eventually. That took some doing, but Rachel had actually met her once and spoken with Greyson's…*memories* of her.

"And how much of my administration do you plan to annihilate, Detective Leigh?" the Metropolitan asked in an equally hard voice.

"Maybe everyone not in this room, Your Honor," he said.

Rachel watched both women and an Investigator flinch.

Nothing like playing for all the marbles, was there?

"Not planning it, by the way," Greyson continued after everyone had a moment to breathe. "Just wanted you aware that it might come to that before I was done."

"And when you are done, Leigh?" Ricia asked. "Then what?"

"Then I go home," he said. "You can blame everything on me if you want. I'll carry all that bad karma back to Earth and wear it like a cloak against any idiots who think they want to say something to me."

"That doesn't bother you?" she asked.

"The Hunter Bureau was created to deal with dangerous aliens," he replied. "Sometimes, we have to kill them. Anybody who travels all that distance to cause me trouble has it coming."

They all shuddered. Rachel was watching body language, having spent enough time around G'schtack now to better understand them. Folks were just not prepared for having a Greyson Leigh in their lives. It was like an earthquake. Little warning, massive rearrangement, damage to clean up afterwards.

"And you, Detective Asher?" Ricia turned this way now. Probably needed a break from bashing her head against Leigh's impenetrability. "What do you think will happen next?"

"We go capture some more bad guys," Rachel grinned at the women. "Hopefully, they don't want to put up too much of a fight in the process, so we can haul them all back down to Judge Rankev and all you lovely folks can deal with prosecuting them. Personally, I'd take Leigh at face value, and start looking at how you might need to rebuild everything from scratch. If shit's gone so badly already, probably past time you folks cleaned things up. Have you considered asking the Guild leadership to step in, or do we think they are just as badly compromised?"

What was it Leigh had said about high score this morning? And should they count this one as part of that or start a new sheet? Metropolitan Ricia and her deadly assistant hadn't given any thought to the fact that the Guild elite, of which she was a member, might have knowledge of said crimes.

Might want to cover them up as well.

"The Guild?" Ricia managed to ask in a tone that wasn't a gasp for air, however barely.

"Somebody decided to make clones of existing people," Rachel reminded them. "We've had only the faintest idea as to what they might have been used for, based on Human imagination and our own history of thinking about such things. If you are going to allow shit like that, you need to be up front about it. Or you need to drop an angry anvil on those people who might think they can get away with it instead. Squash them like bugs and make sure the next batch understand that they can get an anvil just as easily."

Long pause. Like somebody had to reboot everything. The day had been like that for these poor folks.

"Anything else we should prepare for?" Ricia finally asked the room.

"No," Greyson said. "I'm going over to talk to Rankev now. Then maybe go cause some trouble, so you might want to get dinner sooner rather than later, as this might be another long night."

He rose, so she did as well. Arymo took a moment to recover, but he'd been something of an innocent bystander from the beginning, though he'd held up his end just fine.

Metropolitan Ricia rose and moved around the desk to shake their hands before they left.

She'd gotten all the warning she was going to get, and it was out of her hands.

Other than battening down the hatches for Hurricane Greyson.

TWENTY-SEVEN

JUSTICE

Greyson watched Murphely Rankev enter the conference room and had to appreciate that she was still in pretty damned good shape for a past-middle-aged G'schtack, and that they aged like Humans did. He'd compare her to somebody like the actor Dame Helen Mirren, back when he was a kid. She'd been a complete babe in the 1960s and 70s, then kept right at it until she was in her eighties and after.

Murphely wasn't as top-heavy as the Englishwoman, but she had a way of moving that drew the eyes to those generous hips in appreciation. And a subtle smile as she moved past him and took a seat, like she was reading his mind.

"You've got more trouble brewing, Greyson?" she asked as she sat.

Across the way, Rachel and Arymo just watched, like innocent bystanders at a traffic incident.

"Do," he grinned back. "Maybe the piece that really unravels Anic as a government and possibly shatters the local Metroplex so badly that folks finally have to pay attention. Maybe the whole of Brees, depending on how many hands get caught in this cookie jar. Maybe more."

"I knew you were trouble, the first time you walked into my court room," she laughed. "Now you have to top it?"

"Somebody gave me the name of a brothel employing copies of creatures we found at Aeon," he said simply.

All the levity flowed out of her in a heartbeat, revealing the killer underneath. That just made her all the more amazing. And sexy.

"Where?" she asked.

Across the table from him and Murphely, Rachel and Arymo perked up. Game time.

Greyson pulled an Affidavit of Findings from his inner pocket and set it down between him and the judge, along with the unsigned versions of the Warrant for Entry and the Expected Arrest Warrant, this time with four pages of blanks appended, for names to be added as he rounded folks up.

Murphely opened them and read the paperwork. He could tell when she got to the good part because she gasped and looked up at him.

"You're certain?" she asked.

"My informant was," he said. "Claims to have personally…*witnessed* such a person employed there."

"Witnessed," Murphely replied with a tone of such disgust that suggested she understood how personal that particular *interaction* had gone down.

He grinned.

"There are likely to be a lot of…*interesting* folks available, as it is a weekend night," Murphely continued. "Do you plan on arresting everyone there, or just rescuing your lost children?"

"I'm of two minds," he replied. "On the one hand, I might manage to arrest everyone except the Captain of Detectives or the Metropolitan with a raid like this. That's likely to sell a lot of newspapers tomorrow. And employ an extraordinary number of criminal defense attorneys next week as folks get arraigned. On the other hand, there might be nobody interesting there at all and we just shut the place down and rescue all the sex objects from slavery."

"Do you care?" she asked.

Rachel laughed before he could shrug.

"Okay, poorly framed question," Murphely nodded to his partner. "Do you think he'll let that stop him?"

"You want everyone in jail, or just frightened out of their wits?" Rachel countered. "As he told Ricia, we're going home at some point and letting you poor saps sort this out amongst yourselves. Nothing about this suggests that we're going to get anything but the blame for riding into town like a pair of cowboys and causing trouble."

"Cowboys?" Murphely asked.

"Human cultural reference," Rachel nodded. "Big scary dude comes in, ends a bunch of bad folks violently to save the day, then rides out again."

"You two have covered that rather well," Murphely chuckled. "I find it a bit of a shame that you might not stay around to cause more trouble to more people. Brees probably needs something like that."

Greyson didn't like the way the woman was smiling at him as she said it. Rachel had explained competence porn to him more than once, but Greyson just didn't buy it.

He was just a hardass killer with a badge, trying to make the galaxy a better place for folks without the power to change things. Maybe that meant he pinned a brass badge to his vest for Act Three of whatever movie it was.

He was still riding off into the sunset when the credits rolled. Fuck that noise.

Assuming he didn't ride into the entire Bolivian Army, one of these days.

The part that concerned him was how many folks might seek him out, back in Boston. Lissa and Murphely probably wouldn't have dire outcomes in mind, beyond maybe fucking him to death.

The others…?

Murphely dropped it, though, when she saw his face. Sobered appropriately and went back to reading. Pulled a pen from an inside pocket of her jacket and signed everywhere necessary to give his bounty hunting the force of legality.

He'd looked up the lodge Ikoshi had mentioned. Nobody on the board of directors of the place showed up anywhere near the list of investors for Aeon Research Financial, but he wasn't surprised. You'd want to obfuscate things like that through many layers of corporate entities that would normally keep carnivorous accountants at bay.

Until somebody like Greyson Leigh tossed fresh chum in the water.

Like now.

"I presume that I shall see you tomorrow in the grand jury chambers?" she asked as she slid the now-executed paperwork back to him.

"Good Lord willing and the creek don't rise," he answered, standing.

She wouldn't get the reference. It was a Human thing. An American thing, at that.

Her Honor understood where he was going, though.

TWENTY-EIGHT
COPS

RACHEL COUNTED NOSES. And recognized faces. All of Team One from the other day was here, along with damned near everybody else.

Someone had mentioned that Greyson Leigh had another target he wanted help taking down, and a whole posse had come out of the woodwork.

She wondered if the boy realized that he could get himself elected sheriff of this one-horse town without a lot of work. Or however many horses the financial center of the most important planet in the Illymus Merchant Guild might have.

Still wouldn't be enough to stop Greyson Leigh from bringing the trouble.

And the justice.

Arymo was organizing things, just like last time. Six larger teams this go round, as the perimeter they needed to secure was smaller.

"You will stun first and ask questions later," Arymo was telling them.

Rachel stepped up beside him, drawing all eyes to her.

"Additionally," she said in the kind of hardass voice Leigh had taught her. "There is some question as to whether or not there might be Phrenic involved."

She paused, eyeballing all these cops who saw themselves as a posse. Citizen band, maybe. Nothing like the Heavy Response Teams she might have on call back home for something like this, not counting the tall Mooz *chicka*.

Ambitious and willing, though, even as her words penetrated.

"Every team will have a heavy gunner with them," Rachel pronounced her own special kind of doom. "If someone doesn't go down when you stun them, hit them a second time. If that fails, you will escalate things. Detective Leigh and I are always armed with nerve scramblers for exactly that reason. Each of your teams has been assigned someone with training and authorization to use lethal firepower. Do not be afraid to call them in if someone resists arrest. Am I clear?"

Long, ugly pause. Posse coming to grips with the fact that this wasn't just another barbecue picnic in the park on a nice day.

Stun rifles were lovely things. Most of the time they just put someone down and didn't hurt anyone. Occasionally, you got bad reactions, but that just meant you kept medical teams handy to deal with a surprise heart attack.

Phrenic, with their second nervous system, shrugged those things off. And anybody here in disguise had to have killed someone in order to take over their life.

On Earth, that was about the only true capital crime left.

"*Am I clear?*" she repeated louder, not to get them charged up, but to make her point.

Folks nodded, a little hangdog now, but that just meant they would be serious when doing things, rather than rambunctious puppies.

She and Leigh were the cowboys here. Everybody else needed to stay in their own lanes.

She turned to Death Himself now, looking to see what kind of pep talk he had in mind.

A change came over the man as she watched. Not unexpected, but the charm and magnetism got cranked up several notches from his usually-introverted self.

That was the thing Murphely Rankev or Lissa Jonez saw and got turned on by.

"You will run into important people when we arrive," he said now, voice pitched to carry to the seventy-odd folks around them. "People you see on the evening news. Politicians you recognize. Famous and rich people you read about. Every single one of them is involved in a crime. And a criminal conspiracy. Some of them might be able to plead some level of ignorance later, but I intend to capture everyone and then let a judge sort them out when assigning charges and listening to plea deals. There will be no mercy tonight. There is never mercy in the darkness. Let that await the rising of Udoth to return light and warmth to the world of Brees. We are Hunters. If necessary, killers, but all of you will show no mercy. No remorse. You will stun at the slightest provocation. Everyone you meet is going to jail tonight. Or hell. That said, *mount up*."

Rachel felt the same chill as passed through the crowd.

It was a damned good thing that boy didn't want to get into politics, because moments like this would carry him far beyond local sheriff if he did.

The tableau held for a moment. Greyson broke it by turning to her and nodding. She joined him walking towards the transport that would shortly carry all of them over the ridge and drop this group on some bad people who thought that money and power protected them from the law.

When they were supposed to be the law.

Was everybody, everywhere, corrupt? Or was it the nature of power that eventually everyone succumbed? Greyson had mentioned more than once the need for punitive taxes on inheritance and electing politicians by lottery.

More and more, Rachel could see where that might not be the worst way to do things.

Far fewer killer-sex-object clones running around, if nothing else, because nobody would have the immunity from prosecution that came with having money and *friends*.

They climbed into the transport. Senior Officer Uliyari Ovin was with them, the Mooz woman pulling rank to lead Team One again. Most of the other faces Rachel could see in here were the same ones as before as well.

Angry posse, in hot pursuit.

They lifted off into the night sky of Brees, the lights of Anic behind them filling the valley as the darkness of the semi-wilderness ahead seemed like a maw opening to swallow them.

Silly mistake on the part of the darkness. Leigh would make it choke, then cut his way out with a knife, bloody and laughing. He was like that. The feeling seemed infectious around them, as Team One started pulling chinstraps tight and locking in.

They cleared the ridge and the lights of a nice, fancy, country club parking lot and suite of buildings came into view out the front window.

Quiet. Pretty.

And about to be subject to hell on Earth.

Or Brees.

TWENTY-NINE
RAID

Greyson had dressed for this like any other day at the office. Shirt that blood could be washed out of with a little work. Pants that would slough blood off of with a damp cloth. Longcoat that would turn a knife. Boots that would stop a bullet.

Absolutely no tie.

Rachel was in her similar outfit, the only difference between them being his browns to her grays.

The cops around them in the transport were wearing the sorts of riot control plastic armor like had been big when Greyson was a kid. When cops didn't answer to anybody in the United States and could attack riots with the kinds of tools and equipment that violated all those fancy Geneva Conventions that everybody had signed.

Ultimate power, right at the end of the American Empire.

He wanted to say good riddance. That the Guild had brought about a Golden Age. Future historians of Earth would probably call it that, glossing over all the dislocations and unemployment that accompanied First Contact. All the shit that required folks like the Hunter Bureau to keep the peace.

Periods of instability brought just as much corruption as periods of peace, just from different directions. What this town needed, to quote the old supervillain in that one movie, was an enema. Break up everything and wash it out to sea, hoping that you could make the law preeminent for a while.

At least until the chiselers came in and started attacking the corners again. Termites and cockroaches in the halls of power never went away.

He held on to a steel bar as the craft fell out of the sky now. It wasn't as bad as an assault drop, but nobody down there was bright enough to open fire or run either. Not yet. That was coming later. Hopefully, his teams could get most of them.

He could always ask the grand jury to authorize him to seize copies of all the flight control logs for this region later. Hell, if he wanted to be a complete and utter shit, he might suggest going back months or even years to show evidence of folks coming to this particular establishment.

You didn't even have to press charges at that point. In fact, he figured he might just do more damage by dangling that sort of thing out there, leaking it into the court of public opinion, without giving somebody the benefit of their day in court to refute things and maybe get off on a technicality.

Not that a younger Greyson Leigh had ever assassinated someone like that without ever harming the body, or anything.

"Ten seconds out," the pilot said in a mechanical voice over the PA.

Below, Greyson could see the parking lot growing, filled with all manner of flashy and expensive vehicles. Only a few would have chauffeurs who might bolt, because it was so much easier to let the autopilot take you to your midnight assignations, without organic witnesses that might gossip about things.

Yeah, he knew these people. Had spent too much time in…*places he didn't discuss*. Watching folks with money and immunity flaunt it in quiet ways.

And occasionally they suffered a terrible accident when their vehicle ran off a cliff or into a river on the way home, killing all aboard because some asshole American had cut brake lines or mucked with the power steering when nobody was looking.

Being raised by gearheads had given him a fantastic appreciation of how to do things like that. Most folks let the cars drive them, rather than the other way around.

The ground rose up. They landed. Not hard, but not the feather-soft touch of an autopilot bringing them in. The machines wouldn't let you push the margins like this.

Greyson had a grip on the handle and jacked the door open in a single motion that ended with him standing next to the transport, already at a jog that would turn into a sprint shortly. Rachel was second out, then Team One.

He left them all behind. Even Rachel could only move at Human speeds, after all.

The other transports weren't landing as close to the front door, each with responsibility for a sector of his target. Greyson drew his palmstunner left-handed and charged the person responsible for the front door. Pimp was an ugly term, as the fellow was really more of a bouncer in a fancy suit than anything.

Greyson shot him cold with the palmstunner as soon as he was sure of a solid hit, then drew the nerve scrambler to calm his soul.

Having death in his right hand brought focus to things. And the big, double door was open to the night, so he didn't have to do handles right now, or have someone else.

A few other kids were starting to react. Young men, either there to help park cars, or assist in ejecting unruly customers or folks without an invitation.

Like him.

Greyson shot the one on the right. Then the one in the center. Rachel got the guy on the left.

He owned the entrance to the country club.

Team One caught up. Only because he had stopped moving. Team Two was right behind them, starting to array to cover this point without penetrating. Team Three would follow on after One. Greyson had folks assigned for both sides, the roof, and the rest of the parking lot, because he wasn't fucking around today.

A glance to confirm he had nearly twenty officers ready to go in with him. And one other cowboy.

Cowgirl.

Killer.

"In," he said.

The hour was close to local midnight, as the planet rotated. Folks who had been in there a while were probably thinking about heading home soon. Others that had been fashionably late were just getting…warmed up, as it were.

In flagrante delicto. With illegal life forms.

Greyson felt like a cowboy in the shootout scene at the end of the movie. And mentally, he had a brass badge on his vest, just like you were supposed to in Act Three.

He spotted an obvious waitress, wearing an outfit that showed off a lot of flesh but wouldn't be that easy to get out of, so not one of the working girls. Antisaur, with her blue scales almost maroon tonight.

Her mouth opened to scream as she processed that a team of armed people was storming the facility.

Greyson shot her with the palmstunner.

"POLICE!" he yelled in a voice intended to be heard and

obeyed. "Everyone here is under arrest! Do not resist or we will use force!"

There. Official and everything. Only employees had been stunned so far. Everybody else from here on in would be provoking him.

Not that it would take much.

The actual pimp arrived now. G'schtack. Small for a male. Fussy. Well-dressed. Probably the man in charge of the pros, depending on how they organized the operation. A pimp, if not THE pimp.

"What's the meaning of this?!?" he shrieked, stomping forward as Greyson took in the room he had just entered.

Lobby didn't do the room justice, as those tended to be a bit impersonal. More like a salon where the prostitutes could hang out and be selected by whoever came along and had an invitation. The furniture was expensive-looking but so overdone that it was almost tacky. Bright and flashy, when real money would have likely done subtle and demure.

All the things these people weren't.

Heads had turned. Mouths in all manner of species were falling open or making hollow sounds as shock overwhelmed rationality. Some of them might have thought they were being robbed or something.

A party of heavily-armed cops at the door would have a negative effect on your libido, he supposed, that one girl he'd dated as a teenager notwithstanding.

The Pimp was full of himself, right up to the moment Greyson socketed his nerve scrambler in the short man's left eyeball.

"Everyone here is under arrest," Greyson said in a much more conversational tone. "That includes you, the staff, the boys and girls, and every single one of your clients. Would you like to do this the easy way, or the hard way?"

Apparently, nobody had ever told this fool no. He

reached up and actually swatted the nerve scrambler away. Greyson let him, instead of pulling the trigger.

Because he was in a mood, Greyson rotated his left elbow in like a bird and hammered the man in the side of the skull with it. One of those hard spots where the bones are designed to take it on a G'schtack, rather than a soft spot where they might rupture and drive shards into the brain.

Line shot up the middle kind of sound. Followed by a sack of potatoes hitting the floor. Rachel shot him with her palmstunner anyway.

"Gonna need a medic on this one," she called, louder than necessary for the closeness of the team, but enough that the rest of the room would absorb the words.

If not the meaning.

Greyson scowled at the fine folks he could see.

"Easy way, or hard way?" he asked, pitched to get into the dark spaces in the back of your head and stick needles into things.

Hands came up. Empty. Surrendering.

"Stun them all," he said, in motion again. "Sort them out later."

He approached a Mooz woman behind the bar. He kept watching the rest of the room in a wide mirror behind her. She'd put her hands flat on the counter as soon as she realized what was happening. Smart lady.

"Anybody in charge besides him?" Greyson asked, nodding to the pimp. Behind him, stunner fire licked the room with quiet hums. Rachel was at his elbow, watching his back.

"He's the floor manager," the Mooz woman replied carefully. "The boss is through the door on your left with a couple of bigshots. You're really cops?"

"We are," Greyson assured her.

"Wow," she answered, still perfectly motionless as mayhem rattled around.

Greyson nodded and turned to one of his people.

"Take her into custody," he ordered. "Keep her awake. Just cuffs for now and be polite."

Nobody else had gotten that sort of order. Nobody else had volunteered to help, either.

Greyson rotated once to his right, just to confirm the woman he'd seen, almost hidden in a back corner where she'd been facing mostly away from him while sitting on the lap of a G'schtack male. She wasn't wearing much clothing, which was pretty much like she'd been the first time Greyson saw her. Or the last.

Except that it wasn't Anais Manel. Just another copy of that perfect woman, decanted and sold into sexual slavery.

She collapsed as somebody fired into that corner, splayed out in all her perfect beauty, just like she'd been on a slab in a morgue.

He growled, mostly to himself. Nodded to the bartender as she started walking around where she could get politely arrested. Turned to Rachel.

"Time to get ugly," he told her.

R ACHEL TRAILED G REYSON THROUGH A HALLWAY. He'd gestured the rest of the team to start down the other hallways to the cribs, though she supposed that instead of flophouse cribs they were fancy suites with gold-plated bathtubs large enough for small orgies, considering the decoration theme in this place.

This hallway, behind the bar, was much more industrial. Simple white walls in a thing that might be the local equivalent of sheetrock. Paintings hung every once in a while, but nothing much. Couple of landscapes. Some flowers.

The carpet underfoot even felt harder. Maybe half as thick as in the reception area. Designed for a lot of wear.

Greyson went by a door marked Bar Storage and continued. She sidled past the same door to keep an eye on it while following. She could see the pretty door on the end of the hallway that should be where the bigshots would hang out.

A place to have money conversations, instead of the good fucking session that the women and men she'd seen out front could provide down the other hallway. Guild culture didn't have nearly as many hangups about sex as American culture had. They were way more French or German that way, frowning on violence but ignoring most consensual things adults did in privacy.

Like the cowboy in front of her, Rachel was two-gunning today. She wasn't as good at it as he was, but she also doubted that there were that many Humans alive in his league. All she had to do was cover his back against surprises, and even then Rachel knew that Leigh's hearing was better than hers.

He had an unfair advantage there, as well, not technically being Human.

Greyson approached the door in the sort of silence you usually only got in horror movies back home. She was quiet enough getting there, but knew that he'd heard her.

Whether anybody else had was beyond her ability to tell. This was when his thirty-plus years as a killer matched up against her five years of being a cop or training to be one, with only barely one of those as his partner.

He nodded to her. Indicated she should stand to one side, again watching both directions. Which really just meant covering the hallway or making sure nobody in the room managed to run past him.

Rachel nodded back. Watched.

Greyson, that tall, skinny punk with an attitude problem, leaned back and utterly shattered the door open with a foot just below the handle. Someone hadn't thought to put four-inch-screws into the strike plate, either, because local wood erupted from the frame with a sound like cloth tearing.

Like Damnation itself, coming for your soul.

An apocalypse named Greyson Leigh.

THIRTY-ONE
MANAGEMENT

GREYSON HAD FOUND a true rage inside himself, watching someone shoot Anais Manel's identical twin sister with a stun rifle. Ethen had something to do with it, as she'd been a victim of gaslighting and sexual abuse as a younger woman. And child.

He couldn't explain to anyone but Rachel where the new fire erupting had originated. Not if he wanted to live long enough to see this ugliness shattered and buried like it should be.

But it was there, hard and pure like a diamond in the process of being forged by immense heat and impossible weight.

The door felt his wrath. Maybe because he'd paused long enough to dial up his strength to inhuman standards. Didn't feel like being Human right now.

Inside the room, in that split second as the door swung away from him, Greyson saw three people. One behind a desk facing this way. The backs of two heads.

Then he was throwing himself sideways into the room, falling for cover on his right without even bothering to return fire, because the man behind the desk had a pistol and was in the act of firing.

However, the suited fool was moving at only Human speeds.

Insufficient, when an avenging devil named Ethen Boli woke up and got involved.

Greyson practically bounced off the floor, like it was the dojo where he'd learned to fall.

The Human behind the desk was slowly turning his way. Greyson was up to his knees, covering the two seated guests with the palmstunner on that side.

"Swear to God, I will end you," Greyson snarled, centering the nerve scrambler on the man and tightening his trigger finger.

The man had a beam weapon of some sort. Not the little palmstunner that always reminded Greyson of a garage door opener, or a Mark-1 hand phaser from the original episodes of Star Trek.

Not a nerve scrambler like Greyson was holding. Bigger. Uglier.

Up in that category of the old-time guy whose fragile ego demanded he carry a .44 Magnum in blue with an eight-inch barrel, when a real killer needs nothing more than a .22 and hours of practice.

Out in the hall, Greyson didn't hear the sound of Rachel's body hitting the floor, so the shot had missed. Hopefully, just blown a hole in a wall somewhere, rather than carrying all the way back into the main room and hurting someone.

In that case, Greyson might decide to get *cruel*. Like they taught you in the old days when you needed someone to tell you what he knew and didn't have the time to befriend him to gain the intelligence.

When a clock was ticking and nobody was likely to prosecute you for war crimes afterwards.

Just one of many things he didn't talk about with anybody, including the Bureau shrink he was required to visit twice a year. Those folks might be required to report any crimes that came up in his past. Even twenty-plus years ago in a country that didn't technically exist anymore.

Human seated behind a desk. Pistol moving so slowly that it was like watching a replay on the television.

"Put it down, or die," Greyson rasped at him, so hyped up right now that he wasn't sure he wasn't actually levitating.

The pistol stopped moving. The eyes continued. Only now were they beginning to register what *inhuman* speed really meant.

As long as Greyson wasn't nude, nobody would be able to tell what he'd done, and he'd shift himself back to a more normal form once this was under control. Original model Greyson Leigh, rather than the improvements he'd needed for something this stupid tonight.

Rage was a terrible mistress. Ethen was so angry she was seeing red. He'd need to meditate on his sins at some point.

Assuming anything that happened tonight qualified as a sin.

Greyson wasn't bluffing. And had a nerve scrambler on the man. The Human lowered his pistol and set it carefully down on the desk top.

The other two were just starting to react.

Inhuman speeds.

Inhuman.

Vengeance.

A woman named Anais Manel who had had no choice in the matter.

None whatsoever.

Greyson rose from his crouch, both pistols unwavering like a circus trickshooter.

"Hands in the air slowly," Greyson ordered the Human male. "Rachel, get the other two."

Out of the corner of his eye, he saw his partner move, but the two folks seated were nothing more than dark spots until they needed to be shot.

Neither had made that mistake.

Human male moved with the careful deliberation that you usually only saw in the extremely aged, when they didn't want to faceplant to the pavement from moving too suddenly. Both hands went up, empty, over the man's head.

Greyson finally looked at him as a person, rather than a moving target dummy on a deadly combat range.

Human. Male. Almost looked English, with that combination of brown hair and pale skin you got. Could be from the mother country. Could be American.

Could be any number of things.

Criminal conspirator covered all of them, as far as Greyson was concerned.

Slaver.

"Stand up slowly," Greyson growled, barely able to keep from just shooting the fucker in the face right now.

Images of Anais and her sister, both dead on the floor, threatened to overwhelm his self-control.

Her self-control.

How many more sisters were there that needed rescuing from the dragons that held them?

For a moment, Greyson and Ethen had an image of themself as St. George.

It was not a pleasant image, but it did put a smile on his face as the Human rose.

Must have been a pretty good smile, too, from the way the man paled even more.

"Rachel?"

"Got them covered," she said quietly.

Greyson holstered the palmstunner. If anybody gave him trouble right now, they were *forfeit*.

He reached out and took the strange beam weapon, careful not to touch the hot end as he ended up covering his new friend with both barrels.

The new one was indeed heavier. Felt less refined in his hand. Like his uncles and cousins back home had made it, instead of putting together junk cars to race. Functional, but ugly.

The nerve scramblers had been provided by senior members of the Guild, when it became obvious that Humans would need something to protect themselves from creatures that went bump in the night.

Other creatures.

Greyson could have made do with a shiv. Had, more than once.

He let those emotions play out on his face as he watched the man.

"Hands flat on the desk," Greyson ordered him.

He'd been emotionally prepared for some important G'schtack industrialist to be sitting behind this desk. Some ancient conspiracy that spanned generations and had wormed its way into the very heart of the Guild itself.

Humans had only been admitted sixteen years ago, and this fellow wasn't even as old as Greyson, from the way the skin on his neck looked.

The suspect complied. He hadn't spoken. Didn't have a lot of options.

Greyson holstered his nerve scrambler and covered the man left-handed with his own weapon. As if that mattered for accuracy.

He stepped around the back of the desk and into the

man, starting to pat him down enough to be sure he didn't have any more firearms in there.

Let the dumbshit pull a knife right now. Greyson/Ethen would feed it to him.

Slowly.

A wallet in the Human style, inner pocket of the Brooks Brothers jacket. Nice suit. Like folks used to get made in Hong Kong, before the Mainlanders destroyed the place. Grey with razored pinstripes.

A fold of bills in the left, front pants pocket. Way more than necessary. The kind of bankroll you pulled out in the movies to tell people you were a bigshot.

Or an easy mugging target. Whatever.

Fancy shoes. Possibly cost as much as Greyson made in a month. He doubted that they would stop spikes or bullets like his, but decided not to find out.

Not yet, anyway.

He felt like a cat with a mouse in paw.

"I'm going to handcuff you," Greyson told the man. "Relax so I don't have to break anything in the process."

As in, resisting gets shit fucked up beforehand, and then you have to go to the hospital before you arrive at jail.

Greyson quietly hoped the man would do something. Anything.

Give him a justification for using *unnecessary* force, when he could do extraordinary things.

Inhuman, in more ways than one.

Utterly Human, in his willingness to do violence to a total stranger tonight.

Apparently, the fool had a survival instinct after all, as he complied. Without physical damage.

Emotional and psychological trauma he could deal with on his own time.

Like Greyson.

The other two turned out to be G'schtack. Nobody Greyson knew. Middle-aged male and older female. Dressed about as expensively as the pimp here. Just about as shocked fucking senseless as they got handcuffed and patted down.

Greyson wondered if he'd interrupted a meeting about catering an event next week or something.

It would all be in the records somewhere. Having Anais's sister on the property just meant that everyone in this room was automatically tied to the rest of his case.

Like an anchor as the big ship entered the harbor at the end of a long voyage.

"Go get Arymo," Greyson said to Rachel. "I'll watch our friends."

The G'schtack male started to open his mouth. Like maybe he wanted to protest this insufferable behavior and demand his lawyers.

Greyson pulled out his badge and flashed it in the fool's face, just accidentally thwapping him on the nose like a puppy.

"You are under arrest for the enslavement and torture of citizens of the Illymus Merchant Guild," he instructed the man in formal tones. The trio. "Feel free to try my patience."

They did not. Some modicum of survival instinct must have kicked in, though none of them had wet themselves. Everything had happened too fast.

Inhuman speeds.

Rachel returned quickly. The sounds out in the main room had fallen off pretty fast.

Having overwhelming force and a willingness to use it extravagantly got results. Most of the folks being rounded up right now were rich bastards who used that to buy sex with slaves. Anything they wanted to say at that point was legally admissible.

Greyson wondered how many lawyers he'd rolled up.

That was one of the best ways to get rich in the Illymus Merchant Guild, since shipping contracts were the lifeblood of the galaxy.

Arymo and two other cops accompanied Rachel. Greyson sent his three prisoners off with the pair.

"Remember to read them all their rights before you stuff them in the black maria," he said with a hard sneer as they went.

The three of them were alone. Somewhere, a forensics team was being called in. Probably all of them, along with medics and counselors.

Greyson was too angry to sit, so he leaned against a wall and studied the office. Photos of the Head Pimp with some Humans Greyson recognized from Earth. Others with a variety of G'schtack and more that he probably should know on sight.

If he cared.

Rachel stood in the opposite corner, next to a potted plant that looked like mutant fern. Arymo took one of the chairs and kind of collapsed into it.

His eyes were nothing but pain when he finally looked up at Greyson.

"How many clones?" Greyson asked.

"So far, we have three of the Human female you called Anais," he said in a shell-shocked, hollow voice. "Two of the male you called Jan Michael. Three of Lissa Jonez. Pairs and triples of most of the women, plus individuals of a number of the males. About half the staff, just eyeballing it, with the other half being all fairly exotic representatives of their species."

"Geisha," Greyson noted.

"Sir?"

"A Human concept, Arymo," Greyson replied. "More than just women employed for sex. Some of the best of them were dancers, musicians, or just fantastic conversationalists who would get hired for something without ever taking their clothes off. I suspect that many of the non-staff employees who are citizens will fall into that sort of category, to provide, as you said, exotic flavor."

"They thought they were immune?" Arymo anguished now. "To just do these things out in the open?"

"They always do," Rachel said. "Above the law because too many of them end up being the very folks that are supposed to uphold it. We got lucky with you and Judge Rankev. This case could have turned out a number of other ways."

"Yeah," the G'schtack man breathed now. "I can see that. Are there that few honest cops?"

"Not all of them are bent," Greyson said. "You can boil a frog so slowly it never knows what happened, and I suspect that some folks around here fall into that category."

"Like Captain Ikoshi?" Arymo asked.

"He saw a path back to righteousness," Greyson said. "Whether they let him fully return is not my decision to make, but tonight will go a long ways towards paying his penance. There will be others who have to make a hard call right about now."

"This kind of scandal might bring down the government," Arymo said.

"If the truth can destroy something, then it deserves to be destroyed," Greyson repeated back at him. "I figure that the Guild will find a way to deal with it. Too many people will likely get off too easy for my tastes, but I'm a cold, hard son of a bitch when it comes to things like this. The ringleaders will be locked in small boxes forever. Hopefully, the lesson will stick for a while."

"Only a while?"

"The next generation will come along without knowing

this shit personally," Greyson said, nodding to Rachel. "She's likely to have to deal with something like this when she's my age, because everyone else will have retired. Your job, Arymo, is to make sure the rest of the cops around here understand and remember that some things are simply too evil to ever be allowed, under any circumstances."

"Because you're going home?" the Investigator asked.

"Earth's got enough troubles," he nodded. "You most certainly don't want me cleaning up a place like Brees. Not if you liked this planet and its people."

The G'schtack shivered at this tone, but the man had been in Greyson's hip pocket for a week now. Front lines, when that meant you saw all the ugly parts as well.

He'd seen firsthand the decisions Greyson had made along the way, just because he'd had to transcend Human to see justice done.

And he would.

"Now what?" Rachel asked after the silence stretched a bit.

"Now, we head back out and maybe fix ourselves something caffeinated so we can stay up all night while this gets processed," Greyson said. "Since the main pimp was Human, I expect we can find it."

"Haul them all off and let the prosecutors and judges sort them out in the morning?" she pressed.

"You don't want me in charge of dispensing justice, Rachel," he replied. "Ever."

She nodded. Of everyone on the planet, only she probably understood what a lethally bad idea that might be.

He stirred, the pimp's funky blaster pistol still in one hand because he didn't want to lose track of it. Probably also illegal, so just one more charge to add to the man when he went down hard.

Extremely hard.

Rachel and Arymo fell in on his flanks as he headed back down the hallway into that main room. Cops, medics, and warm bodies were in the process of rounding up and hauling off folks. Stunners would wear off in a few minutes, which was perfect for this line of work.

He noted the Anais Pleasure Models over in one corner, along with many of the other slaves. Team One had separated them off, once they understood what they were looking at. They'd been with him at Aeon, and many probably recognized the woman.

Women.

Victims.

Slaves.

Greyson turned to Rachel and handed her the pistol before the urge to shoot someone overwhelmed him.

Her.

Them.

Instead, he walked to the bar and located things by label and smell, until he found a cheap whiskey close enough to that taste of home to grind some of the edges off their rage.

If anything could do that.

GREYSON WAS BACK in the Grand Jury room, still smelling of funk from being up for more than a day. Whatever the actual measure was. Back home, somewhere around thirty hours.

Not the first time. Not likely the last, either. Part of being a Hunter.

He wouldn't say a good part. The best part would be no longer needing Hunters at all. Until then, being able to stand up before five judges and swear to the things he'd spent all night writing down so they could bring charges against two hundred forty-seven Johns and Janes and employees he'd rounded up.

That part made him smile. They were way out past pandering charges on this one.

Murphely sat at the center of the group, as before. Same faces. A lot fewer scowls this morning, but that might be happiness that they'd decided to stay home and watch vids last night instead of maybe going out to a specific country club for a night of…*entertainment.*

Leave it at that. If the powers that be didn't want to

investigate all these judges too closely after this, it would be because they'd slam dunked everyone currently implicated and not stretch their writ too far afterwards.

That was when Arymo Moora would have to step up the training of the kids around here.

"Detective Leigh," Judge Rankev spoke now, having finished whatever quiet conversation the five of them up there had been involved with.

He was far enough away to miss anything but the dull murmur.

Still, showtime. Greyson rose and nodded to everyone politely. Rachel and Arymo were seated at the table with him. Nobody else. Not even a Captain of Detectives could make a much more complete and compelling statement when called upon.

Greyson wondered if that would be a deposition or trial testimony. He didn't feel strongly one way or the other about Captain Ikoshi, but the man had given him the one piece that could utterly destroy everything.

Even having illegal life forms could be explained. Selling matched sets to a brothel was going to ruin lives.

The kind that needed torching anyway.

"We have been reviewing the case file this morning, Detective Leigh," Rankev continued, nodding to her cohorts, all of whom looked a little pale by species standards.

He nodded. Smiled even.

"You have used some rather inflammatory language to describe your findings, Leigh," she observed.

His smile got bigger. Uglier. It helped, having decades of expertise with the G'schtack language, to be able to finely parse some of those terms. No other Human he knew was probably nearly as fluent with the subtleties.

Only Rachel was going to ever meet the bar he'd set this

week on Brees. That was fine. His own form of immortality, as it were.

Murphely was just watching him now. Waiting for a statement. Greyson took a breath.

"The evidence speaks for itself, Your Honor," he replied, knowing that these words would be his legacy in the Guild. To the Guild. "A conspiracy to illegally clone intelligent creatures, subject them to secondary programming stripping them of all free will, and selling them into sexual slavery. Stack on top of that the fact that none of it involved paying appropriate duties and taxes, and I'm not sure there is a worse crime currently listed on your books."

He did let his smile turn sour now. A scowl that wouldn't get written down, and none of this was being videotaped.

"Personally, I think there is a larger conspiracy we've only just begun to sniff at, but my original case was to solve how an assassin was brought to Earth to kill a Guild citizen," he continued. "That, I've done. The raid last night was tangential to the rest of my case, while at the same time proving in my mind that the people responsible were willing co-conspirators who should be brought down, charged maximally, and put in prison for the rest of their lives, without possibility of early release."

The other four stirred angrily at that, but he waved them all off. Perhaps a bit rudely.

"That's neither here nor there," he continued. "I have solved my case, and made it possible for local authorities to identify and detain all other illegal life forms that were known to be created by Aeon Research Financial, as well as prevent new ones from being created. I'm going home. You people get to decide how badly you want law and order versus stability."

"Stability, Leigh?" the other G'schtack female judge asked.

"Justice, as I might embody it would be righteousness itself," he replied, using a G'schtack term that invoked their equivalent of the Archangel Michael and his terrible sword. "But it would also be devastating and I doubt that most of Brees or the Guild has the stomach for that sort of introspective ugliness. You might find all sorts of things about yourselves that you didn't want to know."

"And if we fall short of your definition of a successful prosecution?" the woman pressed.

"That's on your conscience." He stared hard at her now. "Captain Ikoshi decided that he would rather see justice done than let everyone else get away in spite of the stain on his own reputation in the process. The rest of you get to have that conversation with yourselves and your counterparts."

He took a breath and got himself under control again.

"We're new in the Guild, Your Honors," Greyson reminded them. "Humans have only been citizens for about fourteen cycles, depending. I doubt that it is our place to tell you how to run your trade empire."

He wanted to sit, but knew that they would want the last word, so Greyson remained standing. It would be rude to sit now, anyway. Doubly so if he spoke without standing, which might just happen.

He waited.

"You think your kind of justice would be a howling wind that brought devastation, Leigh?" Murphely asked now, quoting some of their own, ancient religious symbolism.

"Only to those that deserved it," he acknowledged. "How many folks are there like that in this town, do you suppose?"

That was a telling blow. He watched the other four metaphorically rock back on their heels as old guilt suddenly woke up and poked them in the kidney.

Everybody has guilt. Things they did. Or didn't do. Should have known better. Should have resisted.

Nobody was as hard on you as your own memory. He could testify to that, but only at that moment when St. Peter was about to toss his ass into hell to burn for all time.

"It might be better if you stayed," Murphely said ambiguously. "To see this through to the end."

"And I might pull down the Guild itself if I tried," he reminded them. "On balance, you folk have been an improvement to the galaxy. Far better than an army of Humans, or Human clones, would have been, had it come to that. Same with invisible assassins or Manchurian Candidates that might protect those who should be in prison forever. I'm not prepared for the responsibility of building something to replace the Illymus Merchant Guild, if I burned your house down, so I'm going home and making sure my corner of the galaxy is safe."

"Would you return if needed?" she asked.

Fuck, this felt like that final scene in a western. He wondered if the cultural connotations carried over, or if she'd just chanced into the phrasing.

He was no King Arthur. No Robin Hood. Not even that guy in the white hat on a pretty horse.

Greyson turned to the right.

"I'm likely too close to retiring," he told them. "Rachel Asher is the one you'll want on that day. She'll be better than me soon."

It was always fun, watching the kid blush. Hard to do, too, which just made it better.

God's honest truth, though. Give them another two years or so and she could step sideways into Ikoshi's spot, maybe.

Wouldn't that be fun?

"And until then, Greyson Leigh?" Judge Rankev asked.

Until then?

"You know where to find me," he said, doubting that anybody would actually come to Boston looking.

Almost anybody. Murphely Rankev might.

She was tough enough.

The woman put her hand down on a stack of printouts that had eaten most of his, Rachel's, and Arymo's night to compile and describe. All the slaves discovered and interviewed.

It had been abundantly clear that they'd been programmed to enjoy that sort of thing. To do *whatever* someone asked of them, once they were alone in a private suite, though snuff films would cost extra and have to be arranged ahead of time.

Greyson still regretted not beating that Head Pimp to death with his bare hands. Wouldn't look good to do it now, and nobody would extradite the fucker to Earth, specifically because the man would be facing a death penalty case if they did.

"In that case, the files are entered as sworn, Detectives Leigh, Asher, and Moora," Rankev said now, only gaveling once. "It is expected that the two of you will remain on Brees for a week or two as things are sorted out, but Metropolitan Ricia has already contacted my staff to assign additional resources, as well as asking other Metroplexes to forward Prosecutors and Investigators to help with the immense case load. Thank you for what you've done."

Greyson nodded and turned to Moora. He'd get the heaviest load dumped on him now, but Greyson had faith that the G'schtack could handle it. And he would have allies like Murphely Rankev and maybe Ikoshi and Ricia as well.

All the bad karma accumulated could go back to Earth with Greyson and Rachel, where he would wear it like a cloak.

He might not save Brees or the Guild in the long run, but they were never forgetting him after this.

Now, he just had to deal with the next issue.

THIRTY-THREE
LISSA

GREYSON HAD MANAGED to get Lissa brought in as something of a consultant. Since she was the source of the genetics for several of the rescued refugees, nobody had really wanted to fight him to the death on the topic.

Not this week, at least. He assumed they would still try to politely brush the woman aside after he was gone.

Greyson found himself looking forward to whatever letters an interested bystander sent to the local news bureaus and reporters, if that blew up. Lissa was a lot tougher than any of these fools understood.

The two of them were in a private office. He'd been assigned one so he could have one meeting after another as folks got brought in from all over the planet and orbit to help. Mostly, he was briefing top level players on some facet of things, and they would take that to their own teams being assembled.

Next door, Rachel was doing the same, while Arymo had an entire space about half as big as the Metropolitan's, because of the expectation that he would need it and a full staff for years.

Greyson could see him possibly replacing Ikoshi, depending on how things shook out. Again, not his problem.

His problem was seated across the desk from him right now, emotionally fragile, but also burning with the sorts of rage Greyson understood, rather than sadness that he was departing in a few more days.

"You don't have to do this," he offered.

Again. Not that he figured he could sway her.

Lissa might be almost as stubborn as him or Rachel.

"No, I do, Greyson," she countered, emotions welling up again. "Nobody else will be able to really speak up for them, and three of them really are my sisters, plus however many more of me there are out there."

"The court can find them guardians," he tried.

"Who will be underfunded and not particularly sympathetic to women who have been twisted to have extreme sex drives and little shame," she snapped. "At least all the slaves were sterilized, so we don't have to worry about that. And we don't have to wonder what their children might be like. Nobody understands whether or not the programming is genetic right now."

"But you'll be responsible for at least thirty people," Greyson said. "All of them extremely bright children with developmental issues. Worse, hypersexualized children."

"I have the money to get them what therapy and protections they need, Greyson," she said, standing firm. "And they can play around within the group without risk. Most of them are physically compatible, so if they get overwhelmed by their needs, there will be others handy. We don't know yet if they truly understand, but that's why I am going to get myself appointed as their Guardian and Conservator. And I can afford it, which even Anic wouldn't necessarily be willing to pay for, depending on how long they are supposed to live."

Greyson shrugged. Would you want your clones living more than a few years? At some point, that first bloom of youth would give way to adulthood. That transformation a woman goes through somewhere between twenty-two and thirty-two as she turns into a bigger and better version of herself.

Maybe that was why they kept getting samples from Lissa, and presumably the other contributors. That would let them see what the future would be like, if they wanted to branch out into other kinks. God knows the sexy mother figure was a thing on Earth. He could only imagine if she remained perfect physically and got overwhelmed by horniness hormones.

Not that such a thing didn't describe Emmy in many ways.

And there was nothing he could do or say. He'd be heading home in less than a week.

Safer, that way, because it wouldn't be too long before someone cracked all the encryption on various datasets and would then know the name and address of the woman who had become Anais Manel.

If Lissa was any example, she'd be almost perfect and still Human. Truly, a frightening thing.

"What about your trip to see the rest of the Guild planets?" he asked, more curiosity than anything.

"That's obviously going to be on hold for a few years," she laughed now, both of them moving away from an unnecessary emotional confrontation. "Though I might be able to hire a smaller ship for my expanded family and continue it one of these days. And we might just need to stay close to Brees for a while because of all the potential medical and legal issues."

Greyson nodded. Up until now, he'd wondered if she might follow him back to Earth. Emmy wouldn't complain much. They had an open relationship where each tried to carve out time for the other, but no claims. She was too busy taking over the world of business, and he was constantly trying to save it from other creatures that went bump in the night.

Worse come to worst, Emmy might want to seduce Lissa. The image of those two women together caused him a moment of panic.

He'd burn that bridge when he got there. Or they would.

"And you are really okay suddenly becoming a rich auntie to a bunch of relative strangers?" he asked.

"Three of them are me," she said, sobering. "I made it possible for them to exist, whether they chose it or not. Right now, they have nothing, at least until the government decides how it wants to handle illegally manufactured life forms. The various others are in the same boat. I've considered starting a modeling agency, for all the obvious reasons. None of them has any hangups about nudity and let's face it, we're dealing with near perfection in every single species."

"That's actually a fantastic idea," he said. "Because that might help you find the other donors faster, if everyone starts seeing their little sister or brother on billboards."

"Always solving crimes, Greyson," she laughed, holding out a hand across the desk.

He took it, reveling in the feel of her skin.

If this was goodbye, that touch promised that it was only for now.

That one day she'd knock on his door in Boston, possibly without calling ahead. Hopefully not a night he and Emmy were trying to set records. Or maybe so. Anything might be possible.

"It's what I do," he said quietly.

"I know that," she nodded. "And better than anybody. I've been hearing gossip around the building as I met with people and explained my connection. They have almost elevated you into demigodhood."

He shrugged. Partly, that was on purpose. If folks around here feared him, the bad guys out there would hear eventually, and stay away from Earth.

Win/win, as far as he was concerned. And that just meant that Rachel would inherit some of that manna when she came back.

Because he knew that Scotland Yard simply wasn't going to be all that interesting after this.

"So now what?" he asked.

"Now, I want you to take me to lunch, then we're going back to the hotel and fooling around for a while, before you have to go catch more bad guys."

"I can do that," he decided.

A break for himself.

Then back to the Hunt.

RACHEL STOOD in the departure lounge and watched as Greyson got a kiss goodbye. And then some. Lissa might be putting on a performance. Leaving her perfume all over the boy, so to speak, to keep anybody on the starliner from making moves when she wasn't around.

Or at least giving him a reason to open the door, the next time Lissa Jonez knocked.

When she finished, Lissa turned, grabbed Rachel, and kissed her on the cheek as well.

Then just like that, turned and walked away.

Greyson had been muttering about his cowboy movies all week. This felt like the moment when the music swelled and the credits rolled, but honestly, they always left out the hard part about riding on to the next city instead of taking the easy way out and hanging around.

Rachel found herself alone with Greyson and about a hundred new fellow travelers, about half of whom were Human, since this ship was on the run back to Earth eventually. Not Cirri Heavy Irregular, so she supposed that

Captain Sheedo would be a little pissed that she didn't get her shot at Leigh.

Of course, everyone here would know where to find him eventually. How many would have friendly intentions when they did remained to be seen.

Quickly enough, they opened the doors over there and everyone began filing aboard. The news shows on Brees had been one scandal after another as the story broke, but she and Leigh had done a pretty good job of staying off the evening news after that first raid. Arymo Moora was handling a lot of publicity now, along with Information Officers from various jurisdictions and the Metropolitan's office.

They got aboard and Rachel dragged Greyson to a bar not that far from their cabins. Everything would be delivered by bellhops and those folks didn't need anyone in their way right now.

Other old pros had done the same, so this particular bar was a little crowded, but not bad. Weeknight, down at the corner joint, rather than weekend.

"So I have been sounded out," she said as they got glasses delivered and were left alone.

Greyson nodded like he'd expected it. You never knew with him how much of it was for show and how much he was that far ahead of everybody else in his thinking. Rachel figured it was about fifty/fifty, most of the time.

"Good enough offer to consider?" he asked as he sipped some of the bad whiskey he'd probably gotten used to by now.

Rachel had ordered herself a little rum, just to be different today.

"Not right now," she nodded. "Like London, I'd rather have the degree and the ability to climb into management pretty quick."

He held out his glass and they touched in a quick toast.

"A half-century ago, London might have been the best gig on Earth," he said. "When I was a kid, they were still part of Europe and had an economy worth discussing. Before they went and blew it all up about the same time the US also finally decided to drive off a cliff."

Rachel nodded. Modern history, measured as that period from about 1980 until the aliens had officially landed in 2042 and freaked everyone the fuck right out the window. The end of the American Empire as a thing.

Good riddance, too.

"But, you know, grass is always greener," he continued, sipping slowly at his glass.

"Is it any greener on Brees than in Boston?" she asked.

He shrugged. Predictable. All relative, he would normally say, but right now he was exceptionally quiet. Maybe a little sad at leaving Lissa behind. At least until he started looking forward to the reception he'd get from Emmy after nearly four months apart.

"It is all a matter of scale," he said now in a precise, laser-focused voice. "Boston is an old city facing new problems. The Metroplex Culture is still settling on some people and awkward. Plus, not all the folks in the Guild have gotten the news to try their stupid bullshit somewhere else, so we'll be dealing with punks and fools for probably another decade or so."

"And Brees?" she asked. "Anic?"

"New York City on its best day," he nodded. "London, same. Paris as well. Hong Kong, when it was the pearl of the entire Orient, to quote the old salts. The social and intellectual center of a culture that spans light-centuries in every direction and is thousands of years old. Sure, the grass probably is greener, but it brings a whole raft of other issues."

"Like they don't need Hunters," she noted.

"Not like Earth does," he shook his head. "There are still

bad people in all species. Worse, as Humans start going out, the Guild probably needs more Human cops to keep our kind in line, because most of the Guild don't grok violence like we do. Nor crime."

"The Head Pimp," she nodded. He had a name. They only referred to him by his job title.

Head Pimp. That was all he was, at the end of the day. A Human who'd been willing to go places and do things that the more genteel folks of Guildspace might not want to initiate.

An awful lot of them had been willing to sample the fruits of his endeavors, though.

"So do we need to talk to folks like Ikoshi and Ricia about creating a thing like the Hunter Bureau out there, but protecting the Guild from our kind?" she asked. "Maybe get Rankev involved?"

She expected a snort of disgust or a deprecating smile like a pat on the head. Instead, his eyes got serious. Deadly, dangerous serious.

Hunting by a game trail with loaded crossbows and poisoned bolts serious.

"That is not the dumbest idea I have ever heard," he said slowly.

High praise, considering his usual attitude.

"You think it has legs?" Rachel asked, suddenly engaged.

"Humans are dangerous predators," he said. "At least some of them. Earth needed the Bureau because of the Phrenic and some of the other folks who might have technology so far advanced as to be indistinguishable from magic. Now I wonder if the Guild needs its own Bureau to protect the citizens of the various worlds from us deranged barbarians."

"They have cops," she noted.

"We have cops," he countered. "Ninety-nine percent of

the time, a uniform and a badge is sufficient to handle things. Inside that last percent, most of those cases just need heavily-armed rescue teams to handle assholes that have barricaded themselves with hostages. Stun cannon work wonders for that."

"But you still need the Bureau," Rachel said.

"You still occasionally need professional killers," he said, sipping again. "Folks willing to walk into a dark warehouse with a nerve scrambler,"

"Only on Brees, it might be against Humans gone wild," Rachel nodded.

He nodded back.

"I want to take my badge off for a few weeks," Greyson announced. "Pretend to be a nobody civilian on an extended vacation. But yeah, we need to circle back on this when we're a week or so out. I'm not sure it will stand up in the light of day, and today is nothing but fog and gray."

"But we might need to have a chat with Parsons," she completed the thought.

"The news of Brees, Anic, and Aeon Research Financial is going to get there before we do," he stated. "Probably on a fast courier running direct. Rutherford will have a few weeks to absorb everything we did out there, on top of everything I left behind for her on Earth."

"New day coming?" Rachel asked.

"New galaxy maybe, kid," Greyson said.

She watched him shoot the rest of his glass, slide backwards off his stool and stand there, blinking like he'd just woken up.

He turned and walked away. Rachel let him. The boy needed some downtime.

He'd been on point pretty much since they got that first call to fly to Armstrong Base and solve a weird-ass murder. Long, hard months. So far.

She wouldn't begrudge him a little break.

Because they still had to deal with Captain Rutherford Parsons, and everything that they'd be bringing to Earth when they got home.

And maybe turned around and leaving again pretty quickly, headed back out to the stars to bring the Bureau into rest of the Guild.

Never a dull moment with Greyson Leigh.

COMMANDER, EASTERN NORTH AMERICA DIVISION, EARTH POLICE SPECIAL MISSIONS

Greyson studied Captain Parsons across her desk. Rachel sat beside him in the other chair.

They'd sat. Made small talk.

Gossiped.

Rutherford Parsons had nothing on her desk except a stack of papers nearly a foot thick. And that was likely just the executive summaries.

Conversation had lulled.

"When you left…" Parsons began before halting. Then changed directions. "I read everything you time-delayed, about Anais Manel and her victim. And how you knew exactly where to go on Brees to find the factory making them. I still don't understand how you got the Phrenic to tell you those things."

"I can be extremely persuasive when I want to be," Greyson smiled tiredly. "It was trying to bargain with us for its life at that point."

"And you still killed it," Parsons said.

"Honestly, trying to send a message to the rest of them,"

he said. "Anyone. Anywhere. Come to Earth, kill a Human, and nothing will save you from me."

"Think it will work?" she asked.

"I think it will now," he countered. "We made something of a splash on Brees."

Parsons erupted in bright laughter. She had a pretty laugh. Beautiful woman, if you liked them cold like marble statues animated by magic.

"I have reports from the Metropolitan of Anic," Parsons finally said after she got herself under control. "And a Judge Rankev. Plus stuff from their Captain of Detectives. All of them point out that you broke open a conspiracy a decade or more in the making, capturing or implicating hundreds of people with incontrovertible evidence. By now, some of them are already probably being offered plea deals if they admit everything and behave."

"Lots of little fish swept up in my net," Greyson shrugged. "That's usually how it works."

"But a Human was behind it," Parsons noted.

"That part of it," Rachel leaned forward. "The whore house. Brothel. Whatever fancy euphemism you want to use. The factory was still a G'schtack thing, predating Humans as Guild members. The Head Pimp was just that. And he was only a symptom."

"You could have stayed longer," Parsons said. "I have notes from folks that they would have welcomed you for at least a year, digging and prosecuting."

"They didn't want my idea of justice any more than you usually do," Greyson countered. "It would have been Zielinski all over again, but this time I might not have been willing to stop short."

Parsons nodded tightly. Her predecessor had retired under a deal where everyone ignored each other and lived out their lives peaceably.

Zielinski had later broken that deal, so Greyson had hunted him down and destroyed him. Man was in a small box for the rest of his life. The kind that didn't have outside windows.

And, like he'd said, Greyson had burned all that blackmail evidence once he had gotten the confession he'd wanted out of Zielinski. The one that put him away forever.

A lot of folks had breathed much easier when rumors started going around that Detective/Hunter Leigh had burned everything in a trash barrel, then stirred the ashes with a length of fence post.

"There is also an open invitation to go back," Parsons continued.

Greyson turned to Rachel now. She perked up.

"So we had an interesting idea on the flight home," Rachel began.

Parsons didn't ignore him as Rachel began to talk, to explain, but shifted her attention to his partner and let him lean back. He really needed some downtime in Boston. Walk the Commons now that spring was here.

Even in his youth, the winters in Boston had apparently not been as bad as the mid-Twentieth Century. Might not return to anything normal in his lifetime.

His Human lifetime. Like Lissa's clone siblings, he was on borrowed time without any idea what was left on the clock. Greyson Leigh was fifty-one on paper. Twenty years Army pension. Technically he was earning extra points on top of a Bureau pension that had been granted equivalent to twenty-year's-service when they made him retire, since they hadn't taken that away from him when he came back.

A comfortable living, if he wanted to quit now and live quietly. Not that Emmy would let it be quiet, but that was a part-time thing. He didn't fit well in her world and wouldn't be happy to be kept.

He needed prey. At least he was adult enough to admit that, thirty-three years on from enlisting.

He was a Hunter.

At the same time, the Human Greyson Leigh would presumably be old in another decade. Physically worn, though every day Guild scientists working with Human counterparts were inventing new ways to stay young.

Ethen Boli was nearly one hundred years old, but Phrenic were adults for centuries, only breaking down as they got close to three hundred. And that end happened quickly.

He could claim a fountain of youth or something. Those assholes on Brees had originally hooked Lissa with the possibility of taking her old lady mind and putting it in a teenager's body.

Most people would probably kill for that opportunity. He had, in a weird way, but he wouldn't recommend it.

One of these days, Greyson Leigh was going to have to die. They didn't know when or how. Probably in a decade at most, and that if everything else went right.

What would Ethen do with her life at that point? Or would Greyson have to hire somebody to make him a new set of identity papers? Maybe tell someone like Quinton Laux that he'd been bit by a vampire or something, and was immortal?

Except that the man would demand that Greyson bite him, more likely than not.

Immortality. The impossible dream.

That thing that separated Human from Inhuman. At least today. Eventually, they might find the right combination of whatevers to pull it off.

But Greyson Leigh would be gone by then. Ethen would revert to base form, most likely, and go through life with bio-restraints to keep her from taking on any other shape.

She would never kill again. He only did because there were folks out there that needed it.

In the back of his mind, Greyson was listening to Rachel explain the possibility of a Hunter Bureau on Brees, whatever they called it.

"Do you think the Guild would go for it?" Parsons asked, turning back to face him now, those hard, blue eyes focusing.

Deadly, dangerous woman, but really only the third most in the room. Fifth deadliest in the building, depending on who might have gone down the street for coffee.

"I think we could make a case for it," Greyson replied. "As Rachel said just now, the species of the Guild are as much at risk from Humans as Earth was from them. The difference is that they were bringing us technological magic, and we're just violent psychopaths with sharp sticks."

"And they have asked if both of you might be available," Parsons noted, finally putting a hand on that stack of papers that had been weighing her desk down.

Greyson shrugged. He could hide just fine on Earth, as there were few places with the kinds of scanner equipment that might show him to be more than he seemed. Or less.

The worlds of the Illymus Merchant Guild were better at scanning randomly. And it only took one unlucky day, one moment of unfocus, to kill him.

But it only took one idiot with a beam pistol firing as soon as someone kicked open a door, too.

A Human cop would have been dead. Greyson Leigh wasn't Human anymore, and wasn't willing to lie to himself about it.

Inhuman.

Hopefully in a good way. The kind of protector that made the galaxy a better place, when corruption and crime seemed to be more the rule than the exception.

"I think I'm an old dog and not really one to learn new

tricks," Greyson offered. "Rude, opinionated, and set in my ways. The kid here might be who they need, in order to build something new. She'll be around long enough to see it done. You might need to go because they'll need folks used to hardheaded punks like me."

"Me?" Parsons flinched back in surprise.

She'd been a Lieutenant/Hunter in Los Angeles who took a lateral and got promoted to Boston when Zielinski went away the first time. And had been a pretty good boss, as they went. Not the best. Far from the worst.

A consummate politician, in a political job. That was why he'd never wanted to go beyond Detective/Hunter. First off, they'd fucking make him start wearing ties again, unless he instituted new rules about cravats or something equally weird from Human fashion history.

Most of modern men's fashion could be blamed on that asshole Beau Brummel, at the end of the day.

"You," Greyson said. "I can make her a better Hunter than me in a few more years. Always planned to quit and go work for her, wherever she ended up after that. Somewhere in the last four months, that stopped being Scotland Yard and maybe became Anic, on Brees."

"Are those folks ready for you, Leigh?" she asked. "Or Asher, for that matter?"

"No," he smiled. "That's why it might work."

READ MORE

Be sure to read the next books in the Hunter Bureau series!

Mirrors
Latency
Pleasure Model
Inhuman

Available at your favorite retailers!

ABOUT THE AUTHOR

Blaze Ward writes science fiction in the Alexandria Station universe (Jessica Keller, The Science Officer, The Story Road, etc.) as well as several other science fiction universes, such as Star Dragon, the Dominion, and more. He also writes odd bits of high fantasy with swords and orcs. In addition, he is the Editor and Publisher of *Boundary Shock Quarterly Magazine.* You can find out more at his website www.blazeward.com, as well as Facebook, Goodreads, and other places.

Blaze's works are available as ebooks, paper, and audio, and can be found at a variety of online vendors. His newsletter comes out regularly, and you can also follow his blog on his website. He really enjoys interacting with fans, and looks forward to any and all questions—even ones about his books!

Never miss a release!

If you'd like to be notified of new releases, sign up for my newsletter.

http://www.blazeward.com/newsletter/

Buy More!

Did you know that you can buy directly from my website?

https://www.blazeward.com/shop/

ABOUT KNOTTED ROAD PRESS

Knotted Road Press fiction specializes in dynamic writing set in mysterious, exotic locations.

Knotted Road Press non-fiction publishes autobiographies, business books, cookbooks, and how-to books with unique voices.

Knotted Road Press creates DRM-free ebooks as well as high-quality print books for readers around the world.

With authors in a variety of genres including literary, poetry, mystery, fantasy, and science fiction, Knotted Road Press has something for everyone.

Knotted Road Press
www.KnottedRoadPress.com